Murder in Misdirection

Anne Cleeland

ARTEMIS
—PRESS—

The series in order:

For Archbishop Padilla, who was always willing to step into the storm; and for all others like him.

Chapter 1

He left to pick her up at the church,
and hoped the subject had not arisen.

"I imagine," Father John ventured, "your husband would prefer that there be no newspaper coverage."

"You imagine correctly," Doyle replied. She was seated in the front pew of the church—empty, as it was mid-afternoon—whilst the good father stood before her with his arms crossed, rocking a bit on this heels as they discussed the weekend's activities.

She continued, "It's probably somethin' that's best kept quiet—although it's not as though he's in line to inherit the throne, or anythin'." Doyle's husband, Lord Acton, was to be confirmed at St. Michael's Roman Catholic Church, and—since he was a peer of the realm—this would incite no little interest, particularly as he was famous in his own right for fighting crime and corruption. More correctly, he was a crimefighter when he wasn't committing his own crimes and corruption on the side—Detective Chief Inspector Acton was something of a vigilante, beneath his much-beloved public persona, and despite his much-aggrieved wife's repeated attempts to sway him from this course.

"A small notice, only," Father John suggested. "But in the front-page section, perhaps."

Doyle had to laugh at his persistence. "Give over, Father; it's not as though anyone's goin' to think religious conversion is all the rage, nowadays."

But the good Father cast a calculating eye over the little church's interior. "In these times, any good publicity is appreciated, lass. I was able to refinish the pews, after the Everyday Heroes program made the papers."

Doyle refrained from mentioning that it was a murder at the church program that had made the papers, and not necessarily the program itself, because she could see that Father John had been bitten by the fund-raising bug, and the next thing you knew he'd probably be selling naming-rights to the holy water fonts. "And here I thought you took a vow of poverty, Father."

The priest ducked his chin and peered at her over his spectacles. "I did indeed, lass. But there are so many worthy causes—and a bit of extra money is always appreciated."

But Doyle—who'd rotated through larceny-by-trick when she'd trained at the Crime Academy—tended to be more cynical. "It seems to me that whenever some charity starts makin' a bit of extra money, they run into trouble by convincin' themselves that they deserve a better reward."

"There can be only one, eternal reward," the priest agreed firmly. "And those who fall into the mortal sin of greed are foolish indeed, if they throw it away."

She glanced at him sidelong, from her position in the pew. "I imagine Acton's goin' to make it all well-worth your while, whether it makes the newspapers or not." After all, her generous husband had already paid for the church's new roof and the new heating system—not to mention a new stained-glass window, which had been destroyed under best-be-forgotten circumstances.

At this reference, Father John looked a little conscious, and nodded. "Well—as to that, he's mentioned a project, but I'm not at liberty to say more, just now."

"A-ha," she teased. "A bell-tower, with a gold-plated bell, within." Father John had long admired the impressive bell tower

2

that graced Holy Trinity Church—or used to grace it, more correctly. The large church—in a posh London neighborhood—had recently burned to the ground.

The priest sighed with regret. "Bell towers are too old-fashioned, nowadays—the city wouldn't want us ringin' it, and makin' noise. And to have such a heavy weight on the roof can be a hazard, as we've learned to our great sadness." He shook his head. "That poor woman."

"What poor woman?" Doyle asked in surprise. "Never say someone was killed?"

Father John raised his brows. "Ah—you haven't heard? They found a body in the rubble, days later. Burnt, of course—but the police believe it is the charwoman; a longtime parishioner." He paused, and his troubled gaze rested on the altar for a moment. "They think she's the one who set the fire, and got caught up in it, somehow."

This was disturbing on several different levels, most notably because Doyle's better half hadn't thought it worthy of a mention to her. "Was it arson, truly? Faith, I didn't know—why would she be wantin' to burn the place down?"

With an air of sadness, the priest brought his gaze back to Doyle. "She was an immigrant—from the Philippines, I believe—and was strayin' a bit from the faith." He paused, and sighed. "It's hard to compete with the evangelicals—all that fire, and passion."

But Doyle frowned, not following. "You'll not be tellin' me that the evangelicals are preachin' arson?"

"No—no, of course not. But they do tend to inspire extraordinary devotion, and sometimes that devotion can take an unhealthy turn."

"More often, it takes a healthy turn," Doyle added fairly. "No one can fund-raise like the evangelicals."

He smiled. "True, and more power to them—we all seek the same aim, after all. The poor woman was not in her right mind, of course, and so I've been prayin' for her soul. It's a terrible thing, to destroy a church."

Doyle paused, because her scalp had started prickling, which was what happened when her intuition was prodding her to pay attention. Although she kept the fact well-hidden, she had an extraordinary perceptive ability that was a crackin' nuisance in her everyday life, but was sometimes an enormous help with her detective work, mainly because she could sense the emotions of the people in her vicinity, and could tell—usually—when someone was lying.

In addition, her instinct would occasionally prod her into paying attention to something that was important—even though the reason for it wasn't clear to her—as it was doing right now. Father John said it was a terrible thing to destroy a church—no arguing with that—so why would her scalp be prickling? Of course, Holy Trinity Church had a bit of a cloud hanging over it, due to its association with the massive corruption rig that had been recently rooted out, but since the place was now a smoldering ruin, one would think that it didn't matter, anymore.

Frowning slightly, she tried to catch at the elusive feeling. "Are they goin' to rebuild, d'you know?"

The priest raised a significant brow at her. "'Tis another blow, hard on the last. They thought they had insurance, but as it turned out, the facilities manager was pocketin' the premium money, instead." He paused, thinking about it. "I suppose I should pray for him, too. Greed is a terrible sin."

"Worse than listenin' to the evangelicals?" Doyle teased.

"Now, lass; not a laughin' matter," the priest scolded. "I've pledged to take up an emergency collection for the rebuildin' effort, but I haven't high hopes."

Doyle nodded in resigned acknowledgment. St. Michael's was a small parish in Chelsea, and rarely had two pence to rub together—that was, until Acton had chosen the mackerel-snapping Doyle to be his unlikely bride, and then had decided to convert to Roman Catholicism. Therefore—as a happy result of the caprices of his lordship's affections—the church's fortunes were now looking up.

She offered, "Well, mayhap the DCS will punt up some of his cash; he's got quite the flock, I hear." The former Detective Chief Superintendent of Scotland Yard was currently serving a prison sentence as a result of the aforementioned corruption rig, but he'd supposedly seen the error of this ways, and had started evangelizing for the prison ministry. Due to this high-profile conversion, the man had attracted a large following, and Doyle had barely managed to dissuade Father John from donating to his ministry, being as she did not believe for one moment that this particular leopard had changed his spots.

"I know you're jokin', lass, but God's ways are mysterious. What we mortals see as a terrible tragedy, is all part of His perfect plan."

Again, Doyle's scalp prickled, and she wondered why it would.

While she was thus distracted, the priest circled back to the topic at hand, which was the planning of Acton's confirmation ceremony. "Would your husband object to a small reception in the hall, d'you think? The bishop will be here, after all."

"Kissin' up," she teased. "It's shameless, you are."

Again, the priest ducked his chin, and regarded her with a serious expression. "Now, my motives are a bit purer, Kathleen. We've a matter before him, and I rather wondered if you could—" here he paused, delicately. "'Intervene' is perhaps too strong a word."

With some amusement, she quirked her mouth. "You've got the wrong girl, Father, if you think I can come up with the right word. Just tell me straight-out what's afoot."

Slowly, the priest began, "I'm not one to be second-guessin' the police, as you know."

Doyle immediately perked up, because whilst she was normally a Detective Sergeant for the CID, at present she was on maternity leave, and having a very tedious time of it. "Oh? What's happened?"

"A couple from Holy Trinity parish came to ask for my assistance, since their own pastor is a bit distracted. It seems that their son was workin' in an investment firm in the financial district, and—sadly—he took his own life."

"A shame," she said sympathetically. "I'm that sorry for it."

"Yes, but they are convinced he'd never have done such a thing. Apparently, he'd been embezzlin' a great deal of money, and was driven to despair when he was caught out. But his parents tell me he was a good RC, and never would have killed himself. So, they're hopin' for a funeral mass, and absolution."

Doyle, who wasn't up-to-speed on such things, asked, "Oh—is he not allowed a funeral mass, then?"

Father John sighed. "It's left up to the bishop, and much depends on whether the poor soul was in his right mind, at the time. But in a case such as this one—where the suicide appears to be the result of an underlyin' crime—it's a bit harder to believe the victim was not aware of the sinfulness of his act. Instead, the church assumes he freely took his own life, in defiance of God's will. The bishop must consider the matter very seriously."

Doyle thought about it for a moment, and then ventured, "I suppose it's hard for a parent to believe the worst—especially if you've raised your child in the church."

But Father John fixed his gaze on hers. "Now, before you say anythin' else, lass, hear me out. They told me there was a bloodstain beneath the gun on the floor—even showed me a photo, from the police file."

Her interest caught, Doyle stared at him. "Was there indeed?" This was something they taught you at the Crime Academy—often murders were staged as suicides, and one of the tell-tale signs was a bloodstain where it shouldn't have been. A shot to the head caused instant collapse, and any short-lived bleeding would occur only after the weapon hit the floor. "Surely, the Met has looked into it?"

"They have indeed, but apparently the evidence was such that it was clear he'd done it to himself. The net was closin' in on him, and he was soon to be exposed."

Still frowning, Doyle mused, "You know, now that I think on it, there's been a rash of suicides in the financial district."

"Oh? Is that so?" The priest shook his head. "Greed, again. A terrible sin."

She glanced up at him. "Have you mentioned this to Acton?"

The priest hesitated. "Well, I would have, Kathleen, but I didn't want it to appear—" his voice trailed off.

The penny dropped, and Doyle offered, "Oh—it's like one of these 'quid for prose' things. You don't want him to think he's obligated, just because you're confirmin' him."

"Exactly." The priest nodded.

"Then I'll have a look-see, myself," she assured him. "It sounds like somethin' I can handle, so long as it doesn't involve walkin' more than ten feet at a time."

The priest reached to place a soothing hand on her shoulder. "Not much longer, lass. And when the babe is born, it will all be well-worth it."

"Faith," she groused, "I would sell my own soul, just to take a deep breath again."

They both looked up as Acton himself entered from the annex door, and approached. "Ho," Doyle greeted him. "We're stagin' up the scene o' the crime."

"Then I am a willing felon." He bent to kiss her, and shook the priest's hand. "Father."

"Michael—it's that grand to see you. I'll leave the two of you alone." The priest gave Doyle a significant look, before he strolled away.

Acton slid in next to her as he tilted his head toward the retreating priest. "What was that about?"

Doyle leaned her head against the arm that rested on the pew behind her, and sighed as hugely as she was able. "He's turned into a money-hound, my friend, and is wantin' to garner some publicity for this wretched church." She glanced over at him. "I told him you'd be perfectly willin' to grease his palm on the quiet, but I think his plan is to give the evangelicals some competition, in the jostlin' for hearts and souls."

"Whatever you will," Acton replied in a mild tone.

"What I will," she retorted a bit tartly, "is not to be put on display, like a raree show."

He nodded in sympathy. "Then we'll have to think of some alternative to a raree show. May I take you home?"

"You don't even know what a raree show is," she accused, frowning at a crack in the ceiling overhead.

"All too true," he conceded. "You must take me to see one."

"There is not the smallest chance, husband. You'd think it vulgar, and look askance through your—your—" Searching for the right word, she made a gesture.

"Opera glasses?"

"Yes—thank you. Your opera glasses."

Gently taking her hand, he advised in a meek tone, "I regret to say that I do not own a pair of opera glasses."

"There's a point in your favor, then."

There was a small silence, until Acton gently squeezed her shoulder and leaned his head in toward hers. "Sooner or later, we'll have to go home."

"I'm avoidin' home," she declared bluntly. "For the love of all that's holy, Michael, please tell me that you're plannin' to break Savoie out of prison."

He smiled for a moment, and then admitted, "Of course I am."

She sat up and laughed aloud, because—wonder of wonders—it was true.

Chapter 2

Snap, went the trap.

Doyle sat on the sofa at home, watching in bemusement as Reynolds, their servant, instructed Emile Savoie and Gemma Blakney on the proper way to poach an egg. The two children were abiding at the flat, because Emile's father was currently cooling his heels in prison and Gemma's mother was working. Gemma went back to her own home at nights, but Emile had taken up residence here, because—in a moment of extreme stupidity—Doyle had agreed to stand in as next of kin for Philippe flippin' Savoie, a promise that she now repented fasting.

"Do you see, children? The color has changed to white."

Nodding solemnly, the two earnest observers—standing on chairs—gazed at the boiling egg, their eyes wide.

"We will now ladle it carefully—like this—onto a slice of buttered toast for Lady Acton. We will add a small garnish to entice her—just so—as she is not very fond of eggs."

"You're a sly one, Reynolds," Doyle called out. "I'm on to you, now."

"I'm going to be a chef, just like you," Emile pronounced importantly.

"My mum won't let me touch the stove," Gemma admitted.

"I am not a chef, Master Emile. I am a butler." Doyle could hear the faint rebuke in the servant's words, even if the child could not.

"Then I'm going to be a butler," Emile amended enthusiastically, as he jumped off the chair and landed with a crash. "Can I carry it over?"

"*May* I carry it over," Reynolds corrected, as he lifted the tray. "And no, you may not."

"Your father would slay me, if he heard you sayin' such a thing," Doyle warned Emile. "There's to be no more butler-talk."

Emile turned to her, his eyes alight. "I'm going to visit Papa, tomorrow."

This was a surprise, and so Doyle replied, "Are you indeed? Reynolds, bake a cake, quick-like, with a file within. Opportunity is knockin', and I'm not one to say nay."

"That is a misconception, madam. A file would be inserted only after baking."

She eyed him, as he set down the tray before her. "Fine, then; whatever's the proper protocol—I think you're missin' the main point, here."

"Protocol for what?" Acton came in from the far bedroom, where he'd relocated his desk ever since Emile had moved in.

"I'm to bring a cake, when I visit Papa tomorrow," Emile informed him importantly.

"You must address Lord Acton as 'sir'," Reynolds reminded him.

"Sir," amended Emile, straightening up.

"Just like the army-man," Gemma offered in her soft little voice. She was younger than Emile, and tended to support him with a mixture of awe and shyness. Her mother, Mary, was slated to be the unborn Edward's nanny, but the woman's husband had been killed, and until Edward made his appearance, Mary was working part-time to stay afloat. She'd refused monetary assistance, but had gratefully accepted their offer to watch Gemma whilst she worked. Doyle had actually hit upon this plan because Emile was a bundle of energy, and it was sincerely hoped that Gemma would serve as a playmate-and-distraction. Thus far, however, this plan had not worked out as hoped, mainly because both children were fascinated by Reynolds, who was doing a journeyman's job of keeping them entertained.

"We were hopin' to break Emile's Papa out of prison—Reynolds and me," Doyle explained. "The reasons for which will go unmentioned."

"Are you going to eat your egg, ma'am?" Emile hovered by the sofa, hopeful.

Acton intervened in a voice that brooked no argument. "She is, indeed."

"I will, I will," Doyle replied crossly, and lifted a fork.

"Come, Master Emile," Reynolds pulled out a chair at the kitchen table. "It is time to practice your sums."

As the boy bounded away, Doyle made a mighty effort to cast off her sulks, and smiled up at her husband. "You never thought you'd be runnin' a daycare. Confess."

"We'll manage," he soothed, and rested a hand on her head.

"I shouldn't be havin' children, Michael; I've no patience for it."

"Nonsense; you are an excellent mother." Absently, he ran his hand over her head, but she could tell that he was distracted, for some reason, as he glanced over toward the children.

As a distracted Acton did not necessarily bode well for her peace of mind, Doyle asked, "Who's takin' Emile over to visit Savoie tomorrow?"

"Lizzie Mathis."

She stared at him in surprise. Lizzie Mathis was a young woman who was related to the steward who ran Acton's estate, and who was therefore devoted to the House of Acton. She also worked in the forensics lab at Scotland Yard, and, on the side, she served as one of her husband's minions, willing to do dark deeds on his behalf—with this visit to Savoie apparently serving as an excellent example. "Holy Mother, Michael; is that wise? What if Savoie works his charm on her, and convinces her to turn coat against you?" This said in jest, as Mathis was all-business, all the time.

Acton smiled at the absurdity of the suggestion. "We shall have to take our chances, I suppose."

Emile's father, Philippe Savoie, was a notorious international criminal who'd masterminded a smuggling rig whereby illegal weapons were sold throughout the country. Currently, he was being held at Wexton Prison without bail, since his major-crimes list was as long as your arm. However, the whole set-up made Doyle uneasy; Acton himself had been up to his neck in the illegal smuggling rig, also—the two men had been partners, in the underworld operation. It was a shrine-worthy miracle that Acton's participation hadn't come to light, else he'd have landed in prison next door to Savoie. But Doyle's husband did not seem at all worried, even though Savoie's case was moving through the system with glacial speed, and even though they were minding Emile-the-wild-child in the interim. Instead, he seemed—well, he seemed *pleased* about something, which was another miracle, since he couldn't buy a moment's peace in his own home, not to mention that his wife was a sulking walrus.

Doyle considered the Lizzie Mathis development as her husband watched the two children settle into their activities at the kitchen table. "Can Mathis even talk to Savoie, without counsel present?"

"Mathis is not law enforcement; she is a civilian."

She nodded, having forgotten this. The lab people, like the Scene-of-Crime Officers, were independent contractors, and not law enforcement personnel. No doubt this was one of the reasons Mathis was going—no one would recognize her, and she wouldn't be constrained in her communications with Savoie. In fact, Doyle would be very much surprised if the girl's task wasn't to pass information along to the prisoner, under the guise of bringing the boy for a visit.

With some uneasiness, Doyle eyed her husband, who hadn't sat down beside her, but who was instead gazing thoughtfully toward the kitchen table, where Emile was bent over his worksheet, and Gemma colored with crayons. "Come clean, husband; what's afoot?"

He turned his attention back to her, and confessed, "It is probably for the best that you not know, Kathleen."

This was undoubtedly true—particularly if he was masterminding some plan to break Savoie out of prison. Presumably, he had some scheme in the works that would turn her red hair grey, if she knew of it, and so it was best that she didn't. Nevertheless, she warned him, "You've had a lucky escape, my friend; don't be temptin' fate."

"No," he agreed. "I won't."

This answer gave her pause, because it was said with a nuance that didn't seem fitting, somehow—Doyle's husband was well-aware of her ability to sort out the truth—but before she could follow up, he'd moved on to the next topic.

"I must visit Layton tomorrow; Nellie has requested a copy of my baptismal certificate. You are welcome to accompany me, of course."

Doyle made a face; Layton handled Acton's financial affairs, and Doyle had visited the man's posh offices once before, under best-be-forgotten circumstances. "No, thank you; you'll have to dig through the vault all on your own. Are you sure you have a baptismal certificate? I wouldn't put it past your mother to neglect such a thing."

With a small smile, he leaned down to remind her, "Indeed I do; I needed it to marry you."

"Holy Mother, Michael, but you were organized. I was like a lamb, bein' led to the slaughter."

"Just so. I could leave nothing to chance."

Meeting his smile with her own, she held his hand against her head, and watched the others at the table for a moment. When she'd first met Acton, she'd been serving as his support officer and was completely unaware that beneath his very reserved exterior there lurked a burning—and slightly fanatical—devotion to the aforesaid support officer. As he was well-aware she'd balk at any romantic overtures, he'd therefore done the only practical thing and ambushed her into marriage on a moment's notice. It had all turned out rather well, actually, if you didn't count the various brushes with death, and the extra children underfoot.

"Speakin' of Nellie, I should go visit the church again tomorrow, so I may as well make the trip whilst you're at Layton's." For reasons that she could not explain, she didn't want to mention the suicide-may-be-a-murder case to Acton; it could turn out to be nothing, after all, and she was dying to do something other than stare at the four walls. Reminded, she lifted her face to his. "Did you know that they found a body, in the Holy Trinity rubble?"

"Yes," he nodded. "The report indicates an Asian woman—possibly the charwoman. Forensics has done some testing, but so far there's no DNA to run a comparison."

Doyle's mobile pinged, and she glanced at it. "There's Mary; we can send Gemma home."

"I will ring for the driving service, madam." Reynolds helped the little girl rise from the table. "Come, Miss Gemma, let's pack up your rucksack."

"In a moment," said Acton. He then walked over to crouch down before the little girl in a friendly fashion. "If you would, Gemma," he began with a small smile, "tell me about the army-man."

Chapter 3

No luck—she'd heard. Nevertheless, it was unlikely she'd piece it together.

"Can you tell me what this is all about, husband?"

Evening was falling, and Reynolds had taken Emile along to drop off Gemma—the driver was a kind man, who was willing to indulge the boy by telling him tales from his own boyhood in Nigeria. As a result, the flat was blessedly quiet for a few minutes, and Doyle had hoisted herself off the sofa to come over and stand beside Acton, where he stood gazing out the windows, deep in thought.

That his attention had been caught seemed obvious; the little girl had blushed and stammered—she tended to be intimidated by Acton—but she'd managed to tell him that there'd been an army-man who'd come to see her father, on occasion. The girl's deceased father had been a pawnbroker, and it seemed clear that Acton found the existence of the visiting army-man very interesting.

Doyle leaned against him, and ran a fond hand across her husband's back. "Mayhap Blakney had an old army friend."

Acton glanced down at her. "Her father called him 'sir', which makes a friendship seem unlikely. And there is no record that Blakney was ever in the armed services."

Interesting that Acton would know this, off the top of his head. Of course, Acton tended to know everything, so there was that. "Mayhap she's confused, Michael—mayhap it was someone who always wore fatigues, or somethin'."

But his next question surprised her. "Did you ever catch the sense that Giselle and Blakney had a child together?"

With a knit brow, Doyle considered this question, since Blakney and Giselle would have been little Gemma's parents, and it seemed an odd question for Acton to be asking. Giselle had been a victim in an earlier homicide case, which was how they'd met Blakney-the-pawnbroker in the first place; he was the victim's ex-husband, and they'd questioned him as part of their investigation.

Doyle shook her head. "No, I didn't—but that doesn't mean much, Michael. A lot of the villains we meet aren't pattern-card parents, after all."

He did not reply, but continued to gaze out the window.

Puzzled, she ventured, "D'you think she's not their child, then?"

"I haven't enough information to create a theory, as yet." He turned to face her. "Would you mind finding out as much as you can about Gemma from Mary?"

She nodded—Acton wouldn't be interested unless he felt it was important, for some reason. "I will. Shall I ask about any stray army-men, while I'm at it?"

"If you would."

Absently, he drew her against his side, whilst they watched the street lamps light up on the street below. As he offered nothing further on the subject, she prompted, "How soon d'you need to know?"

"No great hurry. I don't want to alarm Mary."

"Aye, then. Am I the one who should be alarmed?" She was half-teasing; when Acton's attention was caught, Katy bar the door.

He glanced down, and squeezed his arm around her. "It seems unusual, is all."

With a nod, she acknowledged this—although she hadn't picked up on it, of course. Her husband's reputation as an extraordinary solver-of-crimes rested on his amazing ability to notice details that eventually turned into case-breakers; details that didn't seem of interest to anyone else. There was good reason the younger detectives nicknamed him "Holmes" behind his back.

"Would you like to sit down?"

"No; it's a relief to stand up, for a bit."

He rested a gentle hand on her belly. "How does Edward?"

"Never better. I can't decide if I want him to get here, already, or if I want him to stay where he is, so that I'll never be put to the test."

Smiling, he leaned to kiss her brow. "I believe testing is supposed to be a good thing. Father John mentioned something about the purity of gold."

Surprised, she laughed aloud. "What's that from?"

"The Book of Proverbs, I believe."

"Yes, well—you're an Old Testament sort of person," she observed, giving him a sidelong glance. "If you know what I mean."

"I suppose there's some justice to that observation," he replied mildly.

She laughed again, and leaned into him. "So—you're to be spoutin' scripture at me, now? Faith, I've created a monster, which is nothin' more than what I deserve."

He rested his head against hers. "Just so you know I'm paying attention."

"Well, watch yourself—Father John will try to wheedle you into payin' more than attention, and we're already runnin' a free daycare."

"We've plenty of money to spare," he replied, and it was true.

As usual, Doyle was reluctant to speak of the Acton family fortunes, in that it always made her feel as though she were a pretender to the throne. Therefore, she tugged lightly at his waist and turned the subject. "Well, I hope we're payin' Reynolds enough. Wouldn't want him to throw down his oven mitts, and storm out the door."

"I believe Reynolds rather enjoys the children."

She lifted a corner of her mouth in acknowledgement. "I've a sneakin' suspicion that you're right. But it wouldn't hurt to shovel him some more money, anyways; I don't know where we'd be, without him."

"Already taken care of—please don't worry."

Thoughtfully, she gazed down on the scene below them, because there was something niggling at her—something about what he'd said, and this conversation they were having. "You know, you're a very generous man, Michael, considerin' all the commandments that you don't mind breakin', when it suits your fancy."

Teasing, he drew her to him. "Not so very many, surely?"

"Well, now that you're spoutin' scripture like the curate's cat, I'll say no more—except to say that even before you were reformed, you were always generous, even with your miserable relatives. It's a point in your favor, I think."

But he tilted his head in a disclaimer. "I take a more practical view, I'm afraid. Money tends to smooth over any perceived grievances."

This seemed irrefutable, and she idly watched the pedestrians walking in the park below, wondering what it was she was trying to understand. "I suppose that's true—although in our business, we've seen plenty of people who can never get enough money. Father John was just sayin' that greed is a terrible driver."

"A primary motivation for murder," he agreed.

"That's what they tell you in the Crime Academy—it's almost always about money, or sex."

"There's a lesson, there." This said with a great deal of meaning, as he bent to rest his mouth against her neck.

Laughing, she took his hand, and willingly turned toward the bedroom. "Then come along, husband; I haven't any money, so you'll have to settle for the next best thing."

"We don't want to bring on childbirth," he warned, although his protest was clearly a sham, as he was unbuttoning his shirt with no further ado.

"I'm willin' to test it."

And so she was, if for no other reason than to take her mind off their conversation. There'd been something there—something unsettling, in what Acton had said about the Old Testament, and money being a prime motivator. And on top of that, there was something in the way he'd spoken of the dead charwoman, who'd been caught in her own fire—surely, he'd known that the wife of his bosom would be extremely interested in the Holy Trinity arson case, but it seemed he'd been hoping the aforesaid wife wouldn't catch wind of the particulars, since she was stuck here at home, watching Emile bounce off the walls.

Mother a' mercy, she thought with some annoyance, as she tried to wriggle her jumper over her head—please tell me that I'm not slated to unravel yet another Acton-scheme that may-or-may-not involve a major crime? Enough is enough is enough.

"I'm stuck," she announced in exasperation. "Help me get this stupid thing off, and then tilt me onto the bed."

"In a moment; I'm asking Reynolds to take the long route home."

She giggled as she peered at him though an armhole. "He'll be scandalized, Michael."

"Let him be; he's getting paid enough. Now, raise your arms, please."

Chapter 4

All was in readiness, and they'd only to wait.
Hudson had prepared a room at Trestles to use as a
surgery, if necessary. The Caesarean rate was over
twenty-five percent, for first-time mothers, and she was a
small person.

The following morning, Acton was reviewing the morning's updates on his caseload. Because it was quieter, his desk had been moved into their bedroom, and Doyle watched him sleepily from the bed whilst Emile and Reynolds could be heard in the kitchen, preparing breakfast.

She offered, "I thought I'd walk over to have a coffee with Williams, before goin' over to the church."

Acton tended to keep track of her movements through her mobile phone's GPS function—especially now that she was full term—and she didn't want him to worry about what she was up to. Firmly, she quashed down an ironic acknowledgment that she was indeed up to something; she was only looking into the suicide so as to help out a grieving couple, and bestow absolution if it was warranted. Doing the work of the angels, she was, and if it happened to give her a much-appreciated project, that was only an added bonus. No need to burden Acton, who was busy enough.

He shut his laptop, and turned to face her. "Best do it first thing, he'll be needed to testify, after lunch."

She nodded in acknowledgement. Detective Inspector Williams had been a key player in bringing down the corruption rig that had devastated the ranks of the CID—although Acton had been required to extricate Williams from a trap he'd fallen into, in the process. It was another shrine-worthy miracle that Williams wasn't currently spending his days shackled-up in Detention, alongside the other blacklegs, and Doyle thanked all available saints and angels that everything had worked out so that the correct people were in prison, instead of her nearest and dearest.

Williams could probably be described as Doyle's closest friend; they'd come up together through the Crime Academy, and it was only after her hasty marriage to Acton that she'd discovered Williams had been romantically interested in her, himself. Fortunately, the awkwardness of all this had more-or-less smoothed itself out—although the poor man often had divided loyalties, in that he was Doyle's friend but he was also Acton's henchman in helping him manipulate evidence so that the proper people went to prison. Despite all this, Doyle trusted Williams; trusted him so much, in fact, that he was the only person aside from Acton who knew about her perceptive abilities, because she'd had to save him from Morgan Percy's wiles, once—the same Morgan Percy who'd got herself murdered, recently. Percy had been knee-deep in the corruption rig, and so it was truly no surprise that someone had decided to silence the young woman—the old saying about lying down with dogs came to mind. It was a shame, though, because despite everything, Doyle had rather liked her.

Williams wasn't the one who'd killed Percy—or so Doyle stoutly assured herself—but it wouldn't hurt to see if he'd heard anything new on the young woman's unsolved case, and that was one of the reasons she'd wanted to meet with him today.

Acton rose from his desk, and came over to kiss her goodbye. "Shall I come home for lunch?"

She brushed her tousled hair away from her face. "Faith, that would be grand, Michael—so long as you're not too busy.

Gemma's not here today, and Emile will be drivin' 'em mad at Wexton Prison, so it should be peaceful, for a change."

"Is there anything special that you'd like Reynolds to prepare?"

"No—you may suit yourself." She hadn't been very hungry, these last couple of days.

Her husband left for work, and, after stretching for a moment, Doyle sat herself up, then maneuvered down to sit on the foot of her bed, and look out the windows for a bit. Nowadays, any activity had to be done in stages, and anyways, she was reluctant to get up. Something's up, she acknowledged to herself a bit crossly, and I'll be happy to put off the next flippin' crisis for as long as I possibly can.

Emile bounded into the bedroom, and announced, "Reynolds said to tell you that the cinnamon pastries are ready."

With a mighty effort, Doyle cast off her sulks. "I guessed this," she acknowledged with a smile. "They smell lovely."

"I helped ice them," he declared importantly. "I used a spatula."

"Well, good on you, for convincin' the man that we need to eat somethin' sticky, now and again."

Grinning, the boy dropped onto the foot of the bed beside her. "I like the way they smell—they remind me of St. Petersburg."

"Do they indeed?" Doyle had forgotten that, until recently, the boy had lived in Russia.

Emile nodded, as he gazed down into the park across the street. "We'd walk over—the boys in my school—to buy *bulochki* from the vendor, by the pond. Sometimes they'd let us feed the ducks."

Doyle leaned back on her hands beside him, and considered the view. "Aye—there's nothin' like a scent, to bring back a memory. I was raised in Dublin, myself. My mother used to take me to feed the ducks in the River Liffey, but they were a different sort of duck than the ones they have here."

The boy turned to look at her, curious. "What sort of ducks were they?"

As Doyle didn't know, she improvised, "Irish ducks. Dublin's in Ireland."

He considered this. "Do you ever go back to visit? I'm going back to St. Petersburg, soon."

Diplomatically, Doyle did not cast cold water on this fond hope, but instead replied, "No—I've never been back since I left, one fine mornin'."

Reynolds appeared in the doorway to prod the window-gazers along. "Madam, if you are hungry, we've prepared a treat for breakfast this morning."

"That is excellent." Doyle hoisted herself up just as the concierge buzzed, to announce that a Miss Mathis was in the lobby.

"She's early," noted Reynolds, with a tinge of disapproval. "I haven't packed Master Emile's rucksack."

"Don't throw any contraband in there," Doyle warned, as she wrapped her robe around her expanded girth. "We'll wind up in the soup."

"Certainly not, madam," said Reynolds, the tinge of disapproval still in evidence. Reynolds was not a joking-about-prison-visits type of person.

"What's 'contraband'?" asked Emile.

"Oh—just some things that your Papa's not allowed to have," Doyle said vaguely, wishing she hasn't brought it up.

The boy suddenly looked conscious, and ducked his head, his face the clear picture of guilt.

Alarmed, Doyle asked, "What is it, Emile? Did your Papa ask you to bring him somethin'? Don't be afraid, you can tell me."

Stricken, he raised his head to meet her eyes. "I'm not supposed to say," he whispered.

Adopting a joking demeanor, Doyle laughed, and ran a hand over the boy's head. "Cigarettes, I imagine."

Relieved, the boy nodded. "Lord Acton told me it was all right, that the guards wouldn't mind, but I shouldn't say anything, since they could get in trouble."

"Where're they hidden?" asked Doyle casually. "In your socks?"

Looking from Doyle to Reynolds, the boy confessed, "My jacket pocket."

Amused, Doyle lifted her brows. "Oh? Must be a whole pack, then."

The boy nodded. "I'm not to open it, or to say anything."

Of course, not, thought Doyle, because I'll bet my teeth there's a mobile phone in there—or plastic explosives, or something—heaven only knew. "Well, your secret's safe with me and Reynolds, Emile. Mum's the word."

Mathis knocked on the door, and Reynolds hurried over to let her in. Mathis was a young woman about Doyle's age, and since she was miles smarter than Doyle—and didn't have much of a sense of humor—the two girls had little in common.

"Hallo, Master Emile," the girl offered, in her grave voice. "Do you remember me?"

"No," said Emile bluntly. "Are you going to take me to see my Papa?"

"Not until you mind your manners, Master Emile," Reynolds warned.

Self-consciously, the boy amended, "How do you do?" and offered his hand.

"I am well, thank you," the girl replied. "Have you your jacket? We mustn't forget it."

With a mighty effort, Doyle refrained from exchanging a glance with Reynolds, as the servant fetched the contraband-jacket from the hall closet, and then handed the boy his rucksack.

"There are cinnamon pastries within, Miss Mathis, and an apple," the servant informed her. "He tends to be hungry."

"I drew a picture," Emile reminded the servant.

"Ah; yes. Here it is—it is a dragon," Reynolds offered smoothly, as this fact wasn't at all clear.

The boy had made an attempt to sign his name, and Mathis said kindly, "That is a very good 'E'. My name starts with an 'E', too."

"Sometimes, I'm Jonathan," Emile confessed, looking conscious. "That's my old name."

"Right, then," said Doyle brightly, and ushered them toward the door. "Give us a warnin' when you're headed back." Emile may have been adopted by the imprisoned Savoie, but his true father had been a Russian underworld kingpin named Solonik, who'd been killed—coincidentally—in Wexton Prison, where Savoie now resided. Savoie had changed the boy's name, and it was not clear if the adoption was legal. Honestly, if Doyle had known that she'd be trying to keep all the various international underworld figures straight—including her own husband, she might add—she would have stayed in Dublin, feeding the stupid ducks.

After closing the door behind them, Doyle advised, "Best not to mention the cigarettes, Reynolds. Acton wouldn't like bein' found out so easily."

"It is already forgotten, madam," the servant assured her with a wooden expression, and ushered her toward the breakfast table.

Chapter 5

It was very satisfying, to settle all outstanding accounts.
Snap, went another trap.

When Doyle arrived at the local coffee house—which was a bit snobbish for her taste, but needs must, in this posh neighborhood—Williams was already there, a small cup of coffee at the ready. She'd taken to drinking coffee again—her only vice, truly—now that both Reynolds and Acton seemed to have tacitly decided it was too late in the game to make much of a difference to the anticipated heir. That, or they'd realized she tended to be even more cross without it, and that such a state of affairs was to be avoided at all costs.

"Hey," she greeted Williams, lowering herself into the chair.

"Hey, yourself. It's good to see you, Kath."

One of the reasons Williams was such an exemplary friend was because he knew she was pig-sick of everyone's asking questions about how she felt. "And it's good to see you, Thomas. Mainly, I'm dyin' to hear about an interestin' homicide case—it's utterly *wretched*, bein' sidelined like this. I wasn't cut out to be one of your idle-rich, and I don't know how they bear it."

Williams sat back, and thoughtfully sipped from his own cup. "Can you help Acton with his caseload? He could probably use it."

"He's lettin' me work his cold cases, which makes sense, since I'm not able to go out in the field, but it's *so* flippin' tedious, Thomas—readin' dull reports, and followin' up on social media, to see what the suspects are up to, nowadays. I do think I unearthed a misdirection murder, though, so there's a small feather in my sidelined cap."

With a show of interest, he leaned forward again—a solved cold case was always good for department morale. "Oh? What was the gambit?" A misdirection murder was where the murderer set up the situation so as to mislead law enforcement with respect to the true nature of the crime.

"Acton suspected the husband had killed the wife, but they couldn't prove it, and they couldn't find a body. The suspect had a greedy girlfriend, on the side, and it was the usual story—faith, we've seen it a hundred times—but the CID couldn't come up with enough to nick 'im. Since the heat was on, he took the girlfriend and moved to the Bahamas, but I noticed there were never any snaps of her on his social media—and that he still wore the same weddin' ring, even though there was no record he'd married again."

Williams whistled in dawning comprehension. "So; it was all a debt-avoidance scam?"

"Aye—it was all a sham. He'd a business that was goin' under, and so he and the missus cooked-up her murder, and then used the insurance money to bankroll their retirement in the Bahamas."

"Good catch, Kath. Did they nick them?"

"They did—the insurance company was on it in an instant." Bemused, she shook her head in wonder. "Hard to imagine, that someone didn't mind bein' thought a wife-killer, just so as to have some extra money in the bank."

But Williams took a more cynical view. "News flash, Kath; a lot of people are greedy. Especially if they don't feel that they're stealing the money from anyone in particular—that's why insurance scams are so tempting."

Doyle frowned as she contemplated her cup, because her instinct was prodding her yet again, and she didn't know why.

"Yes—I was just talkin' about it with Father John. Greed is a terrible driver."

Williams shrugged. "I'll second that. Although a lot of times the end game is the power that money can buy, and not necessarily the money, in and of itself."

She looked up. "Speakin' of such, Acton says you're testifyin' in the corruption pre-lims, later today."

"All too true. I'll be glad when it's all over."

A trace of constraint could be discerned in his manner, and she reached to touch his hand sympathetically. "Amen, Thomas—and then you can get back to doin' what you do best, which is muckin' about, knee-deep in corpses."

He smiled. "Now, there's a pretty picture. But unfortunately, I don't think this firestorm is going away anytime soon—if nothing else, we'll be feeling the effects left by the vacancies in the command hierarchy."

She made a disapproving face. "You sound like Acton—he hates all the disruption that will be wrought upon our poor system, and he hates the bad PR for the department, too. I think if it were up to him, everyone in the corruption cases would be quietly fired, and we'd move on. Least said, soonest mended."

"I think that's probably true."

She eyed him with a touch of exasperation. "We have to see that justice is done, Thomas—no matter who, and no matter the consequences. And the public has to see it, too." She'd always suspected that Williams was of the same bent as Acton, which was not much of a surprise, all in all. They liked their justice swift and rough, and the criminal justice system was anything but.

Seeing that he was politely refraining from comment, she insisted, "No matter the direction it takes us, and no matter the cost, Thomas."

"If you say so," he teased, and tapped his cup to hers in a mock-toast. "These trials are taking up a huge part of the budget, though. No raises this year, and the public doesn't think we're worth it, in the first place."

"Oh—sorry; that's heapin' misery upon misery." Suddenly struck by this thought, Doyle paused. "You know—that's a good question, come to think of it. What's happened to all the money?"

Williams raised his brows. "What's happened to what money?"

"All the money from the corruption rig; remember? There must be tons of it—what with the sex slavery, and the blackmail, and such. They were passin' along fat envelopes of cash at Holy Trinity Church, remember? We caught them red-handed."

"I don't know. I'm no longer on that case."

This was said in a neutral tone, because the worthy DI Williams had been caught up in the web, and so she hurriedly changed the subject. "Have you heard anythin' about Morgan Percy's murder? Is there a whisper of a clue, yet?"

"Not that I've heard."

She gave him a knowing look. "It has to be connected—to the corruption rig, I mean. She knew too much, and tended to switch sides, dependin' on who seemed the best bet at any particular moment."

Stiffly, he offered, "I didn't kill her, if that's what you're asking."

Aghast, she leaned in, and took his hand in hers. "*Of course*, you didn't. For heaven's sake, Thomas; it's only me—don't be so bristly, if you please. You know I tend to blurt out things, willy-nilly, and if you're goin' to have hurt feelin's every time it happens, you're goin' to wind up like Elijah at the broom-bush."

"Can't have that." He smiled, and relaxed a bit. "Sorry. I guess I'm a little sensitive, right now."

She leaned back, relieved because she'd indeed been probing him, and he'd told the truth when he'd said he hadn't killed Percy—let it be said that she could wrangle a misdirection play herself, when it was needful. "Confess; you've no idea who Elijah is."

"I'll do you one better; I've no idea what a broom-bush is."

She laughed, and he chuckled in return, and they sat in companionable silence for a few minutes, sipping the coffee. Better, she thought, idly looking out the window. But he's still a bit wound-up. Unfortunately, I've got to undo all my good works, and wind him right back up again.

Casually, she asked, "D'you know anythin' about Gemma's real mother? I'd feel a bit foolish, askin' Mary about it."

Immediately, he was wary again, and small blame to him, since it was a touchy subject. Williams's interest had been caught by Mary-the-nanny, until the mysterious death of her husband cast a cloud over this promising-but-forbidden romance. Paradoxically, now that Mary was an eligible widow, Williams had turned gun-shy—although that was probably a poor turn of phrase, in light of the situation.

"No; I don't think Mary's ever mentioned Gemma's real mother."

Doyle fingered her cup. "Well, Acton's wonderin', and I suppose it would be a good thing to find out—since both her parents are dead, she may be entitled to benefits, or somethin'. Mary's a little short on money, I think."

Williams gave her a look. "On the other hand, you've got to be careful. You don't want to be forced to send her to some shady relatives, since Mary doesn't have much of a claim."

Doyle nodded thoughtfully. "I suppose that's possible— although they should have come forward before now, if they exist. After all, Gemma's such a sweet little thing—never a moment's trouble."

He smiled. "Not like Emile?"

Doyle lifted her head, and declared, "It's exhaustin', is what it is, and I don't know how the human race survives this whole procreation business."

He chuckled. "I think boys are a little harder to handle than girls. I have some younger cousins, and I'll be happy to take him to the zoo with them, if you'd like."

"You'd do that?" she asked in surprise. "Willingly?"

"I would. I was a little boy myself, once."

"Oh—that would be grand, Thomas. Run him like a racehorse, will you? I'd love to see what it looks like when the wretched boyo's tired."

Smiling into his coffee, Williams said, "I'll set it up."

With a pang of guilt, Doyle offered, "I know I sound like an archwife, and it's not as though I don't like him, Thomas. I'm just not used to always havin' people underfoot."

"No need to explain, Kath."

She smiled, suddenly. "Although I do have a bit of a break today—Lizzie Mathis took Emile to visit Savoie."

Astonished, he raised his brows and couldn't help laughing. "Did she? Now, there's something I'd pay good money to see."

Doyle could only agree. "It boggles the mind. Do you know why Acton's sendin' her, of all people? I think he must be hatchin' some plot, and I'm not sure I even want to know the particulars."

Sobering, Williams examined his hands, on the table. "No. I'm not privy."

But Doyle wasn't having it, and scolded, "Oh, spare me your hurt feelin's, Thomas. You can't be the one waltzin' in to talk to Savoie—you're a copper. And besides, you can't blame Acton for puttin' you in his black book." As a result of Williams near-brush with the corruption rig, he'd got himself into a spot of trouble with Acton, and was now suffering the consequences.

He raised his eyes to hers. "Does he ever say anything?"

"I'll not be grassin' on my own husband, Thomas, and anyways, you know he never tells anyone anythin'—which is probably just as well, all in all. But if you're lookin' for a project that doesn't involve noisy little boys, I could use your help, this very mornin'."

He smiled. "Say the word, Kath."

"Well, there's a couple who've come to my priest, because they don't think their son committed suicide—they think he was murdered, instead. I'm to meet with them this mornin', and I'd appreciate it if you'd have a listen-in, to see what you think."

"Is there a case on file?" Williams was wary for good reason; it was important that they respect the hierarchy, and work only on the cases assigned to them. The Met didn't need officers meddling in each other's cases, and second-guessing.

"No—at least, Father John says they've already decided it's a suicide. But I'm curious to hear what the parents have to say, because the victim worked in the financial district, and was accused of embezzlin' funds."

This garnered his interest, as she knew it would. Williams was working on a series of complex embezzlement cases and making little headway, thus far. "So—you're wondering if the suicide was actually a misdirection murder?"

"Somethin' like that." She played her trump. "Father John says there's a photo that shows a bloodstain on the floor, beneath the weapon."

Williams cocked his head. "Let's go, then. Maybe you can solve another one, while you're sidelined."

"Let's not get ahead of ourselves," she cautioned, as he helped her rise. "We can't be seein' misdirection murders pop up behind every bush."

"Behind every broom-bush," he corrected her.

Chapter 6

Good; Williams had given her a lift to the church.
She shouldn't be alone, now that she was so close to term.

Doyle was sitting in Father John's office with Williams and the grief-stricken couple, who were trying to convince those listening that their son would not have committed suicide, and therefore deserved absolution, and a proper burial. The man and the woman were middle-aged and upper class—as Holy Trinity parishioners were wont to be—and they'd brought along a small folder that contained a copy of the police report. An aura of grief hovered around them, and Doyle gritted her teeth against the raw misery—she'd felt that way when her mother died, and the memory was not a good one.

The dead man's father continued, "Father Gregory has his hands full, what with the terrible fire, and so we were hoping—"

His wife offered, "Father John mentioned that Lord Acton might have a chance to bring the matter before the bishop—"

"We'd want to keep it quiet, of course—"

"If it looks like it's murder," Doyle interrupted gently, "we'd have to open a case—we can't allow a murderer to get off. And you'd want justice for your son, wouldn't you?"

There was a small moment of profound silence.

"Of course," the father agreed, with little conviction.

Father John had his own perspective on these matters, and offered, "And if there is enough evidence to open a case, surely it's much more likely that the bishop will allow absolution immediately."

"There's that," the father agreed tentatively, and glanced at his wife, who was clenching her hands rather tightly. "But we were hoping—I know it's not the proper thing, but we were hoping that Lord Acton could put in a good word with the bishop, so that we could have a funeral mass next week." He paused, and then added heavily, "It would mean a lot to us."

His wife reached to take her husband's hand. "He was a good boy; despite—despite what the police say. And he had a lot to live for, no matter the trouble he may have been in—we would have paid for a good lawyer, after all. And he had a new girlfriend—a lovely girl; he was so proud."

Williams, who'd been listening without comment, spoke up. "Is the girlfriend's information in the file?"

The woman knit her brow. "Oh—oh, I don't know. Tasza, her name was—we met her, the other day; we all met for drinks."

"Have you heard from her, since his death?"

The decedent's parents were apparently oblivious to the implication behind Williams' questions, and the mother shook her head. "No, but they hadn't been dating very long—it was early days." She paused. "He was a good boy—a little shy, and—and foolish, sometimes." Overcome, she bent her head, and pressed a handkerchief to her eyes as Father John gave Doyle the high sign that they should leave the grieving couple alone with him.

"I'll put it before the Chief Inspector," Doyle assured them gently as she rose. "I'm truly sorry for your loss."

Williams followed her out, and they walked down the quiet hallway for a few paces, neither making a comment until he broke the silence. "They know something."

"Indeed, they do," Doyle agreed thoughtfully. "And they're very much afraid of whatever it is. So—they know why he was murdered, and they don't want it to get out. On the other hand, suicide denies him absolution, and if they can show he was murdered, he's back in God's good graces—not to mention they're no longer shamed, before their friends. It's a thorny dilemma—small wonder they're so upset."

Williams, who wasn't a believer, could only shake his head in confusion as he held the door for her. "Isn't this a moot point? Wouldn't God already know that he didn't kill himself?"

Doyle sighed, and wandered over to sit on the wrought-iron bench that was situated outside the church's side door. "Aye—but it would be a comfort to these people if God's earthly representative verified that fact—and they're bearin' a heavy load of shame, themselves. I know it sounds a bit strange to someone not steeped in it, but suicide is a mortal sin. Your life belongs to God, and you're supposed to accept what he's planned—lumps and all— and not decide that you'd rather not bear it. It's a shameful thing, to commit suicide."

Williams stood before her with his hands on his hips, reviewing the lichen-covered stone wall. "Especially if you do it because you're worried about getting caught for stealing."

She quirked her mouth in acknowledgement. "Another mortal sin, while we're countin'. His parents seemed to concede that he was committin' the crime, did you notice?"

"I did. And the mother had a very nice diamond bracelet."

Doyle glanced up in surprise. "Oh—did she? You've sharp eyes, Thomas Williams. Ill-gotten goods, d'you think?"

"I'll wager it would cost as much as a new automobile."

"Saints—that much?" asked Doyle, who wouldn't know. "That's interestin'. And another interestin' thing is they didn't approach Father Gregory about this—which is odd, regardless of the fire."

They were silent for a moment, thinking over this point. Williams ventured, "Priest shopping? They think your priest is a softer touch?"

But Doyle shook her head slightly. "That's not how it works—your parish is your parish, and your priest is your priest." Almost reluctantly, she lifted her gaze to meet his. "But recall that Holy Trinity was a meetin' place for all the villains in the corruption rig."

Williams tilted his head in implied skepticism. "So, your working theory is they dare not approach their own priest, because he may fear exposure, himself? Do you really think he's a player?"

Conceding that this seemed doubtful, Doyle leaned back, and blew a tendril of hair off her forehead. "I don't know what I think. But on the other hand, if you didn't notice who signed off on the suicide report, I'll wash my hands of you, DI Williams."

"I noticed," he replied, and offered nothing more.

The report had been signed by Chief Inspector Drake, who was Acton's equivalent at the CID, although he operated under a different Operational Command Unit. That DCI Drake had been hip-deep in the corruption rig was inarguable—mainly because he'd been photographed meeting with the other villains at the aforesaid Holy Trinity Church, now reduced to a pile of rubble.

However, it was unclear whether Drake was a willing participant, or whether he'd been blackmailed into compliance by the other players—and to be fair, there was much that was blackmail-worthy in Drake's past. But Drake hadn't been prosecuted along with all the others, and since Acton had never said anything to her about it, Doyle concluded that Acton wanted to protect Drake for some reason—which was not surprising, in that Acton tended to substitute his own judgment in the place of twelve fair-minded jurors.

And not to mention he'd hate any further disruption to their already-beleaguered department—and if Doyle remembered her evil schemes correctly, Drake was being blackmailed over a love affair, and so perhaps he wasn't quite as black-hearted as the other co-conspirators. Still and all, Drake's signature on the suicide report was another reason she was rapidly coming to the conclusion that she should lay the whole before her better half.

Williams interrupted her thoughts. "What's the protocol?"

With a sigh, she gathered her feet beneath her, and made ready to rise. "Let me speak with Acton, and see what he says—if it involves Drake, he may want to tread carefully."

"All right; let me know if you need my help, otherwise I'll stand down."

But as she took his arm to gain her feet, her scalp prickled, and she paused. "Would it be worth lookin' for a link to your cases? If this fellow was embezzlin' from his clients, mayhap he was connected to that embezzlement scheme you've been workin' on. It just seems so coincidental—that financial people are committin' suicide willy-nilly, and meanwhile there's a lot of money gone missin' from the corruption rig."

But Williams shrugged, as he helped her down the steps. "You'd be surprised how much white collar embezzlement is going on, Kath—it's practically an epidemic. And besides, the one I'm chasing is a cascade scheme, which is probably beyond this victim's pay grade."

She squinted up at him. "Tell me what that means, Thomas, in plain language."

"It's called 'running a cascade'. There are multiple connected accounts set up, and as soon as law enforcement closes in on one, those players disappear and the money is funneled into another account—often carried over as cash, and by hand, so it's difficult to trace—and other players pick up where the first ones left off. It can keep building up indefinitely."

She grimaced. "Faith, it sounds like blind man's bluff, with the Met as the blind man."

He nodded in acknowledgement. "Similar. It's frustrating; just when we think we're getting close, the trail disappears, and the money just keeps building up at another location. So, instead of the usual case—where we trace the missing money electronically—whenever we think there's a cascade scheme, we try to find a player who is willing to grass, instead of wasting our time trying to trace the funds. We look for the money only after we've ID'd the suspects, and can apply some pressure on someone."

Gazing into the distance, she said slowly, "But you can't even do that, if the people who would normally be the grassers keep turnin' up dead-by-suicide."

They'd stopped before his car, parked on the street, and he thought this over for a moment. "I suppose it's possible, but it seems unlikely, Kath. Embezzlers at this high level tend to be white-collar, savvy financial people, and—most importantly—they tend not to be killers. And besides, someone would have connected those dots before now—it would have been obvious."

"Not if these financial district suicides are really misdirection murders."

To his credit, Williams was willing to consider this possibility, as he helped her into the passenger seat. "All right. I'll have someone see if there's any kind of correlation. Munoz, maybe—she's working on known associates, already."

But Doyle could not hide her sidelined dismay at this revelation, and stared at him in surprise. "What? Munoz is workin' on financial crimes, now?"

Williams shrugged a shoulder. "We're short-handed, and she's good with numbers."

"I've never met a number that didn't hate me," Doyle admitted in a glum tone.

He closed the door, and came around to slide in the driver's seat. "Cheer up; she'd change places with you in a heartbeat."

Somewhat comforted by this thought, Doyle asked, "Has she said anything about Savoie's bein' in prison?" Detective Sergeant

Munoz had been dating Savoie, before he'd landed himself in the nick. The relationship had necessarily been kept rather quiet, being as a DS at the CID probably shouldn't be dating someone who figured so prominently on the Watch List.

But Williams would not be drawn. "If you think I'm going to bring up that subject with her, you've got another think coming."

Doyle ventured, "Well, I think Officer Gabriel rather fancies her."

Amused, he met her gaze for a moment, as he pulled out of the space into the street. "I don't think that means much, Kath—everyone fancies her."

"Except you."

"Except me," he agreed, as he navigated into traffic. "And besides, Gabriel's got a live-in girlfriend."

Doyle frowned for a moment. "That's what everyone keeps sayin', but have you ever met her?"

He laughed, as he turned toward Kensington. "Do you think he's making it up?"

"I don't know what I think," Doyle admitted a bit crossly, and as usual, it was true.

Chapter 7

Perhaps in a few days he'd suggest,
very gently, that they retire to Trestles.

Doyle was relieved to find that her husband had beaten her home for lunch, and that Reynolds had prepared some sort of quiche before making himself scarce, so that for a few blessed minutes it was just the two of them.

"Like old times," she teased, as he helped her sit. "Never to return."

He smiled slightly, as he seated himself across from her. "I am given to understand that those who've had children are the happier for it."

"I don't doubt it, Michael, but you have to admit they expect you to take a giant leap of faith, in the meantime."

"They do," he agreed, and lifted his fork.

They ate for a while in companionable silence—it was one of the things she missed about their former life; she and he were not the sort of people who needed to fill the silences. Thinking along these lines, she glanced up at him. "Do you play chess?"

Surprised, he met her gaze. "Not as of late. Why?"

"Edward's goin' to want to play chess with you," she pronounced. "So, best be ready."

He raised his brows, and re-addressed his meal. "I will have to brush-up."

"Not right away, of course," she cautioned. "He has to learn to talk and such, first."

"Understood."

Doyle bent to her own meal again, satisfied. Whilst she was not the social type, Acton was an out-and-out recluse—faith, he was still adjusting to her presence, in his life. She'd hit upon the chess-playing idea as a means to rope him in to spending quality time with his son, just in case he wasn't naturally inclined to do so. Besides, chess seemed like something the aristocrats liked to do, if the shows on the telly were any indication. She could watch, and keep score.

Pausing, she glanced up at him again. "I think Williams is worried that he's still in your black book."

Her husband reached for his glass. "No; Williams is not in my black book." It was true, and he knew that she would know it was true, and it was overall a huge relief—although why it would be a huge relief remained unclear; it had something to do with her conviction that her husband was up to something.

Watching him for a moment, she asked, "Is Drake in your black book? He's been layin' low, lately."

Acton cut another piece—he was the sort of person who would use a knife on quiche—and offered, "Drake is lucky he is not in prison."

She ventured, "Thanks to you, I think."

He paused in lifting his glass, and glanced out the window for a moment. "There were extenuating circumstances."

This was true, and Doyle bent to push her quiche around with her fork. "Well, I hope he's learned his lesson, and will stray no more. The last thing we need is another brass officer in the nick—can't imagine he'd start evangelizin,' like the DCS."

"Unlikely," Acton agreed with a smile. "Although the DCS was an unlikely candidate, himself."

"A gallows conversion," she agreed with a touch of derision, and then hastily decided that perhaps she shouldn't raise the subject of insincere religious conversions—after all, the jury was still out when it came to her better half, here. Therefore, there was no time like the present to bring up the primary topic to be addressed. "Whilst I was at the church, Father John wanted me to meet with a bereaved couple who were worried that their son's suicide was actually a homicide."

She had the immediate sense that he was not pleased, and so she hastened to assure him, "I'm not workin' the case, I promise. It's more that they're lookin' for the bishop to grant absolution, so that their son can have a funeral mass."

"What is the name?"

She told him, and he pulled his mobile to make a note of it. "I will look into it."

Tentatively, she suggested, "Father John hinted that if a murder case was opened, it may be enough for the bishop to allow absolution straightaway."

Lifting a brow, he glanced up at her. "Do we want to put a thumb on the scales?"

"No," she admitted. "If it's truly a suicide, then the bishop's hand shouldn't be forced—he answers to a higher authority. But I felt sorry for them—the parents, I mean; I think they knew he was guilty of his crimes, and couldn't decide which was more shameful, that he was murdered for his sins, or that he was unshriven."

"I will do a review, and see whether a follow-up is necessary," he assured her, and sheathed his mobile.

That's odd, she thought; he didn't ask who'd handled it, and since it was Drake, it meant he'd be meddling in another DCI's file. Not that the protocols mattered much to Acton in the first place, of course.

Before she could fill him in, however, he'd moved on to the next topic, and leaned back to regard her thoughtfully. "I am wondering if we should arrange for Gemma to attend the same school as Emile, when the fall session begins. St. Margaret's has a pre-school program, and Gemma would benefit from socialization with other children, I think."

Rather surprised that he'd even considered it, Doyle considered it in turn. "All right, Michael, I'll mention it to Mary." She made a wry mouth. "It goes without sayin' that she'll be all afret about your payin' for it."

"Then she must be convinced it would be no burden, but instead a benefit to us. Mary would be free to concentrate on Edward, and Gemma can be amongst other children her own age. It would be for a few hours, only."

"Gemma's very shy," Doyle agreed. "I hope it won't traumatize the poor thing, to be pitchforked amongst the toffs." Doyle could relate, having been pitchforked amongst the toffs, herself.

Acton contemplated this aspect for a moment, but concluded, "If she is unhappy, then we will reconsider. But we will be sponsoring her, and so surely the staff will smooth her way."

Doyle couldn't help but smile, as she reached for his hand. "So; we find out that you are as kind as you are generous."

She expected a teasing response, but instead he held the hand in his, and met her eyes with all seriousness. "I suppose her situation reminds me of your situation, when you were growing up in Dublin, with your mother."

Touched, she pulled his hand toward her to kiss its back. "My 'situation' turned out very well, I'm thinkin'."

But she caught a glimpse of deep unhappiness, as he continued, "You suffered so many hardships. I wish I'd been able to smooth your way."

Gently, she reminded him, "My mother never made it seem so, Michael. We always had each other, and it always seemed enough. And besides, you've forgotten your scripture about purifyin' the gold—you're supposed to look at hardships as part of the grand plan."

"No more hardships," he pronounced with certainty. "I will see to it."

"If you say so, Michael," she returned diplomatically, and wondered why her scalp was prickling; it was not as though he could wave a magic wand, and make it so. "And I will agree with you in that it seems no one's paid much attention to poor little Gemma—save Mary, of course."

Acton nodded. "And even Mary's not been long in her life."

"I suppose not, if Gemma only went to live with Blakney and Mary after Giselle was murdered." She glanced up at him. "Although you're not sure Giselle was her mother in the first place, I think."

"No, I'm not," he agreed, and contemplated the glass in his hand. "Although I'm not certain it's worth untangling."

Doyle teased, "It's that wretched 'army-man', again, isn't it? He's thrown you off, but I'll bet a penny to a pound that he and Blakney were just mates, and Blakney called him 'sir' as a laugh."

"I might agree with you," Acton replied, "except for the interesting fact that Gemma attended their meetings."

Doyle blinked, as this did seem strange—and again, trust Acton to have noticed it. "Then mayhap the 'army-man' was her true father, who wasn't able to raise her, for some reason. He was married, or stationed overseas, or somethin'."

"Perhaps," Acton agreed.

His mobile pinged, and all further discussion was put paid by the arrival of Lizzie Mathis and Emile, who did not seem at all fazed by the fact that his father was incarcerated in a Category B prison, and instead described the visit with a great deal of enthusiasm. "The guard pinned my drawing up on the wall, so that everyone could see it. He wore a gun, but he wouldn't let me hold it."

"No?" said Acton. "You astonish me."

"They played football with me in the hallway—I scored the most points."

"Faith, Emile; you're supposed to be visitin' your poor Papa," Doyle reminded him.

But Emile only laughed. "Papa played, too. He was on my team."

"Ah," said Doyle.

"He said I was to be nice to you, because you were being so nice to me." He paused, and then added, "He told me I wasn't going back to St. Petersburg—that was all a mistake."

"I am that happy to hear it," Doyle replied gamefully. "We'd surely miss you."

"I'll be going, then," Mathis advised, as she headed for the door.

With some alarm, Doyle watched Mathis ditch them, and asked Acton, "When's Reynolds due back?"

"I will call him," Acton offered, and walked into the bedroom, toward the sanctuary of his desk.

"Watch this, watch this," Emile called out excitedly, and then proceeded to do a dramatic re-enactment of one of his prison-hallway goals, using an imaginary ball.

Doyle sank into the sofa to watch him for a moment, and then offered in a loud voice, "D'you know what, Emile? I know someone who wants to take you to the zoo."

Chapter 8

He was quite looking forward to his confirmation.

That night, Doyle had one of her dreams.

She had them, occasionally—only they weren't truly very dream-like; instead they usually featured some person—oftentimes a dead person—who was trying to convey some sort of message. The message never seemed to be straightforward, and the dreams were—truth to tell—a bit frustrating, because the message invariably concerned some dire event that was unfolding or about to unfold, and Doyle always felt as though she wasn't quite up to the task of deciphering whatever it was that she was supposed to be deciphering. Nonetheless, she was never anxious or frightened by these dreams; mainly, she was resigned to paying attention, even though it was never very easy.

This time, the person who confronted her was entirely unexpected; the small, slight figure of a priest smiled at her benignly. His hands were clasped before him, and he appeared to be of an Asian race—Pacific Islander, perhaps.

Since he made no attempt to speak, Doyle ventured, "I don't believe we've met."

"Oh, no," the priest shook his head, slightly. "No."

He smiled his serene smile, and didn't seem motivated to continue the conversation.

"What's happened to you?" This seemed the appropriate gambit to get the dire-warnings conversation started; she had some sleep to catch, in miserable snatches, and this fellow was breaking up her fitful rhythm.

"Yellow fever," he explained. "I was part of the immunization outreach, in Togo."

"Oh—I'm that sorry for it; it hardly seems fair."

He bowed his head. "I vowed obedience."

Doyle frowned doubtfully. "I don't know as I'd be any good at obedience."

"Oh, no," he agreed again, with a smile. "No."

She wasn't certain whether it was a sin to be impatient with a priest, and so she decided that instead, she would be as subtle as a serpent. "Tell me, Father, is there anythin' that I can do for you?"

Thus prompted, the man's expression grew a bit grave. "Your husband is paying my sister, and she is troubled by it."

There was a small pause, whilst Doyle wondered if she'd heard him aright. "He—he is?"

"Oh, yes." He nodded. "Blood-money."

Doyle stared at him, astonished. "Why—whatever d'you mean? Who's your sister?"

But instead of hearing an answer, she found that she was staring at her darkened bedroom wall, and listening to the sound of her accelerated heartbeat, echoing in her ears.

Doyle slept deeply the remainder of the night, and woke the next morning feeling more refreshed than her usual. As she lay in bed and watched Acton review his caseload updates, she debated her options. Apparently, her better half was paying blood-money to a dead priest's sister—talk about your improbable scenarios, there was the corker. But the priest seemed sincere, and the fact that he was willing to haunt her dreams about it meant that she should shake her stumps and find out what it was he was talking about, no matter how fantastic the idea.

No point in asking Acton; if it was something he hadn't yet told her, it was something he wanted well-hidden. Besides, sometimes these dreams seemed to center on the proposition that Acton needed to be saved from himself—with Doyle as prime saver—since she was literally the only person on earth who could persuade her renegade husband to veer from his chosen course. With this extraordinary talk of blood-money, this seemed to be one of those times.

So; Acton was paying the mysterious sister blood-money— and for a mysterious purpose, since you didn't just throw blood-money around like penny-cards on the bar. She could try to ask Layton, who handled Acton's finances—it would come as no surprise that Layton knew more than his share of secrets, both of the bloody and non-bloody variety. The problem, of course, was that Layton wouldn't give them up to the likes of the fair Doyle, and instead would grass to her spouse at the first opportunity— he'd regret having to do it, but Layton was nothing if not loyal.

She paused, because Acton had been at Layton's yesterday—ostensibly to pick up his birth certificate—but clearly that was an excuse, and if Doyle didn't have overly-pregnant brain, she'd have seen right through it. After all, there were probably a hundred suited minions at Layton's who'd be only too happy to deliver Lord Acton's birth certificate wherever he directed them to.

So, the remaining option would be to investigate from the other end of the stick—discover who the sister was, and why she was troubled about whatever it was that she was troubled about.

With this object in mind, she ventured in a casual tone, "I'd like to meet Nellie for coffee today, just to make sure we have all our ducks in a rope for the confirmation."

"Of course," Acton agreed, and turned his chair around to face her. "I only ask that you don't venture too far afield."

But she'd caught his flare of amusement, and with a smile, she teased, "Knocker. You should correct me when I get somethin' wrong; I'll never learn, else."

With his own small smile, he bent his head, and contemplated the floor. "The ducks are in a row."

Frowning, she considered this. "Truly? I think it makes more sense to put them in a rope."

He tilted his head. "A rope seems a bit cruel."

"They're Irish ducks," she declared. "They're used to it. Not like your St. Petersburg ducks, who're fed cinnamon pastries all day, and would probably faint if someone shook a rope at them."

At this, he raised his brows, amused. "What is this?"

Smiling, she sank back into the pillows. "Just a conversation I was havin' with Emile, during one of the rare times he was sittin' still for more than a minute at a time. He thought he was going back to St. Petersburg, and was tellin' me all about feedin' the ducks."

"I can't say I'm sorry I missed it." He turned his wrist to check the time on his watch.

Why, she thought in surprise; there's something here—something he doesn't want me to know. Watching him from under her lashes, she casually stretched her arms over her head. "He misunderstood somethin', of course. Small chance of his goin' back to Russia, even if Savoie weren't coolin' his heels in the nick."

"Small chance," he agreed, and closed his laptop with a click.

Ah. Doyle considered the ceiling, and wondered what it all meant. It must have to do with Savoie's escape, she realized; and wouldn't it be crackin' grand if Savoie was planning to take Emile, and flee to Russia? After all, Solonik—the boy's real father—had tried to muscle in on Savoie's operations, and so Savoie might want to return the favor, and muscle in on the Russian operations. Although from what she knew of the Russian underworld, they wouldn't take kindly to foreigners trying to muscle in on their turf—and besides, with Solonik long-dead, no doubt the vultures had already descended on that particular carcass.

She repositioned a pillow, and tried to remember what it was like to lie comfortably in bed. So, that probably wasn't it—Savoie wasn't planning on fleeing to Russia. Mayhap he was worried about stashing the boy somewhere safe, whilst he was imprisoned? It was no secret that he doted on the boy, and Savoie had a basketful of enemies. Although—although that didn't make a lot of sense, either. Presumably, there was no safer place to stash Emile than here at castle Acton, seven stories up in a Kensington security building.

Acton rose. "Have we a full contingent, today?"

"We do. Best make your escape whilst you can, my friend."

He leaned to kiss her, and rest a fond hand on her belly. "Let me know if anything is needed."

"Courage," she teased. "Along with a side helpin' of patience."

"I have every confidence," he replied, and—rather to her surprise—it was true.

With a small frown, Doyle stared out the window for a moment, listening to him take his leave of Reynolds and Emile. Now, here was another interesting little wrinkle; she'd been so busy being a crosspatch that she hadn't considered the extraordinary fact that Acton was in good spirits, and—knowing her husband as she did—he shouldn't have been, what with the corruption trials mucking up the system, and the baby about to be born. She knew that he wasn't putting up a brave front just to reassure her—instead, he was genuinely content, even with the daily chaos in the flat, and the unwanted attention on his religious conversion.

He's got some sort of gambit going, she concluded, and it appears to be going well—so well that he's not putting away a bottle of scotch each and every day, which would be much more in keeping.

The mysterious blood-money? Could that be at the root of her husband's good mood? Although—although she didn't get the sense that he was pleased because he'd covered up something; instead, she'd the sense he was pleased because he was outwitting somebody—the same sense as when he was on the brink of solving a thorny case. There was nothing Acton liked better than turning the tables.

With a small sigh, she decided that whatever-it-was would have to wait until after the confirmation—one crisis at a time, and besides, the crisis with the priest-ghost should probably take precedence over all non-religious-themed crisises. Rising to her feet, she resisted the temptation to peek at Acton's laptop, and instead headed to the shower.

Chapter 9

He spoke with Hudson about the furniture delivery for the nursery, and the need to distract Williams.

Because Reynolds wanted to do some housecleaning, Doyle decided that she would take the two children with her when she walked over to the coffeehouse to meet with Nellie. In general, Emile behaved himself in public—Savoie's influence, no doubt—and Gemma was too shy to act up.

Nellie was already waiting for them, and had saved a table by the window. She was a capable Filipino woman who volunteered at St Michael's, and generally acted as Father John's administrator, since the parish hadn't sufficient funds to hire anyone in that capacity. As an experienced mother of nine, Nellie sized-up Emile at a glance, and commandeered the boy to assist her in placing the order at the counter, leaving Doyle and Gemma to watch the passersby out the window.

As the little girl seemed disinclined to speak, Doyle offered, "We were thinkin', Gemma, that you could go to Emile's school, in the fall. It would only be for the mornin's, and it might be fun for you, to play with the other children."

"Oh," the girl replied, her dark eyes gazing up at Doyle. "Will my mum be at the school?"

Hearing the thread of anxiety in her voice, Doyle reached over to cover the little girl's hand. "Your mum will be at my flat, helpin' with baby Edward. But you'll come home to be with us, and we'll all have lunch together."

The small face brightened. "Will Reynolds make lunch?"

"Indeed, he will. Never doubt it."

Gemma ducked her head and smiled. "All right."

With a pang, Doyle squeezed the girl's hand. Small blame to her, for worrying about any coming changes; her short life had been nothing but upheaval, starting from day one.

Nellie and Emile appeared, Emile carefully balancing the cup-holder that held Gemma's cocoa. "Here you go, Gemma," he said, and only spilled it slightly, as he laid it before her.

"Thank you," the girl replied in her soft voice.

"*Spasibo*," the boy corrected, with a gleam.

"*Spasibo*," she amended.

"*Pazhalooysta*," he replied.

Grand, though Doyle; Emile is teaching Gemma to speak Russian. Better she improves on her English, first—although I suppose I'm not the one to cast that stone.

Nellie doled out the coffee, and took her seat. "Have you heard? The bishop will stay for the reception after the ceremony." Her voice held equal parts gratification and dread. "I wish we'd thought to have the floors refinished in the hall, when we were refinishing the pews."

Doyle blew on her cup impatiently. "Paint a mural on the ceilin', like they do at the Vatican. He'll never even look at the floor."

But Nellie was in a fine fret, and wasn't about to be distracted. "I'll have to use plastic ware—we haven't enough china plates."

"Nellie, for heaven's sake, if he's any decent kind of bishop, he won't care. Not to mention Acton will gladly stand the ready for a new set of plates."

But Nellie shook her head with resolution. "Acton's the honoree, Kathleen. I cannot ask it of him."

"Suit yourself," Doyle advised, and smiled to herself; Nellie was a wily one.

"Father Gregory will attend, also."

"Ah—now I see why you're so worried about the plates," Doyle teased. Father Gregory Brown was the pastor from the now-defunct Holy Trinity Church, and was generally known to appreciate the finer things—it was often the case, with a priest from a wealthy parish; the parishioners tended to spoil their pastor, and it was a hard thing, indeed, to resist such treatment. "Hope we're servin' somethin' worthy."

"Punch and cake," Nellie advised, not quite concealing her disappointment. "Father John asked that we keep it simple."

Doyle couldn't help but laugh. "You mean Acton did; Father John would have barkers out front with megaphones, if he thought he could get away with it." They shared a smile, and Doyle sipped her coffee—it was still too hot, but well-worth the scalded tongue. "It seems a little odd that Father Gregory is comin' over for the confirmation, after all that's happened. I wonder if he wants to put Acton to the touch for the rebuildin' fund, since there was no insurance."

Nellie suddenly looked stricken, and lowered her voice. "I'm not sure there is a rebuilding plan, Kathleen."

Doyle stared at her in surprise. "What? They're not goin' to rebuild Holy Trinity?"

"There are—" here, she glanced around, "there are rumors of criminal wrongdoing."

"Faith, I could have told you that, Nellie; the place was brimful of villains. But it seems strange that they're not plannin' on startin' afresh—that's a crackin' big parish to shut down." She slid her companion a glance. "Hope they're not just goin' to turn it over to the evangelicals, and concede defeat."

"Father John knows something about the plan, going forward," Nellie admitted. "But he's not saying."

The children had finished their treat, and so Nellie instructed them to guess how many women would pass by the window before they saw one in a red coat. While they were thus occupied, Doyle decided she'd best get to finding out what she needed to know before a red-coated woman wandered by. "Speakin' of priests, I'm investigatin' somethin', and I came across the snap of priest who looked as though he might be Filipino. A small man, fiftyish—d'you know who it could be?"

"There are many Filipino clergy," Nellie observed with no small pride. "Which parish?"

"I'm not sure, but I think he was part of the immunization outreach in Africa." She paused, trying to remember. "Gogo, or someplace like that."

Startled, Nellie met her eyes. "Oh—could it have been Father Danilo? He died on the African mission."

"Why—yes," Doyle agreed, suppressing her satisfaction. "I think that's the one."

Nellie nodded a bit sadly. "I knew him well—he was the associate pastor for Holy Trinity Church, before he left to lead the medical mission, in Africa. A very good priest—many thought he'd be appointed pastor, when Father Hugh retired, but then Father Gregory was transferred in, instead. We couldn't have an absent pastor, after all, and—" here she lowered her voice in disapproval, "I think some of the congregants didn't want a Filipino pastor to lead the parish."

But Doyle wasn't as interested in church politics as much as she was in following up on her own late-night puzzle. "And then he died, whilst he was ministerin' in Africa."

Hesitating, Nellie lowered her voice. "Yes, but it may have been a blessing. His sister was the charwoman there—the one who started the Holy Trinity fire." She shook her head. "It would have killed Father Danilo—he was so devoted to that church."

There was a long moment of silence, whilst Doyle struggled with this confusing revelation. "Are they certain she's the one who did it?"

Nellie sighed. "Well, I suppose we can never be certain, but it does makes sense. She was—" here, Nellie hesitated. "She was a bit simple. Someone who'd be easily persuaded by the evangelicals."

But this was a bridge too far for Doyle, who openly scoffed, "For heaven's sake, Nellie; the evangelicals aren't tellin' people to torch RC churches."

"Oh, no; no, of course not. But it was very much in keeping—that she'd think it necessary, for some reason." She fingered her cup, and repeated with regret, "She was a bit simple."

Doyle frowned, utterly confounded. "And now she is dead."

"Yes—poor soul."

Hitting on a possible explanation, Doyle ventured, "Did Father Danilo have any other sisters?"

Nellie raised her brows. "Not that I am aware—although his mother is still alive, and lives near Sabu. Why?"

Doyle watched the children breathe fog-clouds onto the window glass, and carefully chose what to say. "I'm just—well, it would help with my investigation if you'd ask around, Nellie. I'm lookin' for relatives."

Nellie nodded, and thankfully didn't seem to think this request was unusual—although if she'd already heard rumors of criminal wrongdoing at Holy Trinity, she would no doubt think it connected.

Much struck, Doyle paused with this thought. *Was* it connected? It did seem an extraordinary coincidence, that the church that had served as a meeting place for the corruption rig players got itself burned down—not to mention assorted priests and charwomen seemed to be dyin', left and right.

After gathering up the children and taking her leave of Nellie, Doyle uneasily pursued this train of thought, as she walked back to the flat, listening to Emile's chatter with half an ear. Father Danilo said that Acton was paying blood-money to his sister, but the only known sister was dead—after torching a church, no less—so perhaps there was a spare sister in the woodwork, somewhere. And why would Acton be paying these people at all? Blood-money, the dead priest had said—and presumably, he would know.

With a sense of growing dismay, she finally examined a thought that she'd been trying to avoid examining. One of the things you learned at the Crime Academy was that committing a successful arson wasn't easy, which was why so many arsonists wound up dead or in prison. The charwoman was a simple woman, Nellie had said, yet she'd done a spectacular job of burning the place to the ground. Acton, himself, had burned down a building or two in his youth—but it was completely unthinkable, that Acton would burn down a church—wasn't it?

"It makes no sense a'tall," Doyle confessed aloud. "I'm lost."

"No, we're almost home," Emile assured her, pointing forward. "Look, there's the doorman."

Chapter 10

Interesting, that the zoo outing incited such interest.
No matter; a worthy opponent made the victory that
much sweeter.

"Y ou should come," Doyle teased Acton. "It's just the sort of outin' you'd prefer."

It was the week-end, and true to his word, Williams was taking Emile on an expedition to the zoo, along with his young cousins. The party had expanded because Officer Gabriel had caught wind of it, and asked if he could bring his younger sister, Marnie, and then Doyle had decided that she may as well come along as an excuse to invite Mary and Gemma. She was rather hoping to re-kindle Williams' romance with Mary—if it could even be called that—and it wouldn't hurt to throw them together again, this time in a situation that didn't involve mysteriously dead husbands.

Acton responded to her teasing with his usual politeness. "As tempting as it sounds, I must regretfully decline."

"Don't forget about the church dishes." They'd decided that Lizzie Mathis was going to deliver a set of plate-ware to the church, and claim they were only on loan from Trestles for the occasion. Nellie, of course, would come to the complicit understanding that they'd never be reclaimed; Doyle was a wily one, too.

"Mathis will make the delivery this morning."

"You're a good man." She lifted her face for his kiss, and noted that he seemed in good spirits, yet again, which apparently came from masterminding some scheme that may-or-may-not involve arson. Arson, blood-money, and the ducks of St. Petersburg.

Startled, she wondered where this last thought had come from—for the love o' Mike, her poor overly-pregnant brain was working as a sad shadow of its former self, if her intuition was dwelling on Emile, and his tales of duck-feeding.

Acton broke into her thoughts. "Do you have any spending money?"

She glanced up at him. "Oh—d'you suppose I'll need it? I have my credit card."

Pulling his wallet from his inner jacket pocket, he produced a few crisp bills. "Best be safe—the children may want treats from the vendors."

"Oh—oh, of course, Michael. Thank you." Thinking about this, she added, "And I suppose I should offer to pay for Mary and Gemma's admission, too. I think poor Mary's pockets-to-let, and I wouldn't want to break her weekly budget."

"It may be simpler to pay for everyone," Acton suggested gently. "And thus spare her feelings."

Seeing the wisdom of this, Doyle confessed, "That kind of thing never occurs to me, Michael, because I never had any money to speak of, before I met you."

He smiled, and rested a palm against her cheek. "You do, now. As much as you'd like."

Laughing, she warned, "Don't try to spoil me, husband—I'll wind up like that wife in the tale about the magic fish, and never be satisfied."

"I disagree," he said softly, and caressed the cheek under his hand. "Instead, you are satisfied with very little."

She clasped his hand, and turned it to kiss the palm. "All I need is you, my friend."

This promising tête-a-tête was interrupted when the concierge buzzed to say that the driver was downstairs, and so Doyle gathered up Emile, and bid her husband farewell.

"Make certain to check in with me," he reminded her as they left, and she winked in acknowledgment. In truth, it was a bit surprising that he was willing to let her wander about at will, the past few days—he tended to keep her close, especially now that she was full term. Of course, she'd have Williams and Gabriel with her, so there would be plenty of loyal help at hand.

And besides, Acton wanted to take this opportunity to sneak off to Layton's, again, even though he'd said nothing to her about it. With an inward sigh, she acknowledged that there was something brewing over there—over in the financial district— and that Acton was in the thick of it, for some reason.

And so, whilst Emile described the St. Petersburg zoo at great length, Doyle braced her back against the wall of the lift, and thought about her husband, who was dyin' to shower riches on his hardscrabble bride, even though she wouldn't know what to do with it, even if he did. Faith, she'd never even asked about his wealth—wasn't very interested, in fact—but she'd always had the sure impression that Acton had buckets of money. His grandfather had married an heiress, of course, but she knew that it was ridiculously expensive to own a fancy flat in Kensington— not to mention an estate like Trestles, where there didn't seem to be anything particularly productive going on, aside from a lot of trimming and flowerbed-gardening.

Of course, her husband had been involved with Savoie in his illegal-weapons rig, and it must have paid well—never a shortage of black-market buyers, after all—but it was clear that Acton was not one to let the grass grow under his feet, when it came to building up the family fortunes.

So—Acton was in cahoots with Layton about something, and, on the side, he was paying blood-money to a dead priest's sister. But until she could discover a potential sister who wasn't yet dead, this seemed to be a dead end, itself.

"Do you think there will be ducks, at this zoo?"

Something in the child's voice pulled her out of her thoughts, and she contemplated the small face that was turned up to hers. Leaning down as best she could, Doyle suggested gently, "Would you rather we avoided the ducks, Emile?"

Sobering, he nodded, and for once, seemed at a loss for words.

"*Saints* and holy angels," Doyle declared in a voice of righteous anger. "Never say one of those black-hearted St. Petersburg ducks haled off and bit you?"

Silently, he nodded, and then hesitated slightly, before pushing up his sleeve to reveal a small white scar, on his forearm.

Taking his arm, Doyle examined it carefully. "Well, if any one of those paltry London ducks tries to come near you, I will shoot him dead, Emile. My hand on my heart."

With a small smile, the boy ducked his head self-consciously. "When I held the bread, they all came in a bunch, hissing at me."

"Not on my watch, they won't."

The doors slid open, and the boy glanced up. "Don't tell anyone."

Doyle nodded solemnly, as they stepped out of the lift. "I won't, but you should—scars are very interestin'. Your Papa has one on his face, and everyone who meets him wonders how it got there."

Brightening, the boy disclosed, "He said it was a knife-fight."

"There you go. He had a knife-fight, you had a duck-fight."

With a bark of laughter, the boy bounded across the lobby.

Nothin' to this havin' boys business, thought Doyle, as she followed him; I don't know what I was so worried about. She nodded to the concierge and greeted the driver, who was examining Emile's scar with great interest.

Chapter 11

"By your wisdom and understanding you have made wealth for yourself, and have gathered gold and silver into your treasures."

The zoo visitors were all assembled outside the giraffe exhibit, and Doyle found it all very interesting, since she'd never seen a giraffe outside of a picture book. As a matter of fact, she'd found many things very interesting this morning, and truth to tell, she was well-tired of it. I keep forgetting that there's a good reason I can't abide crowds, she thought; mental note.

The first interesting thing had to do with Officer Gabriel, who was on indefinite loan to the CID from the MI 5 domestic counter-terrorism people, lending a hand whilst Scotland Yard worked to dig itself out from under the unholy mess that was left-over from the corruption cases. The young man had been assigned to a few cases with Doyle, and although she felt they were friends, of sorts, she always had the feeling that she couldn't read him very well—he played his cards very close to the vest. Indeed, Acton had mentioned that Gabriel was originally called-in to monitor DCI Drake on the sly, but now that Drake was off-the-hook, Gabriel's role seemed to have evolved into helping out where help was needed—they were so short-handed.

To everyone's surprise, Gabriel brought along his elusive girlfriend—a tall, willowy blonde who seemed a bit reserved, in contrast to Gabriel's hail-fellow-well-met likability.

Doyle would have written it off as the attraction of opposites, except that such wasn't the case. Even though there was now proof-positive that the mysterious girlfriend existed, Doyle knew—in the way that she knew things—that the young woman was not, in truth, Gabriel's girlfriend, and that there was no romantic attachment between the two. Exactly why such lengths had been taken in this ongoing pretense remained a mystery, and Doyle decided that she didn't much care.

On the other hand, she was glad to see Gabriel's little sister Marnie again—the girl was in-between rounds of cancer treatment, and her prognosis was now excellent. She was a bit pale and thin, but informed Doyle that she was going back to school in the fall.

"I'm going to school, too," Emile broke in importantly. The older girl was roundly ignoring the younger children, and it was clear that Emile found this type of treatment unacceptable. "I'm going to wear a uniform."

Marnie frowned at the boy. "Where are you from?"

"St. Petersburg," he replied, happy to have garnered her attention. "I was going back to live there, but now I'm not."

Doyle had forgotten that the boy had a trace of an accent—being as everyone who wasn't Irish always had a strange accent, anyways—but she was reminded that she should find out why Emile had believed he was returning to Russia. With Savoie in prison, it seemed a very unlikely possibility—perhaps the boy had misunderstood a chance remark. It was bothering her poor, disfunctioning pregnant-brain, for some reason.

Whilst Marnie and Emile were talking, Gabriel's erstwhile girlfriend took the opportunity to approach Doyle. She was coolly attractive—tall and lean, and as Doyle was currently envious of anyone who was tall and lean, she had to tamp down an impulse to entertain uncharitable thoughts. Although to be fair, there did seem to be a valid basis for uncharitable thoughts; whilst the girl's manner was warm, behind her eyes she was a bit cold, and assessing. In a strange way, she reminded Doyle of Lizzie Mathis.

"I'm so happy to meet you, Lady Acton; I'm a big fan."

This was, of course, in reference to the bridge-jumping incident. DS Munoz had been stabbed—and then thrown into the Thames, for good measure—and Doyle had been in the unfortunate position of coming to the rescue in spectacular fashion. The story had been picked up by the media, with the result that Doyle was now something of a folk-hero, despite her longing to be left alone. It all went to show you that no good deed went unpunished.

Doyle tried to be gracious, even though she knew the other girl's admiration was not exactly sincere. "It was nothin', truly; the papers made it up to be more than it was."

With a fond gesture, Gabriel hooked his arm through his companion's. "Easy, Tasza; the baroness hates to speak of her mighty deeds."

They all laughed—which is what Gabriel had intended—but Doyle's attention had been caught. Tasza? It was an unusual name, but she'd heard it before. Who else was named Tasza?

Gabriel continued, "And speaking of mighty deeds, Lady Acton was there on that fateful night when the DCS was brought down—at Acton's estate, no less. It must have been like a scene from *The Hound of the Baskervilles*."

Doyle didn't understand the reference, and so she merely said, "Well, it was a close-run thing. Horrifyin', to think that the DCS of Scotland Yard was such a blackleg, through-and-through. Lucky that Acton twigged on to it, in the nick of time."

"It is an extraordinary story," Tasza agreed. "But it's not yet been told, since now he's completely turned his life around."

As Doyle was winding up to say something rude and skeptical, Gabriel intervened smoothly, "Tasza follows the DCS's ministry, and finds it very inspiring."

"Oh," said Doyle, very much surprised. "Oh—well, I suppose his is a redemption story, then." She was understandably confused, because Tasza did not, in fact, find the DCS's ministry inspiring—it was not true, and Gabriel knew that it was not true. I wonder what's going on, here, she thought with a flare of impatience; for the love o' Mike, I just wanted to visit the zoo, and do a bit of matchmaking on the side.

Thus reminded, she glanced over to see that Williams was pulling his cousins off the wrought-iron fence, whilst Mary held Gemma's hand at a small distance. A nudge will be needful, and some delicacy besides—although delicacy wasn't exactly the fair Doyle's strong suit.

From the corner of her eye, Doyle noted that Gabriel and Tasza exchanged a glance, and then Tasza immediately addressed Doyle. "I should buy tickets so that the children may feed the elephants—the elephants are coming up, I think."

"That would be excellent," Doyle agreed, thinking that such a task might focus everyone's attention for a moment. As it was, the boys and Marnie were tearing around the elm tree that stood in the pathway, shrieking, whilst Williams watched with a benign eye. He then walked over to stand next to Mary, and the two began talking. Quickly looking about for the nearest bench, Doyle announced, "As a matter of fact, I think I'll sit here and rest for a moment, whilst you fetch the tickets."

"All right—will you help me, Marnie?"

After Tasza and the girl walked away, Doyle was not at all surprised to find that Gabriel came over to join her on the bench, his lanky legs stretched out before him as they observed the boundless energy on display. "What do you think of my Tasza? I'm worried you don't approve."

This was plain-speaking, but as Doyle excelled at plain-speaking, she was not thrown off. "I will admit that she doesn't seem your type."

He laughed aloud. "Wait—is this the part where we gleefully snub each other?"

Doyle had to laugh along with him. "I suppose it is. Although it would all be miles easier if you just explained to me outright what's goin' on, here."

There was a small pause. "I'd like to, but I can't," he offered in his easy manner. "Loose lips sink ships."

"Are you tryin' to sink Acton's ship?" she asked bluntly.

If he was thrown off by the question, he hid it well. "What is his ship doing, that you are worried about such a thing?"

"Never you mind," she replied mildly—as shame, that he hadn't answered the question. But Doyle had already gained the impression that Gabriel was well-aware that the illustrious Chief Inspector tended to sail a bit too close to the wind, and—probably because he was MI 5, after all—that this was not, in fact, objectionable to the young officer.

Teasing, Gabriel slid her a glance. "Big day, tomorrow."

Doyle smiled in response, happy he'd turned the topic. "Faith, don't remind me; the confirmation's timin' couldn't have been worse, what with me as big as a whale, and the Met so short-handed. At least the corruption rig is windin' down—it's hard to believe that it's all finally over and done with."

She then paused, wondering why her scalp was prickling. Truly, the conspiracy was indeed over and done with; all the lower-tier evildoers had twigged out all the upper-tier evildoers—as they always did, faith, you'd think the upper-tier evildoers would learn a lesson or two from history—and now everyone seemed confident that the corruption rig was dust and ashes, with salt sown into the ground, for good measure. Certainly, Acton seemed to think so, and Acton was someone who was warier than most.

Except that Acton was in a good mood, and it shouldn't worry her, but it did; there was something brewing, just under the surface, that he didn't want her to know about. Something that he was very pleased about, and that was apparently going forward at Layton's—although a less-likely fellow schemer than the elderly banker would be hard to imagine.

"Any chance I can attend? Or is it an exclusive event?"

Smiling, she shook her head. "Anyone can come witness a sacrament, Gabriel—they're not allowed to keep it private."

"I wouldn't want to offend."

She quirked her mouth. "You'll not fool me, my friend—you love to offend. But please come; Tasza too. Cake and punch in the church hall, after."

"Exactly the type of offerings I most enjoy. I'll bring my gun." This, in a sly reference to a best-be-forgotten occasion, where each of them had discovered that the other was carrying an illegal weapon.

"Well, don't shoot my poor priest, he's a vanishin' breed."

"Then I'll shoot all the evangelicals, instead, and even out the numbers."

This seemed a provocative comment, but Doyle was not about to delve into the Tasza-the-evangelical ruse, and merely quoted Father John. "We all have the same aim, Gabriel."

"That's as may be," he replied in an equivocal tone, and then rose to greet Tasza and Marnie as they approached; Marie having the look of a child who knew she had to be nice to her brother's girlfriend, but was not so inclined.

Mother a' mercy, but I hate crowds, thought Doyle, and went to seek out Williams, who'd wandered from Mary's side.

Chapter 12

The furniture was ready to be delivered,
with no one the wiser.

"Ho, Thomas," said Doyle. "Are you regrettin' your kind offer, yet?"

"It's going exactly as expected," he admitted with a smile. "And I don't mind at all—I'd forgotten how much fun the zoo is."

Doyle stood beside him, and watched the unbridled energy on display. "D'you think when Edward is this age, he'll be wantin' to climb up on everythin'? Faith, I'm goin' to have a daily heart attack."

Williams laughed. "A few cuts and bruises go with the territory, I'm afraid. If you're anything like my mother, you'll learn to take it in stride."

In an offhand manner, Doyle noted, "And Gemma's such a timid little thing—I wish we could rub some Emile-energy off on her."

"Very shy," he agreed, glancing over at the girl, who was clinging to her mother.

"Acton wants to send her to Emile's fancy school—there's a preschool, there. I haven't yet broached the subject with Mary, though; she may not like the idea."

Williams immediately gave Doyle a look that told her he was aware that she was trying to draw him out on the subject of Mary, and that he refused to be so drawn.

Smiling at being so easily caught out, Doyle rested a hand in the crook of his arm and squeezed. "Sorry."

"Allow me to handle my own affairs, Kath."

"Right-o," she agreed. "Instead, tell me why Gabriel would be angling for an invite to Acton's confirmation."

"Is he?" Williams thought about this, and shrugged. "I suppose it wouldn't hurt his career—maybe he'd like to transfer in on a permanent basis. I'm coming to it, myself, in the hope that I can work myself back into Acton's good graces."

But Doyle disagreed with this assessment. "You're not in Acton's dog house, Thomas, my hand on my heart. Instead, I think there's somethin' brewin', and he wants you well-away from it, for some reason."

Frowning slightly, he met her eyes. "What sort of thing?"

"I wish I knew." For a moment, she teetered on the edge of asking if he knew anything about the blood-money, but decided against it. Unlikely he would know, since Thomas was being kept out of the loop, and anyways, it sounded too ominous to say aloud—as though Acton was up to something truly evil, which he wasn't; please God, amen. Honestly, the ghost-priest needed to make it all a bit clearer, and not be so caught-up in contemplating the eternal mysteries.

"Oh? Are you expecting any trouble at the confirmation?"

Doyle could tell he was half-hoping; never one to shun a fistfight, was our Williams. "I hope not; the bishop will be there, and I hear that he's a righteous bishop, with a no-nonsense attitude. Which doesn't bode well for our poor suicide-embezzler, come to think of it."

She caught a sudden flare of emotion from her companion, and turned to him in surprise. "Why—what is it? What about the bishop?"

There was a small pause, and then Williams replied, "Nothing, Kath—it's probably nothing. I just want to look into something, is all."

Thoroughly alarmed by his reticence, she shook his arm impatiently. "Look into what? Thomas Williams, if you know somethin' about the bishop, tell me this instant."

"No—it's not about the bishop." He offered slowly, "It's about the embezzler—the suicide, who may-or-may-not be a misdirection murder."

She waited, then prompted, "And?"

He dropped his gaze to the pavement for a moment. "The parents said the son's new girlfriend was named Tasza, remember?"

There was a moment of alarmed silence, whilst Doyle resisted the urge to turn and stare at Gabriel's pretend-girlfriend. "Holy *Mother*, Thomas. What does it mean?"

But Williams was a good detective, and not a leaper-to-conclusions. "It may be a coincidence. I'll see if I can get a description from someone, to find out if it was really her. If it was, then she was two-timing Gabriel, and it's probably none of our business."

"Well, Gabriel was two-timin' her with Morgan Percy, lest we forget," Doyle noted fairly, "although I think that was strictly business." She decided not to mention that she also had the sense that the Gabriel-Tasza connection was strictly business, too; first, she had to decide what it all meant.

He shrugged slightly. "It may be nothing."

But she knew that he thought there was something there, and couldn't help but agree—it seemed too much a coincidence. "Tasza will be at the confirmation," Doyle disclosed with some alarm. "Do we warn anyone?"

Again, he shrugged. "I vote for no. It's none of our business."

Doyle decided she had to speak the thought aloud. "Unless she murdered the embezzler-suicide. Then it's our business, in spades."

But Williams only rested his thoughtful gaze on the rest of their party. "Let's not ruin Acton's confirmation with wild accusations, Kath."

She could only agree, and rather glumly contemplated the coming sacrament, which was supposed to be a joyous occasion, but which was fast devolving into a crackin' minefield, what with a potential murderess having open access to the punchbowl. "I hope it's not like one of those Agatha Christie stories with that funny little detective, where everyone's gathered together—all nice and polite—and then—bang—the boom gets itself lowered, when they least expect it."

He laughed. "I hope not, too, Kath." The conversation abruptly came to an end as he moved forward to separate two of his cousins, who had started shoving at each other with wild abandon.

Almost as soon as he walked away, Doyle was much heartened to see that Mary came forward, bringing Gemma, and smiling upon the sight of Williams separating the two tusslers.

"Such energy," she observed with a smile. "Their mother must appreciate this day off."

Doyle agreed whole-heartedly. "Williams is a semi-saint, to volunteer for this outin'. It was his idea, in fact—Emile was drivin' me mad." May as well openly boost Williams' stock; unlikely that Mary would give Doyle the let-me-handle-my-own-affairs snub.

Emile, who'd managed to stay out of the current round of trouble, called out to Gemma to join him at the railing, and Doyle noted—and not for the first time—that beneath the boy's madness-inducing energy he had a kind heart; he'd no doubt noticed that the little girl was outmanned and outnumbered.

Very pleased, Gemma hurried over to join Emile, after glancing back to make certain her mother stayed nearby.

"She's such a sweet little thing," Doyle offered.

Mary sighed. "She's so timid, though. I should join a play-group, but I'm not sure if that would only make matters worse."

This seemed to be an appropriate opening, and so Doyle ventured, "Acton was hopin' that you'd allow us to enroll her in Emile's school for two mornings a week. They've a preschool, and it may be just the thing for her."

Mary looked upon Doyle with alarm. "Oh—oh, I couldn't possibly—"

"Before you say no," Doyle interrupted, "remember that it would be to our benefit, too. You'd be able to concentrate on baby Edward, without any distractions."

Silently, Mary contemplated the small girl who was listening, wide-eyed, to whatever Emile was telling her about the animals presented before them. "She might feel out-of-place."

But Doyle already had a rejoinder prepared. "The church runs the school, Mary—I can't imagine they'd make her feel unwanted. And she's a bright little thing—it would give her an amazin' opportunity."

There was a small pause, whilst Doyle could sense Mary's desire to capitulate, but the woman's next words were a surprise. "I'm worried—I suppose I'm worried about filling out the necessary paperwork. I've never done anything to adopt her."

Doyle drew her brows together, surprised, but at the same time, not surprised—Blakney wasn't long dead, and Mary wasn't the sort of person to put herself forward. "Well, you could start the process now, and that would count for somethin' with the school, I would think. You were married to her father, after all—and besides, she's got no one else. It's not as though they'd take her away from you, Mary."

Mary pressed her lips together for a moment. "I think—" She paused. "I'm almost afraid to mention it, but I think she may not have been Bill's child—I think she was one of those foreign adoptions, that you hear about. Gemma used to speak a few words from other languages, once in a while, although it's happening less and less. I recognized a bit of French, I think, although I don't speak French, myself—and neither did Bill."

Now, there's a wrinkle, Doyle thought with all due surprise. And it does go to show that everyone speaks French but me. "But you're not sure? Faith, if she was a foreign adoption, it seems a bit odd that he'd never mentioned it to you."

She shook her head. "No—which is one of the reasons I'm a bit worried about starting a formal proceeding. Why would it be such a secret? And he was genuinely fond of her, there was no question about it. So, I suppose I can't be certain, it was just— just the feeling that I had. That, and the foreign words."

Thinking this over, Doyle's gaze rested on the children for a moment. "Did you ever run into Bill's ex-wife, Giselle? She hung about with some shady characters at a racecourse—a lot of them were French or Russian, with some shady Irish thrown in, for good measure. Mayhap Giselle took Gemma in from one of them, for some reason."

But Mary shook her head. "We never saw Giselle—she didn't seem to be involved with Gemma at all. It was another reason that I had the feeling I did." A bit stricken, she met Doyle's eyes. "I'm afraid to say anything that might alert the Child Protection Board."

But Doyle stoutly assured her, "If you think Acton's goin' to let anyone come between you and Gemma, you've sadly misjudged your man. Instead, they'll do whatever he asks— there's a different set of rules for the aristocracy—there shouldn't be, but there is—and may as well put it to good use."

"Oh," Mary said, brightening considerably. "Oh—I hadn't thought of that."

"Let me approach him, and see what's best to be done about St. Margaret's." With a small qualm of conscience, Doyle considered the fact that yet again, she was helping to pull the wool over the poor school's eyes, since Savoie had forged Emile's school-papers, too. Faith—it seemed like everywhere you looked, there were loose-end children, having to be buttoned up and put in their places.

She paused suddenly, because her scalp was prickling, and she immediately thought of Acton, although it made no sense. Acton wasn't a loose-end child; there was no dispute about his parentage—although it had practically taken an Act of Parliament to set it all straight, come to think of it. It's my overly-pregnant brain, again, she thought a bit crossly; I've too much on my plate, between the stupid ghost, and stupid Williams' star-crossed romance, and stupid Gabriel's pretend-girlfriend who may-or-nay-not be a murderess. It's truly a wonder I haven't gone barkin' mad.

Williams called out, "Come along, you two; we're going over to feed the elephants."

"Such a kind man—d'you see how he cares about animals?" Doyle dutifully observed to Mary.

Chapter 13

It was a long day for her, but if she were kept busy,
she wouldn't have a chance to look into the murders.

Doyle was sitting in her usual perch on the sofa at home, gazing at the fire and recovering from the day's events. Acton was not yet home, and by some miracle, Emile had been tired enough to consent to a nap, which meant the place was quiet, and Doyle had a few minutes to gather her thoughts together. Try as she might, though, she couldn't decide why her instinct had raised the alarm when she'd been discussing the children's school with Mary.

Loose-end children, she mused—that's what brought it on. And it just so happens that I've got two such children, currently living underfoot. Although—although to be accurate, neither one of them is what you'd truly call a loose-end; Emile's parents are dead, but Savoie has stepped into the breach and seems genuinely fond of the boy—even though the man is in prison for an uncertain amount of time. On the other hand, he'd maneuvered the fair Doyle into taking care of Emile in the meantime, which was—all in all—an excellent strategy, and was paying off like a trump.

And although Gemma's father and mother were also tragically dead, the girl had managed to wind up with Mary, who loved her as though she were her own. And—in a truly amazing coincidence—like Emile, Gemma had also managed to get into the good graces of the House of Acton, and was now reaping the substantial benefits.

I don't understand it, Doyle thought, as she rubbed her eyes with the heels of her hands; I don't know why I think this is significant, in some way. It's not as though any of this was planned, after all. I'm the one who asked Mary to be my nanny, and she'd no inkling it was in the offing—faith, I'm sure she thought she'd never see me again. And although Williams may have presented himself as a potential step-father to little Gemma, Bill Blakney went off and got himself murdered, thereby throwing a spanner into the spokes of that promising romance.

So, what was it? There was no grasping plan afoot to hitch these children to the illustrious fortunes of the House of Acton—and even if there were, the illustrious head of that illustrious house would have twigged onto it, and put paid to such a plan with no further ado. Why was it pokin' at her—aside from the fact, of course, that everything seemed to poke at her, nowadays, including Edward.

Surely, it had nothing to do with the blood-money? It was hard to imagine how it would, but it did remind her that she should do some more digging, since it had been her unfortunate experience that ghosts didn't haunt her dreams without good reason.

Pulling out her mobile, she thought to scroll up Williams, but then hesitated. She'd had the impression that Williams was truly out of Acton's loop on the blood-money matter—whatever that matter may be—but she couldn't be certain, and one thing she did know for certain was that she shouldn't let her husband twig on to the fact that she was digging into a dead priest's relatives—not yet, leastways. Because if Acton didn't want to her find out whatever it was she was trying to find out, suffice it to say that he'd take steps to ensure that she never did; she was no match for her wily husband.

So instead, she'd have to recruit someone else who had access to the general database. It couldn't be Lizzie Mathis, since she'd grass to Acton in a heartbeat, and probably with a great deal of satisfaction. Gabriel would be a candidate, save for this whole unfortunate fake-girlfriend-may-actually-be-a-murderess problem—faith, another tangle patch laid before the fair Doyle, who was already awash in them. Therefore, there was but one option left, and Doyle regretfully rang up Detective Sergeant Isabel Munoz.

"Doyle. What's up? I'm busy."

"That's not very friendly, Munoz. How d'you know I'm not callin' to say I had the baby?"

"Everybody here would probably know before you did."

Doyle smiled. "A fair point. But I was wonderin' if you could do me a favor—on the down-low, so to speak. I'm tryin' to help my church-friend track down the sister of a dead priest, and I told her I'd take a peek into the general database, since she's not havin' any luck."

"We're not allowed to do that sort of thing, Doyle. They're very strict about it."

But Doyle had already foreseen this protocol-skirting problem, and had come up with a plausible tale. "It's for a good cause, though—it has to do with payin' over some money."

"It always does," countered Munoz, unmoved.

Delicately, Doyle offered, "This one's truly connected to a Met case, though, so it's not as though I'm fishin' for random information. It's that arson investigation, with Holy Trinity." She'd been hoping not to disclose this connection, but stupid Munoz was being a stupid stickler.

"All right," Munoz conceded with poor grace. "Let me pull up the clergy database—I can't get into as much trouble if I use that one. What's the name?"

"I only know the first name—Father Danilo. He was the associate pastor at Holy Trinity; or he was until he left, leastways."

There was a small pause. "Oh. Well, you may not want to hear this."

"Is it about how his sister was the arsonist?"

"That's the one."

"Yes—well, I already know about her; we're lookin' for another sister."

But Munoz replied, "No record of another sister—or any other siblings, for that matter. It does list his mother, who's still alive, but looks to be quite old. She's in the Philippines—want an address?"

"Surely, I do," Doyle said, all bright with pretend-gratefulness. "Now we'll have someone to send the money to—thanks a million, Munoz. And I'd appreciate it if you didn't mention it to anyone until we find out if we can reach her—we don't want anyone else to catch wind about the money."

"Already forgotten. I've got too much to do."

It suddenly occurred to Doyle that it was a Saturday; since she'd gone on maternity leave, every day seemed like every other boring day, and it was easy to lose track. "You're workin' today?"

"No rest for the weary. And besides, I haven't any plans." This, of course, was because Philippe Savoie was her current beau, and he spending his Saturday nights in Wexton Prison, larking about in the hallways with the guards.

Doyle was alive to the underlying nuance in the other girl's remark, and on impulse, offered, "Come to Acton's confirmation tomorrow, then. I know Drake and Williams will be there; mayhap you can flirt up a storm, and forget about Savoie for a while."

Rather to Doyle's surprise, Munoz agreed, and as she was giving the other girl the event's particulars, Acton came in through the front door.

Doyle immediately covered the mobile and hissed, "Stay quiet; Emile's asleep."

He nodded as he hung up his jacket. "Reynolds?"

"We're back from the zoo early, so he's not here yet—I've a million things to tell you; let me ring off with Munoz."

Doyle said her goodbyes as her husband sank into the sofa beside her, and when she'd put the mobile down, he promptly began kissing her neck. "Don't get any ideas," she giggled. "We don't want to traumatize Emile, if he walks in unexpectedly."

"Or Reynolds."

She lifted her chin to grant him greater access. "Reynolds probably wouldn't turn a hair; he's too well-bred. Faith, if someone had told me when I moved to this stupid city that I would wind up with servants and loose-end children always underfoot, I'd have laughed in his face."

"Not much longer," he soothed, and moved southward to bestow a lingering kiss on the mole near her collarbone.

"Which?" she teased. "Not much longer for Reynolds, or for the children? Or both?"

He smiled, and placed his hands on either side of her as he moved to kiss the other side of her neck. "It would take an act of war to dislodge Reynolds, I think."

She giggled. "Mainly because there's an earldom on the come. He's probably crossin' his fingers and checkin' the obituaries, each and every mornin'." Aside from holding a barony, Acton was set to inherit an earldom from Lord Aldwych, who was nearly ninety.

"Hmmm," said Acton, whose mouth was otherwise engaged.

"You've got to stop," she laughed. "I'm powerless to resist, as my hormones are runnin' amok, and you are one handsome man, my friend."

"Right then." With some regret, he pulled himself away, and stood. "What might I bring you?"

She brightened. "Coffee."

Smiling, he stepped toward the kitchen. "Water, perhaps. We've got to keep your amniotic sac hydrated."

"Faith, that sounds nasty—like prison slang, or somethin'."

Amused, he looked at her over the refrigerator door. "I'll add some lemon, to make it more palatable."

She was aware that he wanted something stronger—a scotch, perhaps; he was in a good mood—but he poured his own glass of wretched water so as to commiserate with her, which was very much appreciated.

After dutifully accepting her glass, she gave him a look, as he settled in beside her. "Tell me, Michael; d'you ever get tired of bein' right?"

"No." With a small smile, he sipped his water, and it was the truth.

"Well, you were right about Gemma—Giselle wasn't her mother, apparently. In fact, Mary thinks Gemma may have been a foreign adoption, and so she's worried about our preschool plan, since she may have to prove she has legal custody."

He contemplated the glass in his hand for a moment. "I foresee no problem. Mary is providing for Gemma, and the two have a close relationship. It is clear the child has never been trafficked or abused, which would be the main concern. I think we tell the school the truth, and if they balk—which I am certain they will not—I will offer to sponsor her until the legalities are concluded."

Although this was nothing less than what Doyle had expected, it was nonetheless gratifying that he was willing, and so she hooked an arm around his head to kiss him soundly, despite the fact she sloshed his water a bit. "You are a good man. You've only to throw your mantle over Gemma—like Elisha at the plow—and her path will now be made smooth."

He used the excuse to set his glass on the sofa table, and demurred, "It is little enough, surely."

With a fond smile, she traced the day-end stubble of his beard with a forefinger. "You threw your mantle over me, too."

But his mood shifted subtly, as he stayed her hand, and pressed her fingertips to his mouth. "Your path has not been the smoother for it."

Lightly, she teased, "Fah, husband; never had a nicer time, I assure you."

He gathered her to him in a fond embrace, and in the process, she tried to set her water glass next to his, but he neatly intercepted it, and so she was forced to take another drink, and then cradle the glass between them.

"Your way will be smoother, now; my promise on it."

With a sigh, she nestled into his side, and watched the fire. "Are we back to 'no more hardships' again? You can't make it so by declarin' it, foolish man; the reason that they say 'give thanks in all things' is because the 'all things' part is goin' to include a few lumps."

"No," he declared, only half-joking. "No more lumps."

Her scalp prickled, but before she could think about why it would, he'd changed the subject. "How was your visit to the zoo?"

"Well, for starters, Gabriel was anglin' for an invitation to your confirmation. I wasn't sure what to do, so I invited him."

"By all means."

Turning her head, she eyed him. "Williams thinks Gabriel's just polishin' the apple, but I'm not so sure. As a matter of fact, I don't think his girlfriend's his girlfriend; I think she's actually some sort of subordinate officer."

Absently, he fingered a tendril of hair that had fallen onto her shoulder, and observed in a mild tone, "You've had an eventful day."

It was not surprising, of course, that he appeared to be well-aware of this alarming situation, and so she asked the next logical question. "Is the girlfriend workin' for you, Michael?"

"No, she is not."

This was true, and she blew out a breath. "Well, that's rather a relief, because here's a wrinkle; her name is Tasza—which isn't your ordinary, everyday sort of name—and Father John's embezzler-suicide fellow was datin' a girl named Tasza."

There was a small pause, whilst Acton absently rubbed her arm. "That is indeed very interesting."

Watching him, she prompted, "And? Aren't we the least bit worried that the woman's a murderess?"

"Unlikely; Gabriel would have made an easy target."

Hearing the trace of humor in his voice, she reined in her wayward imagination—for heaven's sake, if Tasza was a law enforcement officer of some stripe, she was hardly a murderess. "It just seemed such a coincidence, that the name was the same. Have you had a chance to resolve the suicide's case, one way or the other?"

"I will," he promised. "Very soon."

She turned her head to look at the fire again. "I suppose you have to tread carefully, since you'd have to tell Drake that he mucked it up, in his initial report."

"Yes," he agreed. "Very carefully."

"Nothin' new, there—you're always careful," she observed fondly, burrowing in beside him. "Which is a good thing, I think, since I'm a bangin'-about sort of person, and we counter each other. It's that ying and yams, again."

Fondly, he kissed her head. "You mustn't exert yourself at the event tomorrow—no banging about, if you will. Mathis will be there to help Nellie, so that you may stay off your feet."

"I've no intention of exertin' anythin', husband; instead, I'm goin' to sit back and watch this little holy show unfold—although

I'll keep a sharp eye on Tasza, in case she decides to murder someone else."

"Better safe than sorry," he agreed.

Reminded, she turned to ask, "D'you know about the scary hound—the one from basketville?"

He tilted his head toward hers. "Could you give me some context, perhaps?"

"Well, Gabriel said somethin' about it, and I had the feelin' that he was havin' a private joke with himself. He was speakin' of that night at Trestles, when the DCS was taken down."

Acton smiled, slightly. "He must have meant *The Hound of the Baskervilles.* It is a famous story—a famous story about a misdirection murder."

"Oh—then I suppose it would be 'apt'?" She was teasing him, because she still wasn't certain when one said "apt," which was a funny little word that the nobs tended to over-use.

Amused, Acton considered the fire for a moment. "*The Sign of the Four* would be more apt, perhaps."

Sighing, she tried to brush off the water she'd spilled on her blouse, but it had seeped through, making the wet material cling to her skin. "I'm goin' to have to change."

"Allow me to help," he offered, and began kissing her neck again.

Giggling, she relented, "All right, all right—I'm only flesh and blood, after all. Five minutes, Michael, and keep your ears on the stretch in case you-know-who wakes up."

"Done," he agreed, and lifted her water glass from her hand.

Chapter 14

It should prove to be a very interesting sacrament.

That night, Doyle was visited again by the Filipino priest, who faced her with his usual benevolent attitude and—as before—seemed disinclined to speak.

She ventured, "The ducks are all hissin' for the bread, and I'm worried that Acton is goin' to shoot them all dead."

His expression became a bit grave, but he offered no response.

Although privately she could commiserate with the priest's grave attitude, Doyle felt it was her obligation to defend her better half, and so she offered, "I truly think he's tryin' to tone it down a bit. He's gettin' confirmed, and he's had a scare, what with the ACC, an' all. He didn't kill Morgan Percy, which should go down as a mark in his favor."

At this, the ghost raised his head.

"I know, I know," Doyle offered in apology. "I should look into her murder, but I've too much to sort out, just now, and I can't get around, like I used to. I'm working on your sister, too—I had to wheedle Munoz into the general database, and I can't keep doin' it, so I'm not sure what to do next. I'd like to help your sister, but there's no record of her, and I can't very well ask Acton why he's payin' her the money."

"Why is that?" the priest asked gently. "Why can't you ask him, my child?"

Doyle stared at him for a moment. "I suppose—I suppose I'm afraid of what I'll find out. We're not your usual mister-and-missus, Father, and it's important that I not go probin', overmuch."

She paused, gathering her thoughts, because it was important that he understand. "It's a delicate balance, I guess you'd say. He trusts me not to hurt him, and so I can't just start crashin' about in his doin's, like a cow in a cornfield. I know I'm havin' an effect, and it's a good effect—or at least, a better one—but if I start shovin' at him, this whole house of cards could come tumblin' down, and he'd go back to where he was before he let me in."

Pausing, she lifted her head and met his gaze. "I know it doesn't sound like much of an excuse—everything's black-and-white, to you. But on the other hand, you've never been married."

He nodded, as though she'd made a fair point, but returned no comment.

"I'm goin' to follow up," she assured him. "I know it's important, or you wouldn't be here—but it has to be guilefully done, which is probably another thing you've no experience with."

The little priest smiled in concession, and—although his face was careworn and weathered—when he smiled, there was a startling contrast, in that his teeth were very white, and very uniform. On reflection, it shouldn't have been a surprise, though—Nellie had similar teeth; it was in the genetics, from that part of the world. In admiration, Doyle observed aloud, "You have such beautiful teeth—so even, even though your incisors are shovel-shaped."

He nodded affably, and she felt a bit embarrassed that she'd blurted out such a thing; they taught you in forensics that a dead person's race could often be discerned from the shape of certain teeth. Quickly, she returned to the subject at hand. "I feel as though I should be figurin' it all out, but I can't make heads-nor-tails of it—pregnancy makes one un-sharp, I think. And I've been distracted by the hissin' ducks, and how Emile thought he was goin' back to St. Petersburg."

The little priest offered, "In the end, the only kingdom that matters is the kingdom of heaven."

"Amen," she replied dutifully, and wished she knew what he was talking about.

They regarded each other in silence, and she ventured, "You know, Father, I'm thinkin' that a bit more information wouldn't be out of line."

"My sister is troubled," he reminded her gently. "And money is no remedy for a troubled mind."

There was a pause. "Are we talkin' about Acton, again?"

But her eyes flew open to observe the darkened bedroom wall, and she lay still, listening to her husband's steady breathing, as she stilled her hammering heart.

The following morning was the day of the confirmation, and Acton was showering whilst Reynolds served up yet another helping of eggs to Emile, who was shoveling them in as fast as his hand could lift a fork.

"Your suit of clothes is laid out on your bed, Master Emile, but we will wait a bit before we see you dressed."

"Emile's comin' to Acton's confirmation?" Doyle asked in surprise.

"Lord Acton thought it appropriate," the servant replied, and Doyle could see that Reynolds didn't think it was appropriate, but his was not to reason why.

"Faith, Reynolds; Emile's comin', but you're not?" This was almost too alarming to contemplate.

"Miss Mary will attend, madam, and she will look after Emile. And I believe Lord Acton thought I might enjoy having the day off."

"Oh—oh, I'll bet that's it." Strange, that Acton hadn't invited Reynolds—it wouldn't hurt to have another pair of hands, and Acton would be more interested in making things easy for Doyle, rather than for Reynolds—Emile was a handful.

She turned to the boy, and warned, "You've got to behave yourself, my friend—the bishop will be there."

Emile paused, much struck. "Will he wear his big hat?"

"No doubt," Doyle said. "And he'll have his crook, besides—best mind yourself."

"The bishop will officiate?" Reynolds had perked up because—in the best butler tradition—he was more of a snob than Acton was.

"We didn't warrant an archbishop," Doyle replied with mock-regret. "Acton needs to donate more money."

As the servant did not appreciate this attempt at ecclesiastical humor, he made no response, but instead retreated to the stove to fetch the boy more bacon.

Watching him, Doyle decided that it was an opportune time to ask, "D'you know about *The Hound of the Baskervilles*, Reynolds?"

"Certainly, madam. Another Doyle, if I may say so."

"Oh. Well, be that as it may, d'you remember how it went? Who the real killer was?"

Reynolds knit his brow for a moment, as he deposited a heap of bacon onto Emile's plate. "I believe there was a secret heir, madam."

"Truly?" Doyle considered this with interest. "I like 'secret heir' stories."

"A popular trope," the servant agreed.

"So—how about *The Sign of the Four*? What's that one about?"

"One of the earlier stories." Reynolds straightened up, and thought it over. "A dispute over a purloined treasure, I believe."

Doyle teetered on the edge of asking what "purloined" meant, but then decided that she'd got the gist. "I see—well, I suppose that's another popular whatever-it-was-you-said."

"Indeed, madam."

Frowning slightly, she continued, "Was it blood-money, in *The Sign of the Four*? The treasure that they were fightin' over?"

Reynolds paused over the sink, carefully hiding his surprise that she was interested in this particular topic. "I don't believe so, madam—not in the traditional sense. Instead it was the spoils of war, if I recall correctly." He dried his hands. "Allow me to pull it up, and we'll have an answer."

"No—let's not look it up," she said in alarm, and then wondered what to say; if Acton saw that she was researching the story, the gig would be up—she'd known at the time he made the comment that he was having a private joke with himself, in the same way that she'd known that Gabriel was having a private joke when he mentioned that story about the hound. Improvising, she cautioned, "I'm workin' on a surprise for Acton, and I don't want to tip him off."

Hesitating, the servant ventured, "Are you aware, madam, that Lord Acton already owns the complete Holmes canon?"

"Oh," said Doyle, blinking in surprise. "He does?"

But Emile sprang out of his chair in excitement. "Can we go shoot it off, at the park?"

"I'm afraid, Master Emile, that's not the type of canon—"

But Doyle smiled at the boy. "Let's. We'll aim it at the ducks, Emile—it's nothin' more than what the miserable chousers deserve."

As Emile expressed his extreme enthusiasm for this plan, it was left to Reynolds to throw cold water on the idea. "I believe Lady Acton is joking," the servant intervened firmly. "Instead, we will gather up some stones when we are next at the pond, Master Emile, and I will teach you how to play Ducks and Drakes."

With a slingshot?" asked Emile, still hoping for a bit of violence.

"I know a Drake who can't keep his hands off the ducks," Doyle offered slyly. "He definitely deserves the slingshot treatment."

As Reynolds shot her an admonitory look, Doyle wondered why her scalp had started prickling.

Chapter 15

She didn't enjoy this type of gathering, of course.
A shame, that it was necessary.

I keep forgetting that I hate crowds, Doyle thought. For two pins, I'd duck into the sacristy, and wiggle myself out a window.

The confirmation ceremony had concluded, and she was now positioned next to Acton in the receiving line at the reception, trying to keep up a pleasant front even though she was thoroughly sick of answering questions about her due-date, and equally sick of being buffeted by the undercurrents that swirled around her.

Dr. Timothy McGonigal—Acton's longtime friend—had come through the line, and ordinarily Doyle would have been relieved to see a familiar face; McGonigal had proved to be a staunch ally, through thick and thin. In this instance, however, the good doctor was troubled—an unusual state of affairs for him. Although the man smiled and shook Acton's hand, his heart wasn't in it, and neither was Nanda's, for that matter. Nanda was McGonigal's sweetheart, a nurse who'd originally hailed from Rwanda, but who was now working at the Holy Trinity free clinic—which prompted Doyle to wonder if they would have to shutter it, being as there wasn't any money to keep the parish going.

Usually, Nanda was as restful a person as McGonigal—which was why the couple had always seemed so perfect for each other. Today, however, Nanda was a seething caldron of frustrated rage, and could barely muster up a smile, as she greeted Doyle.

A lover's tiff, Doyle decided, and hoped they could work it out—Acton had opined that an engagement was in the offing, but it certainly didn't appear so, today.

Officer Gabriel then ushered Tasza through the line, and Doyle was immediately irritated, since she didn't much like the fact that Gabriel was presenting his live-in-girlfriend subterfuge to her without confessing to it, and then explaining why it was necessary. Doyle had always felt they were more-or-less honest with one another, she and Gabriel, and it made her think that maybe she'd misjudged the man.

Indeed, when Gabriel had invited himself to the confirmation, Doyle had entertained the uneasy suspicion that Gabriel might be after Acton, which was why she thought she'd best mention his invitation-wrangling to her better half. Acton hadn't seemed thrown at all, though—not that he ever seemed thrown—and on reflection, it didn't make much sense. There'd be no point, one would think, in going after Acton just now; he'd almost single-handedly brought down the corruption rig, and was therefore bullet-proof—not to mention the Met was running out of people to go after him, in the first place. Besides, she'd always had the impression that Gabriel already knew about Acton's doings, and didn't necessarily disapprove.

As Tasza exchanged pleasantries with Acton, Doyle leaned to look down the line, hoping they'd be finished soon, and saw that Chief Inspector Drake was coming through, although she caught her breath at the difference in his appearance. He was about Acton's age, and had always been something of a Jack-the-lad; vain about his looks, and popular with the ladies. Now, however, he'd gained some weight, and didn't look well—he seemed to have aged considerably, since the last time Doyle had seen him. And it had been a goodly while, she realized; although she'd worked with several detectives on Drake's team, she'd never run into him—almost as though he were avoiding her, even though she'd saved the man's life, once.

"Michael," Drake said, shaking Acton's hand. "I'm not certain what one says; congratulations, perhaps?"

"Thank you," said Acton politely. "It is happy occasion, indeed."

Oh-oh, thought Doyle, alarmed.

"DS Doyle; you are looking well."

"Thank you, sir."

Pausing, the man then leaned in to murmur to Acton, "Perhaps we could share a pint, Michael; I'm worried there's been a small misunderstanding—"

"Certainly," said Acton. "I am at your disposal."

Oh-oh, thought Doyle, with acute dismay.

"I'll phone you." Drake put a hand on Acton's upper arm as he moved on, and Doyle could feel her husband's irritation—Acton didn't like to be touched by anyone, save the wife of his bosom.

Instinctively, Doyle reacted to the ominous exchange, although she wasn't certain why she knew it was ominous. "Michael—," she cautioned in an undertone, but before she could say anything further, Dr. Hsu drew Acton's attention, and bowed.

The Chinese coroner expressed his pleasure in his overly-formal manner, and looked nothing like the sort of person who'd drawn a knife on the illustrious Chief Inspector, once upon a time. You have to give it to Acton, Doyle thought; he made the right choice there, in knowing who to forgive, and who not to forgive.

Her scalp prickled, and she thought again about her husband's alarming interaction with Drake. Perhaps Drake hadn't been forgiven, after all? As Doyle shook yet another hand and answered yet another question about her due-date, she glanced uneasily at her calmly-standing husband, and hoped a pitched battle wasn't about to erupt—Acton might be behaving as affably as he was able, but she'd the strong sense that mayhem was lurking just around the corner, and her strong sense was rarely wrong.

Doyle mustered up a smile for the next guest, and tried to convince herself that she was overreacting—it wasn't as though Acton and Drake would start a ruckus, right here in front of God and the bishop. And it had surely seemed as though Acton wasn't the least interested in nicking Drake, for his sins.

Only now—now, she wasn't so sure. Thinking back on it, it did seem a little strange that Acton had never mentioned Drake to her, during these fearsome months when the corruption rig was being taken down. After all, the other DCI had been photographed handing money over to the villains, and he'd orchestrated a shadow murder, to boot; other players were going to prison for far less. And it wasn't as though Acton admired the man; she'd the impression that Acton didn't like him very much at all—although to be fair, Acton didn't like anyone very much. Save for herself, of course.

Her scalp prickled yet again, and she paused for a moment, but couldn't think of any reason why Acton's out-sized devotion to his bride would result in his hands-off attitude with respect to Drake—there didn't seem to be a connection. She'd never been particularly friendly with Drake, and she'd never worked for him, either—with hindsight, she realized that Acton would never have allowed it.

Acton lifted his gaze across the room for a moment, and Doyle realized he was signaling to Lizzie Mathis, who then promptly appeared at Doyle's elbow. "Shall I see you seated, Lady Acton?"

"If you would," Acton said.

Doyle was tempted to refuse, and then decided she was being cross and childish—obviously, Mathis was just following orders, and besides, Doyle was pig-sick of being nice to people, and was ready to sit her weary self down—being nice for an extended period of time was not for the faint of heart.

Mathis escorted her to a comfortable chair that was set against the far wall. "May I fetch you any refreshment, Lady Acton?"

"I don't suppose there's coffee?" Doyle asked hopefully.

"I don't believe so," Mathis replied. "Would you care for a glass of punch, instead?"

"There's usually a pot o' coffee, brewin' in the church office," Doyle hinted.

There was a moment's hesitation. "I'm sorry, Lady Acton, I shouldn't leave my post—but I'll find someone to fetch you coffee."

Thinks I'm a crackin' pain, Doyle deduced; and I suppose she's right. "Never you mind, Lizzy—Nellie needs you, and coffee's bad for the baby."

Mathis walked away, but Doyle saw that she made a quick, quiet comment to Acton on her way over to the refreshment table. Looking up, her husband met Doyle's gaze, and then promptly excused himself to come lean over her. "Everything all right?"

"I suppose it is," Doyle replied, as she fought a mighty inclination to sulk. "But if you want me to sit still and behave myself, you've only to ask, husband. No need to game it out with stupid Lizzy Mathis, ahead of time."

He bent his head for a moment, and then took one of her hands. "Forgive me, Kathleen. I knew you wouldn't be comfortable in this crowd, and I thought to give you an excuse to sit aside, for a few minutes."

This was true—and very much in keeping—but for some reason it only served to further irritate the already-irritated

Doyle. Although she knew she sounded like a baby, she couldn't seem to help herself. "I just hate it when I have the feelin' that Mathis is on the inside, and I'm not."

He met her eyes. "I am sorry. You must know that nothing matters to me but you."

This was true, and she was a gobbin' fool to be throwing a childish fit—shame on her, for making the man scheme to smooth her way. Chastened, she teased, "You're forgettin' the Holy Trinity—that should matter to you, too."

"That, too."

With a mighty effort, she cast off her sulks, and smiled. "I'm that sorry I'm an archwife, Michael."

But their conversation was interrupted, because Emile could be heard to shriek, "Papa!" and Doyle looked up in surprise to see the boy race across the room to be swept up in a bear hug by Philippe Savoie.

Chapter 16

Savoie, on time to the minute.

"Well," said Doyle, blinking. "Now, there's a surprise."

"I believe he was granted a day pass, so long as he wore a GPS device," Acton explained smoothly. "I didn't want to mention it, in the event permission was withdrawn."

"A strange sort of prison," she remarked dryly, when in reality, she was thinking that she'd a strange sort of husband. "Let me go explain the situation to Mary—we can't have her tryin' to wrestle Emile away from Savoie."

But when Doyle approached, she found that Mary seemed unalarmed, and was standing patiently next to Savoie and Emile, holding Gemma's hand as they listened to Emile gave his Papa a lengthy and disjointed recitation of a story the driver had told him on the way over.

Upon seeing Doyle, Savoie set Emile down. "I have the big surprise, yes?"

"You're a rare wonder," Doyle agreed. "Did you break out?"

The pale eyes gleamed. "*Non*, but I could. I have broken out of better prisons, *je vous assure.*"

"Never in doubt," Doyle agreed. "You take the cake, my friend."

"*Non*—it is Emile who eats all the cake." Savoie ran his hands over Emile's head, making the boy's hair stand on end as he grabbed at his Papa's hands, giggling with delight.

"Emile is eatin' us out of house and home," Doyle agreed. "We can't fill him up—I think he has a hollow leg."

The boy threw back his head and laughed, and Savoie bent forward so that he addressed Emile upside-down. "You are happy? Yes?"

"Of course, he's happy," Doyle supplied, since Emile was too busy giggling. "He rules the crackin' roost. And shouldn't you have been charged and released by now? Or are you enjoyin' yourself too much?"

"Soon," Savoie promised. "Soon I will go home, and then I will take Emile to rule the cracking rooster."

Any further conversation was curtailed, as Emile excitedly introduced his Papa to Mary and Gemma, Gemma clinging to Mary's legs, and no doubt wondering how Savoie had earned his scar.

As she watched the little group, Doyle belatedly remembered that Munoz was due to appear, and was probably unaware that her erstwhile beau had slipped his chain. Hastily, she decided that she'd stay well-away from that little tangle patch, and so instead, she cautioned Savoie in a generalized manner, "Behave yourself; I've a bad feelin' about all of this, and I'll not have Acton bounced out of the church the minute I finally get his foot in the door."

Savoie smiled his thin smile—which had the effect of making her very uneasy, when it should have had just the opposite effect. "*Non-non*; me, I am the St. Bernard. I am the helping."

This was true, and Doyle asked suspiciously, "What sort of helpin'?"

She was not at all surprised when Acton suddenly materialized at her elbow, and seemed intent upon steering her away. "If you could spare a moment, Kathleen, we should thank the bishop."

"By all means," she replied. "Lead on."

"It should take but a moment," he apologized. "Then you can return to your chair."

"Not to worry, Michael. I'm doin' fine." She pronounced it "foine" just to tease him. "Truly."

He covered her hand with his own, and she mentally girded her loins to make nice again, even though she was fast running out of reservoirs of nice-ness. She needed to make the effort, though, because it was truly something to celebrate—that Acton had been confirmed—and she shouldn't let the fact that she didn't handle crowds very well steal her enjoyment away from what was important, here. Why, she need look no further than her husband's exemplary behavior; Acton himself was the next thing to a hermit, and yet here he was, making nice, and chit-chatting—

Oh, she thought, as he led her across the room, stopping occasionally to respond to a greeting. Oh—I'm a complete knocker not to have realized it before now, which goes to show you that pregnancy does tend to make you lose a step. The last person on earth who'd consent to a cake-and-punch reception was the man walking by Doyle's side—faith, they could award him the George, and he'd refuse to go to Buckingham. Which meant that the only reason he was here was because he wanted to serve his own purposes, and Acton's own purposes often could not withstand the light of day.

Alarmed by these thoughts, it seemed an opportune time to mention, "Reynolds tells me you have a cannon."

Acton glanced down at her in surprise. "Reynolds is mistaken."

"Oh. Well, Emile will be hugely disappointed—we were goin' to go shoot it at the ducks."

He cocked his head. "You seem very anti-duck, I've noticed."

"Don't you dare take their side against me," she warned.

"Never for a moment."

She eyed him sidelong, because despite all his light and charming duck-talk, he was a simmering pot of—of something; some powerful and ominous brew of satisfaction, and anticipation—he was well-pleased, for some reason, even though Drake had been pestering him, and Acton was not the sort of person to suffer a roomful of well-wishers.

Whilst Doyle was trying to tamp down her alarm, Timothy McGonigal approached them, looking a bit distracted, and apologizing profusely. "Nanda is not well, and I'm afraid we must leave."

This was not true, which came as no surprise to Doyle. The couple seemed to be quarreling, and as Nanda was nowhere to be seen, she'd probably already left—lucky thing. It was a little out-of-character, that the woman would embarrass McGonigal in this way—she was usually so easy-going—but there was no question that she'd been mighty angry, when Doyle had glimpsed her earlier.

Acton expressed his regret, and shook his hand. "I hope she recovers soon, Tim; please come by for a visit."

"Will do." After attempting to muster up a smile, he left.

Doyle noted in an undertone, "They're havin' a tiff, I think."

"So it would seem; she left without him, about ten minutes ago."

Trust Acton to have noticed, but further discussion was curtailed because they were now being hailed by a couple coming in the entry way; a tall, lean gentleman accompanied by an impeccably-dressed young woman, who wore a very stylish hat.

"Acton," said Howard with a smile, offering his hand. "Well met. How do you do, Lady Acton?"

"Howard—good to see you." Acton greeted the other man with what Doyle called his public-school voice, which came out from hiding when he was speaking to members of his own tribe. "Thank you very much for coming—much appreciated."

Howard, now an MP, had been the government official most responsible for taking down the massive corruption rig. He'd done so at no little risk to himself, and was now held in high esteem by the public. Not coincidentally, he was very much a fan of DCI Acton, who'd thwarted a scheme by the villains to have him arrested before he could do them any damage.

"May I introduce my fiancée, Lady Abby?"

They greeted the gracious young woman, and Doyle had the immediate impression that she was nice enough, if a bit self-centered—which, to be fair, was an unavoidable by-product of being an attractive member of the aristocracy. And good on Howard, for hitching his rising star to a such a woman; it would no doubt stand him in good stead, whilst he navigated his bright future.

For her part, Lady Abby was heard to gasp in polite surprise, upon beholding Savoie's party. "Oh—isn't that Grosvenor's little niece? Do you remember her, darling, from the Ascot Gala?"

With an indulgent smile, Howard dutifully reviewed Gemma, still clinging to her mother's hand. "I believe Grosvenor's niece is a few years older, my dear."

His fiancée laughed her captivating little laugh. "Sorry—I'm not good at guessing how old children are." But her eyes strayed over to Gemma again.

They exchanged inconsequentials for a minute, but Doyle knew that Acton was hiding his impatience, and so she was not surprised when he made their excuses, and then they continued over to the bishop's group, where they were warmly welcomed, with hands shaken all around.

Chapter 17

Very soon, he could take her home—she was tired.

Acton expressed his polite gratification to the bishop, who was flanked by the two priests who'd attended the ceremony—Father John, and Father Gregory from Holy Trinity.

Doyle hadn't met Father Gregory before, but when she'd seen him during the ceremony she'd entertained the brief impression that he was rather preoccupied, and small blame to him; his church had burned down, there were no insurance funds to rebuild, and the bishop didn't have the look of a man who thought this sort of carelessness was a trifle, being as money didn't grow on trees—especially trees in London, where the RC population was small and unmighty.

Rather surprisingly, she'd also had the impression that Father Gregory was a bit vain about his looks, which might be appealing to certain female parishioners, but was perhaps not so appealing to the communion of saints, which was, after all, the more important audience. For example, the man wore trendy, dark-framed eyeglasses, which for Doyle was an automatic black mark—couldn't imagine him risking yellow fever in an African outreach, with those sleek frames. He was overly-muscular, too; as though he spent a great deal of time working out, which also didn't seem quite in keeping. Mustn't judge, she reminded herself sternly; different gifts, same spirit.

After greeting the other clergymen, Acton began without preamble, "I hope you don't mind if I inject a bit of business. I've brought along a witness—one of the participants in the government corruption case you may have read about." He raised his head, and his eyes met Savoie's. "I believe he can shed some light on Father John's absolution issue—whether the young man's death was a suicide, or a homicide."

Immediately, Doyle could sense a wave of deep dismay from Father Gregory—he was very unhappy that the subject had arisen, and Doyle was reminded that the dead man's parents had sidestepped Father Gregory, in this matter.

Savoie promptly came over to join them—he'd obviously been awaiting his cue—and for once, he shed his insolent manner, and instead humbly bent to kiss the bishop's ring.

Oh, thought Doyle, reminded; I should have kissed his ring, too. It's setting a bad example for Acton, I am.

Acton continued, "Unfortunately, it appears the dead man was involved in the very same corruption scheme."

There was a moment of surprised silence, and then Father John offered sadly, "Then he did take his own life, poor soul."

"*Non*," Savoie corrected. "He did not take his own life. Instead, he was murdered, to keep him quiet about the money."

This was the truth, and—aside from her own profound surprise—Doyle was treated to a jolt of panic, emanating from Father Gregory.

"Mr. Savoie was kind enough to act as an informant, in the corruption case," Acton explained in his cool voice. "And I would appreciate it if his role in this matter remains confidential, as his life has been threatened."

Gravely, the bishop stepped forward to take Savoie's hand. "Thank you for coming forward, Mr. Savoie. We will ask for absolution from God in good conscience, and say no more on the matter."

Savoie—who was never one not to press an advantage—asked, "You will bless my boy, yes?"

"I will. Are you married to his mother?" This asked in a slightly ominous tone.

Sadly, Savoie shook his head. "His mother, she is dead." He then turned to call Emile to him.

As Doyle watched the bishop make the sign of the cross over a fascinated Emile, she noted that Father Gregory had taken the opportunity to slip away from the group, emanating a panicky sort of dread.

"Shall we find your chair, again?" Acton asked Doyle, as he took her elbow. "This way, please."

Willingly, she let him lead her away, mainly because she wanted to tell him, "There's somethin' smoky about Father Gregory, Michael. I think he was in on it." This, of course, shouldn't come as such a huge surprise—since the priest's former church was ground central for evil doings—but all the same, Doyle's thoroughly RC soul was a bit shocked by the realization that a priest could abet the aforesaid evil doings.

"That is of interest; thank you." Acton's reply was in a neutral tone, and she was not at all surprised to discover that she was—as usual—ten steps behind her husband.

As she was treated to the sight of Lizzie Mathis giving Drake a flirtatious look over the rim of her punch glass, Doyle thought, this is a very strange sort of reception—it's rather a shame that Acton doesn't truly have a cannon.

Chapter 18

Another ten minutes, perhaps.

Acton turned to greet the new deacon, who was hovering nearby, and awaiting an opportune time to express his extreme admiration. As the deacon was the type of man who tended to rattle on, Doyle took this opportunity to cast an uneasy glance over toward the group chatting by the punch bowl—although Father Gregory wasn't chatting as much as he was anxiously touching Drake's elbow, and attempting to draw him away from Tasza, who seemed to be competing with Mathis in the flirting-with-Drake department.

A sorry group, if I ever saw one, thought Doyle; I'm glad I'm over here. And she decided that Acton must be avoiding them, too, since he was patiently listening to the deacon—now joined by the facilities manager—as the men discussed the rise in church attendance since the sad demise of Holy Trinity parish, and not-so-subtly noted that several new pews should probably be added to their own nave, so as to accommodate the new attendees.

Whilst Acton was content to engage in this mundane conversation, Officer Gabriel took the opportunity to draw a folding chair over, and settle in next to Doyle. "Listen, I've been meaning to tell you that I owe you one. Remember when you warned me that you thought I was headed into a trap? It made me think twice about some evidence I'd come across that seemed a little too convenient. Good thing."

Doyle nodded, not at all surprised. "You were bein' set up by the ACC, then?"

"I think so."

He offered nothing more, and so she prompted, "Was it evidence that Acton was runnin' a weapons-smugglin' rig? They tried the same thing with Munoz, but she didn't fall for it, either."

A bit absently, his gaze rested on the group by the punchbowl. "A ludicrous notion, of course."

This was not true, and she had the distinct feeling that he was trying to gauge whether or not the fair Doyle knew that it was not a ludicrous notion at all. Therefore, she decided to change the subject, and referenced the odd assortment of persons who were assembled at the punch bowl. "Are you worried that Tasza is goin' to step out on you?"

He smiled. "Not particularly. Are you?"

She quirked her mouth. "I just think you're a very tolerant sort of boyfriend—Drake has that reputation, you know."

"I'm no match for him," he agreed, and it was not true.

"Well, Munoz should be here, soon, and then you can noodle up to her, and wage a counter-attack." Over the past few weeks, Doyle had garnered the strong impression that Gabriel very much admired the fair Munoz, but was constrained by events from acting on this admiration. Not to mention that the fair Munoz did not seem remotely interested in him, which was a drawback, all-in-all.

Gabriel smiled. "More like she'll elbow her way in for some Drake-action."

"It's hardly fair," Doyle teased. "Drake's in no shape to handle all of them—he should share."

"He does look a bit stressed, doesn't he?"

Doyle could sense a nuance beneath the question, and again, decided she'd best change the subject—irritating, that stupid Gabriel was making her feel wary, when she was always inclined to let her guard down around him. In a small measure of revenge, she decided to throw her own dart. "What does Tasza do for a livin'? She's LEO, I think."

To his credit, he hesitated only for a barely discernable moment. "Yes, she's law enforcement. She specializes in forensic accounting."

Doyle made a face. "Mother a' mercy, but that sounds hideously dull. I'd be longin' for my days at the fish market."

He smiled. "Now, I'll have to white-knight it, here, and tell you that she's not hideously dull at all—far from it." He paused, then added fairly, "Although I can't imagine she'd do well in a fish market."

But Doyle had decided that she may as well throw another dart. "Well, she's got a crush on my husband, so there's that."

Amused, his eyes slid toward hers. "So does Lizzie Mathis."

Not to be outdone, Doyle countered, "So does Munoz."

He laughed aloud. "I can't condemn any of them; I'd have a crush on him too, if I were so inclined."

There—it felt as though they were back on their old footing, and Doyle was relieved; she liked Gabriel, despite his mysterious ways. Smiling, she teased, "No, Gabriel—you think Acton is that frightenin' hound, from that famous story."

Amused, Gabriel shook his head in disagreement. "Not Acton—it's Savoie, who's the hound. Everyone's terrified of him."

Doyle followed his gaze to Savoie, and was much struck, since this—of course—was exactly what Acton had intended. It would not do at all if the blacklegs were to discover that the illustrious Chief Inspector himself was the one who was terrorizing all and sundry, and so a stalking horse in the form of Philippe Savoie had been put into place.

Doyle's gaze rested on the notorious Frenchman for a moment, as he sent Emile over to eat his cake with Mary and Gemma. There was no denying that Savoie was an out-and-out villain, but in this case, he was only serving as cover, and she had to admit that whatever her husband's scheme was, it had been brilliantly executed, so that no one realized who was actually pulling the levers, behind the curtain.

Thoughtfully, she turned her gaze back to Gabriel. "You don't seem terrified of Savoie, though."

Gabriel tilted his head in acknowledgement. "Only because Acton seems to have him in check, somehow."

As Doyle was well-aware of the reason Savoie was held in check, she hastily changed the subject. "Well, now that he's coolin' his heels in prison—most days, anyways—he's not so very terrifyin', anymore."

"I suppose that remains to be seen," Gabriel replied thoughtfully, and Doyle noted that Tasza had looked up to meet his eyes, even though Doyle couldn't discern the message. Frustration, thought Doyle; I think she's frustrated, for some reason. Join the club, Tasza; I've a plottin' husband who can't seem to resist sowing seeds of destruction, willy-nilly.

"Are you expectin' bloodshed?" She was only half-teasing.

"At a confirmation? I hope not. Although in that famous film there was plenty of bloodshed taking place during a baptism, and I think there are definite parallels."

"You've lost me," Doyle admitted. She didn't have a chance to ask him to explain, however, because she'd caught a sudden flare of emotion from him, and, looking for its cause, she saw that Munoz had entered the room.

Oh-oh, she thought, and braced for the Spanish girl's reaction when she realized that Savoie was wandering about at large, but hadn't informed her of this fact.

Munoz, however, casually took an assessing glance about the room, and then made her way over to where Doyle was seated. "Up," the girl instructed Gabriel, and with a mock-deferential gesture, he relinquished his seat to the newcomer.

Not surprisingly, Munoz offered Doyle an insincere smile, but said in an accusatory undertone, "Did you know Savoie was going to be here?"

"No, Munoz—truly I didn't. He's out on a day pass of some sort."

After a moment's consideration, Munoz shrugged a resigned shoulder, and sat back. "Leave it to him to manage it—the rules never seem to apply to him."

As Doyle was well-aware why the rules never seemed to apply, once again she hastily changed the subject. "Good on you, Munoz, for keepin' your dignity. The likes of him doesn't deserve the likes of you."

Glumly, Munoz glanced around. "Where's Williams? I need someone to flirt with."

"Williams may have left already—he's churched-out, I think. And I'll withdraw my recommendation that you flirt with Drake—he's a wreck of his former self."

Munoz slid her gaze over toward the punch bowl. "I think he's drunk, which isn't a good look for him."

Doyle followed her gaze, and it did seem as though Drake was swaying a bit on his feet, scowling as Father Gregory spoke urgently in his ear.

"Well, Gabriel's at hand," Doyle suggested with an overly-casual air. "He wouldn't mind bein' your flirt-target, I think."

The beauty's dark eyes assessed Gabriel, who was leaning against the wall and watching Drake. "I can't, Doyle—his girlfriend's here."

"Oh. Does that stop you?" Doyle was genuinely curious.

Munoz made an impatient sound. "In this case, it does. She's a little scary."

Doyle regarded her companion with surprise. "But not as scary as you, Munoz."

With narrowed eyes, the other girl contemplated Doyle for a moment. "I appreciate that, Doyle—always good to have a reminder." With no further ado, Munoz stood and moved over toward Gabriel, smiling her sultry smile, and never for a moment glancing in Savoie's direction.

Chapter 19

"But let justice roll on like a river."

Acton had finished up his conversation with the other men, and bent to inquire, "May I fetch you a glass of punch, Kathleen?"

"How about coffee?" she suggested hopefully.

"Punch, perhaps," he repeated, and made as though to move toward the punchbowl.

Almost without conscious volition, Doyle grabbed at her husband's hand. "Michael," she said in an undertone, and then wasn't sure why she was worried. "Let's not start a ruckus."

He squeezed the hand in his, gently. "Drake is not himself. I will see that he is taken outside."

This was true, and with a sense of relief, she let him go, scolding herself for jumping at shadows.

As Acton approached, Drake angrily pushed Father Gregory away, and then turned to confront Savoie, who'd made some comment to him, but now backed away, holding up both hands in a placating gesture.

Drake seemed drunk indeed, and as there'd been no alcohol served, this might have been a surprise save for the fact that Doyle had seen this play once before, courtesy of Lizzie Mathis, who was not-so-coincidentally here today. On that fateful night at Trestles, when Acton had taken down the corrupt DCS, Doyle suspicioned that Mathis had given him an assist by slipping some sort of poison into a coffee cup.

Acton took Drake's elbow, and spoke quietly into his ear. Whatever he was saying, however, did not seem to have a soothing effect, as Drake angrily lunged toward Savoie. "You—you *bastard*; don't think I don't know—"

"Hold," said Acton in a firm tone, placing a restraining arm around Drake. "Let's take this outside."

Drake wasn't having it, though, and yanked himself out of Acton's grasp to advance on Savoie, only to pause as he contemplated the switchblade in his own hand, blinking in surprise.

There was a collective gasp, and Savoie held out a warning hand. "*Non-non*; stay back; there are children—"

Warily, Acton moved to stand behind Drake—boxing him in—and command in a voice that brooked no argument, "Drop it."

Drake, however, was past listening, as he dropped the blade, and then staggered into the refreshments table, clutching at its edge as he collapsed to the ground, and pulling a stack of plates along with him.

Doyle could hear Nellie's sound of dismay as the crockery crashed, and then there was a rush of action, as Acton rolled Drake on his back, and the bishop and Father John hurried over to offer their assistance.

"He's breathing. Please call an ambulance," Acton instructed the deacon.

"On its way," Gabriel called out, as he moved to stand behind the others, watching them loosen Drake's tie. "Anything else?"

"Please check to see whether Dr. Hsu has yet left."

Fortunately, the coroner was found outside, and his expression was a bit grave as he knelt, and asked the others to help prop Drake into a sitting position. "Heart," he explained succinctly. "He's had a heart condition for some time."

This wasn't true, but that came as no surprise to Doyle, who no longer wondered why the coroner had attended Acton's confirmation ceremony, even though the Chinese man wasn't remotely Christian.

After taking Emile by the hand, Savoie retreated to stand at the back wall beside Doyle, which necessarily brought him next to Munoz. "Hallo, Isabel," Emile whispered to her, his eyes wide. "Is the bad man dead?"

"Which one?" asked Munoz.

Savoie chuckled, and Doyle devotedly hoped that it wouldn't come to cuffs between the two—she didn't know if poor Nellie's sensibilities could survive any more broken plates.

Fortunately, Munoz's temper was not put to the test, as Gabriel, after taking an assessing glance toward their group, approached to say to Munoz. "Would you mind? I've got to go flag down the EMTs, and I could use a hand."

Doyle thought it interesting that Gabriel hadn't bothered to recruit his girlfriend, but then she realized that Tasza seemed to have disappeared.

Munoz left with Gabriel, and whilst Savoie crouched down to speak in a quiet voice to Emile, Doyle noted that Drake had not died—yet—and that everyone had discreetly backed away so as to allow the coroner to minister to the patient, not realizing, of course, that the patient's fate was sealed, and that he was being ministered straight into the morgue.

The EMTs arrived, and in the flurry of activity, she thought over this carefully-choreographed misdirection murder, wondering what it all meant—that it meant *something* seemed obvious, but she was at a loss. Acton had shielded Drake from prosecution in the corruption case, but now it seemed plain as day that he wanted the man well-and-thoroughly-dead. And not only well-and-thoroughly-dead, but in a public venue, so that this turn of events could be witnessed by the right people. A threat? A warning? But to who?

After a grey-faced Drake was wheeled away, the guests spoke in the subdued voices of people who didn't want to make a hasty retreat, even though such was their inclination. Acton and Father John approached them, and the priest apologized to Savoie. "I'm that sorry the fellow attacked you, Mr. Savoie. And to think you risked your own safety, to come tell us what you knew."

"*De rien*," disclaimed Savoie, in all modesty.

"It was indeed unfortunate," said Acton, in a classic understatement. "But we mustn't leap to conclusions."

"No—of course not," Father John agreed hastily. "Perhaps the less said, the better."

"I must go." Savoie bent to kiss Emile on each cheek. "*Au revoir, mon fils.*"

"*Au revoir*, Papa."

Emile's face looked a bit stricken, as he watched his Papa make his way toward the door, and almost immediately, Mary appeared beside him to take the boy's hand in her own, and speak of their planned visit to the treat shop.

During the discreet exodus of the guests, Howard came over to take his leave. "Never a dull moment," he offered, with a wry smile. "Sorry for it."

"We are fortunate no one was hurt," Acton replied, bowing his head in acknowledgment. "A regrettable situation."

"Quite." The man's gaze strayed over to Mary, as she spoke in a cheerful tone to the two children.

With a smile, Doyle asked, "When's the weddin'? Have you set up a date?"

"Oh—oh, no. No date, as yet."

The bishop approached to draw Acton's attention, and while the officiate took his leave, Howard turned aside to speak with Mary. "Pardon me; pardon me, but I was wondering—I suppose I was wondering if you are Mrs. Savoie?"

"Oh, no," Mary smiled. "I'm Lady Acton's nanny." There was a small silence, as she and Howard looked into each other's eyes, and were mated for life.

Doyle caught her breath in wonder, rocked to the soles of her shoes. I *am* a matchmaker, she thought—it's only that I keep matching up the wrong people. And poor Williams is outflanked, yet again—not to mention Howard's well-bred fiancée; she'll have to go to the next Ascot Gala all by herself, poor thing.

Chapter 20

Trouble; she was angry with him. She must have guessed.

When their party returned to the flat, Mary helped the children change out of their best clothes in preparation for the promised outing to the treat shop, and—rather defiantly—Doyle announced her intention to join them. "I'm goin' to the treat shop, husband, because if anyone is deservin' of a treat, it's me."

Acton regarded her for a long moment, assessing. "May I accompany you?"

"No," she said shortly, and refused to meet his eyes. "You may not."

"Kathleen—"

But she wasn't having it, and instead went to lend a hand to the confusion of activity that surrounded the bundling of the children out the door, since the efficient Reynolds wasn't there, and Emile had left his jacket at the church.

Once they were finally organized and outside, Doyle fell into step beside Mary, and breathed in the evening air, as the children ran ahead on the pavement. Mary was radiating happiness, and Doyle felt a bit humbled by her first-hand witness to the overpowering glory of love, which always found its own way, and always would. I don't know as I ever felt like that, she admitted to herself with a pang of envy, although I should have—Acton and I are a perfect match, too, despite his alarming moral choices, and despite my inability to make the *slightest* dent. Looking up into the darkening sky, she wondered, a bit bleakly, what was best to do.

Mary offered, "Let me know if we're going too fast, Lady Acton—the children are a little lively, after having been so well-behaved this afternoon."

Doyle made a wry mouth. "They were well-behaved thanks to you, Mary, and it's a crackin' shame that the adults weren't as well-behaved."

"It was such a strange place to pick a fight," the woman said in wonder. "Did you know the gentleman? We are lucky he didn't hurt Emile's Papa, right there in front of him."

"I imagine Emile's Papa is well-able to take care of himself," Doyle ventured a bit dryly. "I'm guessin' he knows his way around an edged weapon."

"Yes—well, his Papa does seem to be an—an unusual man. He clearly loves Emile, though."

"Yes," Doyle agreed. "And I suppose that gives us hope for redemption." Her scalp prickled.

"Yes—I'm certain of it," said Mary stoutly. "He'll turn his life around, now that he has a reason."

Doyle watched Emile demonstrate to Gemma how to jump from one square to the next on the pavement. "I was worried that Emile would be a bit down-pin, after havin' seen his Papa again, but he's bounced back like a dandelion."

Mary smiled. "His Papa told him there will be another prison visit, soon."

Doyle case a knowing glance at her companion. "The cigarette supply must be runnin' low."

Mary chuckled. "I must say, Lady Acton, that you are so very kind—to take care of his son, during this difficult time."

But Doyle could not accept the accolade, and retorted in a frank tone, "No—I haven't a kind bone in my body. I wish I did, but kindness doesn't come naturally to me, like it does to you."

Genuinely surprised, Mary turned to face her. "Oh—oh, I must disagree, Lady Acton. You—and Lord Acton—you've both been so generous."

Doyle knit her brow as she trudged along, and considered this. "I don't know, Mary—it's a lot easier to be generous than it is to be kind, I think; givin' away money is not the same as givin' away yourself."

"I'll not hear of it," Mary teased. "We'll agree to disagree."

With a mighty effort, Doyle tried to shake off her melancholy. "I'm sorry I'm such a grouser; faith, it's been a very—" she thought the right word was 'tumultous', but decided she should play it safe "—a very strange day."

In sympathy, Mary touched her arm. "You are tired, and there's none to blame you. In fact, Lord Acton asked if I'd mind taking Emile tonight, since Reynolds is away, and that way you could have a lie-in, tomorrow."

Doyle's sour mood immediately returned. "Did he? Very thoughtful, that man."

"You could say he is kind and generous," Mary teased.

Doyle mustered up a smile, and refrained from pointing out that Acton had no doubt read his bride aright, and was eliminating potential witnesses to the bear-garden jawing that was to come. Instead, she offered in a mild tone, "If you say so, Mary, but he's probably hopin' for a bit of peace, himself."

Right on cue, Emile shrieked like a banshee, and both women laughed. With her gaze resting on the two children, Mary said softly, "I don't mind the noise—in fact, I'd like to have more children, someday."

Again, Doyle could feel a surge of sheer happiness emanating from the woman, who knew, beyond the shadow of a doubt, that she'd met her own future, on this strange and wondrous day. "You'll have more children," Doyle assured her absently. "Three, along with Gemma."

Surprised, Mary laughed. "Now, there's a generous prediction."

Doyle reminded herself that she should practice holding her tongue, and turned the subject. "Here's the treat store, and not a moment too soon—I'm ready to have a sit-down."

"What can I fetch for you, Lady Acton?"

"Thank God fastin', I'll finally have some coffee." Doyle replied a bit grimly, as they herded the children through the door. "And as strong as they can make it, please." She then paused in stricken alarm, because she'd been so intent on ditching her better half that she'd forgot to bring along a credit card. "Oh, Mary; I didn't bring any money—I *never* remember."

"Lord Acton already gave me money, Lady Acton—please don't worry."

Of course, he did, thought Doyle, as she watched the children cling to the counter's edge, jumping up and down in their excitement. Because he always covers for me—always. There's not a soul alive who'd mistake Acton for kind-and-generous, except that's exactly how he is, with me. I think he doesn't know how to simply be happy, like Mary is, right now—he doesn't know how to go about it—and so he makes up for it by taking care of me as though I'm one of those fancy porcelain vases at Trestles. Although I've survived being shot—twice—so I suppose that's not a very good comparison.

She paused for a moment, turning this thought over in her mind. Acton was over-devoted to his unlikely bride—no question about that—and she was at the center of his rather dark universe—although she was striving mightily to make it not quite so dark, so that he didn't destroy himself in the process. However—as today's events had demonstrated—she wasn't exactly covering herself in glory.

I'm not as strong an influence as I thought I was, she admitted, and then was surprised when her instinct prodded her, telling her that she was on the wrong track.

She lifted her brows in surprise. What? The wretched man had Drake murdered right in front of them, with no trace of blame to be discerned. Any influence I have should be ashamed of itself and repent fasting for such a paltry showing.

No, her instinct told her. Look again.

Frowning, she examined this insistence, and was suddenly struck by something that didn't make sense. Drake's murder was a vengeful one—yet again, Acton had meted out his own rough justice—but it didn't quite seem in keeping. Despite her glum sitting-on-the-ash-heap attitude, she knew, down deep, that she was indeed an influence on her wayward husband, and for the better. Faith, one need only look at his recent record of dark deeds to see that his purpose had changed—he might still be masterminding some dark plot, but he was now seeking to eliminate threats to her, or threats to their way of life.

And this was why Drake's murder seemed so out-of-keeping; Drake was no threat to Doyle, and no threat to their lives together. If he'd somehow made himself a target for Acton's merciless vengeance, she didn't know the reason, or why said vengeance had been delayed for so long, compared to all the other evildoers they'd run across.

She blew out a breath, knowing now that she was on the right track. Once again, I am at the center of this—I always am, she thought; there is something here that I should try to understand, and I think it's important, for some reason.

Mary returned with the drinks and proffered treats, and the children ate with gusto for a few minutes, until Emile demonstrated to Gemma how to blow bubbles through his straw, with the result that chocolate milk was spewed all over the table.

As the two women wiped with napkins, Doyle offered, "I keep hopin' that Gemma will rub off on Emile, not the other way 'round."

But Mary only smiled, and wouldn't criticize one of her charges. "If he helps to bring her out of her shell, it is all to the good, I think. Bill used to say that she wouldn't say boo to a goose."

It occurred to Doyle that Mary rarely mentioned her late husband, and wondered if this was because she didn't want to criticize him, either. Doyle offered, "He was fond of her, though, which speaks well of him, since you think she wasn't his own."

"Yes—he was a good man," Mary replied evenly, and Doyle noted that this was not exactly true. "But he tended to be influenced by the wrong people—especially if he thought it might result in a windfall."

Doyle quirked her mouth. "He can join up with the rest of humanity, then."

But her companion disagreed with a smile. "You'll not fool me, Lady Acton; you're not influenced by money in the slightest."

Doyle could only concede this point. "Well, we never had any—my mother and me—but it never seemed to matter much." She paused, lifting her head to gaze out the darkening window. "But now that I look back, I imagine it mattered a great deal to her, but she saw to it that it didn't matter to me."

"A wonderful mother," declared Mary, who knew of which she spoke.

"I hope I can be half so wonderful," Doyle admitted. "We're back to that whole kind-and-generous tangle-patch."

Mary laughed, and herded the children outside so that they could begin their return journey to the flat. They walked for a few minutes in silence, Doyle puzzling over whatever-it-was that her instinct was trying to get her to understand, whilst Mary called ahead to caution Emile to wait for her, before crossing the street.

Twilight was upon them, and they all paused to admire the sunset, more visible now that they'd come to the cross-street. The vivid streaks of deep orange and red were offset in startling contrast to the dull veneers of the tall buildings that flanked the colorful display.

Gemma said softly, "*Rizhaya.*"

Emile laughed in delight, but Doyle stood stock-still, staring at the little girl who'd used the Russian word for "sunset." Doyle had heard the word once before, when it was used in reference to her own red hair—

"*Holy Mother,*" she breathed, in abject astonishment.

Mary took her elbow and asked in alarm, "Lady Acton, are you all right?"

"*Holy* Mother of God," Doyle blurted out, her scalp prickling like a live thing. "I think it may be misdirection murders, all the way down."

Chapter 21

Of course, she knew.
He didn't know why he always underestimated her.

With barely-contained impatience, Doyle entrusted Mary and the children to the driving service, and then texted Acton to let him know that she was on her way up.

When she entered the flat, she duly noted that no lights had been turned on against the darkness, and that her husband was stationed at his desk in the bedroom, where he'd no doubt been tracking her progress on his laptop. She knew immediately that he'd been drinking—even before she saw the bottle of scotch as his elbow—and upon reflection, this state of affairs was not unexpected; when Acton indulged in his behind-the-scenes masterminding, he often retreated into a dark mood that apparently required a great deal of brooding, combined with the consumption of impressive amounts of alcohol. And in this particular instance, he was also worried that she was finally going to ditch him for his many misdeeds, and therefore she beheld a husband who was a strange mixture of repentant and triumphant—although he was trying his hardest to disguise the triumphant part, the wretched man.

She paused at the entry to the bedroom. "I see you've found a way to pass the time. And here I thought you'd be hoverin' by the door, wringin' your hands, and wearin' sackcloth."

He closed the laptop with a soft click. "I am wearing sackcloth in spirit. Tell me what I may do, so that you will no longer be angry."

"You can stop goin' about, killin' people," she retorted, throwing down her coat. "And give me some of that—is there any left?"

After a pause, he handed her the bottle, and with no small measure of defiance, she took a pull, and then grimaced as she wiped her mouth with the back of her hand. "Fah, that's horrid stuff. I don't know how you bear it."

"It's an acquired taste," he acknowledged.

"Like marriage," she countered with a great deal of meaning, and set the bottle down. "We're goin' to talk about this, and there's no shirkin' it." Acton famously did not like discussions, and small blame to him, as a discussion might feature the fact that a fellow DCI's corpse was now cooling in the morgue, the supposed victim of a supposed heart attack.

Somberly, he gazed out the window at the park lights below, his dark hair falling across his brow. "I didn't think you'd guess."

This went without saying, of course. "I know you too well, my friend. And Gabriel seemed to know what was goin' on, too, so best watch yourself."

He contemplated the glass he held in his fingers. "I am unsurprised."

"Well I wasn't 'unsurprised', mister hoity-toity backwards-speak, and I'm that ashamed of you. What on earth were you about?"

He glanced at her, and then looked away again, to review the scene below. "Drake killed Morgan Percy."

Drake did?" She was so surprised that she forgot she was angry for a moment, and sank down to sit on the bed. "Oh—why would he kill her? Because she knew too much?"

"I imagine."

She frowned out the window, thinking this over, although she supposed it made sense. Since Drake was the only player who'd escaped retribution for the corruption rig, he must have been nervous that his lucky streak could come to an end. And Doyle herself had made a mighty effort to convince Percy that she should grass on everyone in exchange for a lighter sentence, so it did seem likely that Drake would want to snip off this particular loose end. He'd already committed a containment murder before this one, so it wasn't as though he couldn't bring himself to do the deed.

She paused, because she realized she was trying to talk herself into this theory when she didn't necessarily believe it. While it was true that Percy had been murdered just as the initial arrests were being made—the timing of her death pointed to a panicked, containment murder—there was the undeniable fact that Drake was a wreck at the confirmation reception; filled with dread, whilst he was pretending to be all friendly-like with Acton. Drake may have killed Percy, but that was not the reason that Acton had killed Drake. There was something else at play, here.

Trying to decide what it was she was thinking, Doyle mused aloud, "So—those times when I caught you burnin' the midnight oil to set a trap, you were settin' a trap for Drake?"

Acton glanced at her, and then looked away. "In a manner of speaking."

Making a derisive sound, she hunched her shoulders in annoyance. "Now, there're some weasel-words, if I ever heard them. Why won't you tell me straight-out what's goin' on, husband?"

He was silent for a moment, contemplating his glass. "I'm afraid it is rather complicated."

Naturally, it was complicated—he didn't have any other mode of action, did Acton; the more complicated the better, so that lesser mortals couldn't possibly keep up. And something in all this wasn't adding up; even if Drake had been served up his just desserts, it didn't explain why it had been done so publicly. Acton was sending a message to someone—she'd bet her teeth on it. But who? And what was the message?

She blew out an exasperated breath, and moved on to the next worrisome subject in what seemed like an unending list. "Well—as usual—I don't have the luxury of combin' your hair with a joint-stool, husband, because we've yet another crisis. Should we put your head under the shower, or can you pay attention?"

Acton was immediately as alert as someone who'd put away a half-bottle of scotch could be. "Why? What has happened?"

"It's about Gemma, Michael. She's—I think—I think she's Solonik's daughter."

For a long moment, he stared at her, frowning. "Why would you think this?"

"Because she said '*rizhaya*'. I know it sounds silly, but she said it just the same way Solonik used to say it, when he was referrin' to my hair."

Still frowning, he bent his head and ran his fingers through his hair. "She must have heard it from Emile, Kathleen. Emile speaks Russian."

"Oh. Yes—that's right; and I think he's tryin' to teach her some Russian words." She knit her brow, wondering why she hadn't leapt to this rather obvious conclusion.

But apparently, Acton trusted her instincts more than she did, and lifted his head, trying to focus. "It must be more than that, or it wouldn't have alarmed you so."

Slowly, she nodded, grateful that he recognized this as an article of faith. "Yes; there's somethin' there. I know it makes no sense, but now I'm worried that Blakney's murder was a misdirection murder, and that Mary might be in danger, too. I know you told me that Solonik is dead, but—but I'm worried he's behind all this, somehow." A Russian underworld kingpin,

Solonik had attempted to muscle in on Savoie's smuggling operations but in the process, he'd got himself into a blood-feud with Acton—never a good idea—and had wound up getting himself killed, whilst serving a prison sentence. The family skullduggery had then been carried forward by the Barayevs— Solonik's sister and brother-in-law—who were hip-deep in the corruption rig, themselves. Barayev had been dispatched by Acton himself, and the missus had been incapacitated by a bout of poison, and thereby satisfactorily sidelined. So—there was truly no reason to believe that the Russian contingent had somehow managed to resurrect themselves and be of any influence whatsoever on the current round of crises. Strange, that Doyle had that feeling, nonetheless.

After a moment's contemplation, Acton shook his head. "I don't see how Gemma is involved, Kathleen. Solonik had no children save Jonathan, who is now Emile." He paused, and ponted out the obvious. "It would be difficult to convince me that Emile and Gemma are related."

Still troubled, she looked up at him. "Are you *sure*, Michael?"

"As certain as I can be. And aside from that, why would Gemma be living with Blakney, if she were Solonik's daughter? After all, the Barayevs were living here in London, at the time."

"Oh. Oh—of course; Gemma would be their niece, if she were Solonik's daughter." Slowly, she shook her head. "I don't know why I leapt on that notion—it doesn't make much sense, to think that there's any connection between Gemma and Solonik." Struck with a thought, she lifted her face. "Although Gemma spoke of an 'army-man', visitin' her; were either Solonik or Barayev in the army?"

"No. Or at least, there is no record."

Thinking it over, Doyle looked out the windows for a moment, and concluded, "There's something there, Michael— somethin' that we're missin'. I think we need to find out about

Gemma—it threw me back on my heels, when she said the word. I thought immediately of Solonik, even though I don't know why I would."

"Right, then. I haven't followed up, but I will tomorrow."

"Don't think I'm lettin' you go off-topic," she warned, and then carefully laid back on the bed, so as to contemplate the bedroom ceiling. "I'm warmin' up to lay into you like the rough end of a jack-saw, but first I have to rest-up."

Carefully, he crawled next to her on the bed, and lay back to contemplate the ceiling alongside her—he smelled of scotch, and remorse. "We could wait for tomorrow, if you are too tired."

"No. I am filled with righteous anger, and if I wait too long, my righteous anger will ease, and I'll start recallin' how very fond of you I am."

"Understood," he said in a meek tone. "Lay away."

With some suspicion, she turned her head to eye him. "I'm not talkin' about sex, you know."

"That is a shame," he admitted. "But I'd guessed as much."

"You're always thinkin' about sex," she accused, turning back to review the ceiling. "That, and who's next to be murdered."

"Surely not," he demurred. "I think about a good kidney pie, on occasion."

"It's not a jokin' matter," she warned.

"No," he agreed.

She pressed the palms of her hands against her eyes for a moment. "Saints and holy angels, Michael, I hate this. I'd rather be havin' sex, too."

"I know."

"I have to try to save your miserable soul. Faith, I'd be that fashed, if you were destined for hellfire, and I didn't at least make a push."

"Understood. You'd feel badly about the hellfire."

In an ominous gesture, she turned her head to eye him, yet again.

Chastened, he took her hand, and held it against his chest. "I beg your pardon, Kathleen. I do indeed understand."

"I know you can't seem to help it—manipulatin' things to suit your own notions," she observed fairly. "I know this, my friend. But I'm worried that you're in for a terrible reckonin', some day, and that I'll be on the sidelines, weepin' and wringin' me own hands."

Slowly, he offered, "Believe me when I say that I am working to secure our future, Kathleen. Ours, and Edward's."

This was true, and seemed a little surprising, as it was unclear how stupid Drake's miserable death did anything to secure the fortunes of the House of Acton. Nevertheless, she explained, "That's not our call, Michael—securin' the future. You're supposed to accept whatever's thrown your way, with all gratitude."

This pronouncement was met with a doubtful silence, and so she lifted the hand that held hers, and squeezed it. "This—this right here—is all that matters, truly. We could be livin' in a box under a bridge, and as long as we have this, nothin' else is needful."

Again, she was met with a doubtful silence, and so she sighed, and contemplated the ceiling again. "At least tell me you'll think about what I'm tellin' you."

"I remember everything you've ever said to me."

This was true, and as a reward for this accolade, she lifted his hand to her mouth, and kissed it fondly. "Well, try to remember this one more than anythin' else, please. And please don't forget about the hellfire."

"I won't."

Reminded, she turned her head toward him again. "Speakin' of which, I think the bishop wasn't at all happy with Father

Gregory. Faith, it didn't look good—him all sweaty and nervous, whisperin' to Drake like he's another in a long line of sneakin' weasels. The bishop's not one to miss much."

"I cannot disagree."

"No hoity-toity backwards-speech," she reminded him absently—when Acton was drunk, his speech tended to revert to House-of-Lords. "Well, it pains me to say it, but I hope that Father Gregory goes down with the Drake-ship, if he's just another villain. Horrifyin', to think he'd wind up in another parish, preenin' somewhere."

"Unlikely," he replied, and Doyle's scalp prickled, because she knew—in the way that she knew things—that Father Gregory was a marked man, too.

With some alarm, she propped up on an elbow, and brushed the stray hair from out of her eyes. "You can't go about killin' priests, Michael—whether they deserve it or not."

"No," he agreed, looking up at her.

"You're RC now; it's just not done."

"Understood."

She lay back down, relieved because she didn't have the sense that Acton was winding up to murder Father Gregory— thank God fasting. "The bishop, now; he's one who might think it justified."

"Very few Christian clergy have managed to survive Nigeria," Acton observed. "He is a rarity."

"A scrapper," Doyle agreed. "Let's not get on his wrong side."

They lay, side-by-side, in the darkened room for a few minutes, until Acton broke the silence. "Are you still resting-up, or may I ask a question?"

"We're not goin' to have sex," Doyle warned. "You have to learn your lesson."

"It's not about sex," he promised.

"Ask away. I'm not sayin' I'll deign to answer you, though—I'm righteously angry, remember."

"Why would Howard want Mary's phone number?"

Despite herself, Doyle smiled. "Because he's fallen in love with her."

His turned his head, and regarded her. "Is that so?"

"It is indeed so. I think that's one of the reasons I'm hesitatin' to pull a switchblade, myself. Something very good came from all this."

He thought about it for a moment. "Extraordinary."

She kissed his hand again. "What's extraordinary is we've got a quiet house. Let's go to sleep, and hope tomorrow's a better one."

Chapter 22

She'd forgiven him, and now it only remained to finish up.

It seemed to Doyle that she was barely asleep before the Filipino priest made his silent appearance.

"Oh," she said guiltily. "I'm that sorry, but your sister's been pushed down in the things-to-get-fashed-about list. Acton's gone and killed Drake."

"Yes." He nodded a bit sadly. "He was next."

She stared at him. "Never say Acton has a list?"

"Oh-oh, no; it is not his list."

Frowning, she regarded him. "Then whose list is it?"

He answered easily, "It is Drake's list."

Doyle closed her eyes for a moment, reminding herself that it was probably a sin to be short with a saintly priest. "I have to say, Father, that you're not the most sense-makin' ghost I've ever met, and I've met more than my share."

He seemed rather pleased, and smiled in a friendly fashion.

As he seemed disinclined to expound further on the subject, she ventured, "Was your sister on the list, for some reason?"

"Oh, no." He raised his sparse brows in surprise, and shook his head. "No. But she has been forwarding the blood-money to the bishop, because she cannot bear to keep it."

"Is it possible," Doyle ventured delicately, "That your sister is no longer alive? Perhaps she didn't wind up in the same place as you, and therefore you're all unknowin'."

He did not reply, but smiled his white, even smile.

"Your teeth," Doyle realized with dawning comprehension. "Holy Mother; of course—I'm that sorry I've been so dense."

Her eyes flew open, and she lay still for a moment, recovering, then drew a deep breath as she carefully shifted her weight—although Acton tended to sleep soundly, when he drank overmuch. Faith, she'd been a clueless knocker not to have seen what the ghost was hinting at—if he'd only the one sister, and she was feeling guilty about gettin' paid blood money, that meant she definitely wasn't the corpse buried beneath the rubble at the church. Or at least, that should be Doyle's working theory, until she could rule it out. And she could rule it out easily, if the coroner's report showed that the victim had Pacific Islander teeth—teeth normally survived even the hottest of fires, and any remaining bones would have been photographed for the report.

So, if the body wasn't the charwoman's, then where was the priest's sister? And whose was the corpse?

Frowning at the bedroom wall, Doyle mustered up her rusty detective skills—such as they were—and tried to create a protocol. It seemed clear there were two separate puzzles, here, and she had best go about solving both of them without her better half twigging on to it—a tall order, since she was homebound, and not what one would call mobile—not to mention when Edward made his grand appearance, she'd be even less mobile.

First, she had to take peek at the charwoman's autopsy—if the teeth were not Pacific Islander teeth, then it wasn't the charwoman. Instead—apparently—it was yet another misdirection murder that Acton was trying to cover up, if he was sending blood-money to the charwoman to keep it all quiet. This fit; the blood-money must be to convince the charwoman to allow everyone to believe the corpse in the church was hers.

Doyle paused, and traced the edge of her pillow with a forefinger, thinking on this. It all seemed so—so far-fetched, and so unlike her wily husband to go to such lengths to cover-up the death of some woman at Holy Trinity Church. He'd bigger fish to fry, one would think.

So; what was he about? Why would he do such a thing?

There was no clear answer, and Doyle reminded herself that—confusing as it all was—Acton's actions always seemed to center around her. I'm squarely at the center of Acton's universe, she thought, and—if the past is any guide—his dark-deeds-doing is always connected to something that he thinks will work to my benefit, somehow. That, or he's taking a bloodthirsty revenge for something that's happened to me.

She thought about the revenge angle for a moment, but discarded it. She'd seen Acton in vengeance-mode—a fearsome sight to behold—but he hadn't been in vengeance-mode, lately. Instead, he'd been pleased—faith, even the chaos at the flat hadn't put a dent in his benign attitude. And he did say that he was working to secure their future—although it seemed a strange thing to say; their future seemed as secure as it could possibly be, what with various hereditary estates all lined up, and a healthy heir on the way.

Try as she might, she couldn't even take a guess as to how the fair Doyle's secure future was somehow connected to the unknown corpse—who'd been killed, in the charwoman's place?

I should follow the protocols for when we're researching an unknown Jane Doe, she decided, and take a peek at the missing persons reports for the pertinent time period—I'll do that next thing, after I establish that the teeth aren't right. Mayhap some woman had some blackmail-worthy material to hold over Acton's head—something he didn't want the wife of his bosom to find out—and that's why she'd been the victim of a misdirection murder.

Doubtfully, Doyle tried to decide if she knew anyone at Holy Trinity Church who could serve as a candidate for an Acton arch-enemy. Timothy McGonigal and Nanda had gone to Holy Trinity, but Nanda was at the confirmation reception, very much alive—and glowering a bit at the bishop, she was; didn't seem to like him much.

Caroline McGonigal, Timothy's sister, had been a Holy Trinity parish member, but Caroline was already dead—no doubt about that, another best-be-forgotten event.

With a sigh, Doyle carefully shifted her weight again. I'm flummoxed, she thought. But first things first; I've got to find out about the teeth, take a peek at missing persons, and go from there.

The second problem was the Drake-puzzle. Acton had taken Drake down—but he'd waited until now to do so. Why? She knew—in the way she knew things—that the delay was significant, for some reason. The ghost had said that there was a list, and that Drake was on the list, but this did not seem helpful, as it made no sense—it was not as though Drake was on his own hit list.

And then there was Acton's explanation—or more properly, his implied explanation—that he'd set the trap for Drake because the man had murdered Morgan Percy. The only problem with this being that Acton had been doing his late-night-trap-setting well before Percy was murdered, and if he weren't drunk, he'd have been a bit more careful with the tale that he'd made up for his righteously-angry wife.

So; she was left with the original question—why had Acton been patiently setting a trap for Drake, and why had it been planned out for now, after Drake had already escaped any retribution for his role in the corruption rig?

Flummoxed yet again; I need more information, she decided. And I should prioritize the priest's puzzle first, since he's the one haunting me, and I should probably make a push to stay in his good graces. She then paused in surprise, because she was given the distinct impression that there was some sort of connection between these two puzzles—that Drake's murder and the charwoman's pretend-death were somehow connected.

This seemed extraordinary, and she decided, after a moment, that there was no point in even trying to find a commonality—she needed to know more. So, some leg-work was needful, and—since her own legs were swollen beyond redemption—she'd have to recruit some other foot-soldiers to do the legging for her.

With a small sigh, she tucked a pillow against her back, and settled in to try to catch some sleep.

Chapter 23

He didn't attempt to phone Layton; if the Commander knew about Drake, he'd have to step carefully.

On the whole, it was not surprising that Acton left early for work the next morning; he was no doubt behind on his caseload, what with the whole confirmation-with-attendant-murder taking up his week-end. That, and he was no doubt eager to duck out because the two children would be arriving soon.

Prompted by this thought, Doyle quickly picked up her mobile where she was seated at the kitchen table. "I think I'll meet Williams for a coffee this mornin', Reynolds. You're on your own, and may God have mercy on your soul."

"Certainly, madam. I thought to take the children on an outing to the park, before it becomes crowded."

Doyle's fingers paused. "Behind all that bravado, Emile's a bit nervous about the ducks, Reynolds. Just so you know."

"Is he? I will be circumspect, then."

As she rang up Williams, Doyle took a guess at what "circumspect" meant, and said with all sincerity, "I truly appreciate all your good works, Reynolds—you're a rare wonder."

"Not at all, madam; I would enjoy an outing to the park, myself." There was a slight pause. "Will the schedule remain the same, madam, after Master Edward is born?"

"Oh." This was, of course, a good question, and Doyle felt a little foolish, because—come to think of it—Acton had never mentioned it to her, and it was rather surprising that he hadn't mentioned it to Reynolds, either. "I imagine that—after I come home from the hospital— Mary will move in, and if she's here, Gemma will be here, also. We'll all be cheek-to-jowl for a while, I'm afraid."

"Very good, madam."

Williams picked up. "Hey, Kath."

"Hey yourself; any chance you can meet for coffee, on your way in?"

"Is Reynolds making breakfast?" This asked in a hopeful tone.

"Faith, Thomas; you're such a bachelor. All right; I'll see if I can convince him to cook somethin' up before he leaves for the park."

"Thanks—only for an hour, though; I have a witness at ten."

Doyle glanced up at Reynolds as she rang off. "Williams is longin' for your cookin'."

"Very good, madam." With efficient movements, the servant began to assemble the ingredients for an egg soufflé. "And before I forget, I must correct myself; the treasure in *The Sign of the Four* was not the spoils of war, as I'd suggested. Instead, it was a stolen treasure."

"Ah," she said. Leave it to Reynolds, to go looking it up when Doyle hadn't given it another thought. "Good to know."

The children appeared in short order, and were happy to have a second breakfast with Williams, with the result that Doyle had no opportunity to speak with him until after the park-outing party had left and the flat was quiet once again.

As he was on a deadline, she began without preamble, "I'm lookin' for a favor, Thomas. It's sort of a no-questions-asked favor."

"Oh-oh," he said, leaning back in his chair. "That sounds ominous."

"It's a DL sort of thing," she admitted. This was a reference to Williams' divided loyalties, which cropped up, once in a while; he was loyal to Acton, but on occasion he'd help Doyle in her quest to spike Acton's questionable plans. "It's nothin' too terrible, I promise."

"That remains to be seen. Do I have to drive somewhere with Lizzie Mathis?"

"She's not so very terrible," Doyle defended, and wondered if Williams was aware that not-so-terrible Mathis had probably poisoned DCI Drake. "And she has a crush on you, despite herself."

"So, I gathered. She definitely didn't want Tasza talking to me at the reception."

This was a revelation, and Doyle was immediately distracted. "Saints, Thomas; we already think that Tasza was steppin' out on Gabriel with that suicide-embezzler; you mustn't muddy the waters, it's not good for morale."

"She was just interested in my cascade case, is all—no flirting or waters-muddying whatsoever."

Doyle was eager to plunge forward with her favor, but found, for some reason, that she couldn't move on from this particular topic. "That seems a little out-of-character for Mathis, to be like a dog, fightin' over a bone. D'you suppose there's bad blood, twixt her and Tasza?"

He shrugged. "I shouldn't have mentioned it, I sound like a puffer."

Doyle decided—in light of the Mary situation—that it may soothe Williams' feelings to have two girls fighting over him, and therefore determined to say no more. "How *is* your pesky cascade case? Are the villains still hidin' the money from you?"

He sighed, and threw an arm over the back of the chair. "We've lost the trail, so now we're waiting for something to surface. But it's bound to happen; that amount of money has to show up somewhere, sooner or later."

Doyle made a sympathetic sound. "Well, that's frustratin'—I hate dead ends. I'd suggest you enlist the fair Tasza to help you, but I wouldn't want to give Mathis an excuse for a fistfight."

Smiling at the picture thus presented, he asked, "Why would Tasza want to help?"

"Oh—oh, I thought you knew. She's LEO. A forensic accountant, or somethin'."

He lifted his brows. "Is she? I suppose that would explain her interest in my cascade case, then." He paused. "And I suppose that means we can rule her out as a potential suspect, if the suicide turns out to be a murder."

Surprised that he didn't already know, Doyle informed him, "It was indeed a murder. Savoie told the bishop that the fellow was murdered. It was Drake, who killed him."

Slowly, Williams leaned forward and stared at her. "*Drake* killed him?"

Doyle was suddenly aware that she didn't really know this—well, she did, but it was an intuitive leap, and not something that could be backed-up with cold, hard facts. A bit lamely, she cautioned, "I think it's bein' kept very quiet, Thomas. That's why Savoie was there, at the reception; he was brought in to tell the bishop that the suicide was, in fact, a murder."

Frowning, Williams contemplated the table for a moment. "Well, I suppose that explains why Drake attacked Savoie at the reception."

Doyle could only reply, "I suppose." The two men hadn't truly fought, of course—it had all been staged by the stager-in-chief. What was immensely surprising was the fact that the stager-in-chief hadn't informed the trusty Williams of what was going forward—Williams had been kept out of the loop, yet again. A strange sort of world, she thought in wonder; where

Savoie knows more about Acton's doings than Williams. Acton must not trust Williams, yet—although when Acton had told her that Williams was not in his black book, it was true.

This thought, however, led to an even more extraordinary realization; why wouldn't Acton mention this very pertinent fact to the wife of his bosom? When he'd told her that Drake had murdered Percy—which was true—why hadn't he also mentioned that it was Drake who'd killed the suicide-embezzler?

She stared out the window without seeing, trying to come up with a theory. Perhaps Acton didn't know it was Drake who'd killed the fellow? But of course he did; he was Acton, after all. Not to mention that it was plain as a pikestaff that the sneaking weasels were having a collective panic attack at the reception—Drake was a wreck, and Father Gregory was sweating like a bowser at closing time—all because Savoie had said it was murder, not suicide.

So—when the corruption rig arrests were playing out, Drake must had gone into panicked cover-up mode, murdering Percy, and then murdering the suicide-embezzler a bit later, for fear of what he'd say. But these containment murders hadn't worked, and Drake had become aware, somehow, that Acton had twigged him out—the man was clearly unnerved in the receiving line, and was being all conciliatory—like a supplicant, begging for mercy. Mercy hadn't been meted out, though; instead Drake had been dispatched by her husband with a great deal of satisfaction, so that all Drake's murdering was for naught. Which led her back to the original question—why hadn't the worthy Chief Inspector mentioned the suicide-fellow's connection, or that Drake had murdered him?

This puzzling contradiction couldn't be examined, however, because Williams had pushed back his chair, after checking the time on his phone. "So, what's the favor?"

With an effort, Doyle returned her focus to the task at hand. "Well, I'm tryin' to find a missin' person—for a friend—but Acton wouldn't be happy with me for lookin' into it, so I was wonderin' if you would." This was more-or-less the truth, save for the relatively significant detail that the friend was a ghost.

He nodded. "All right. What do we have?"

"Female; middle-aged, I imagine. Within the past two months."

"Race?"

"Don't know."

He gave her a look. "You don't know the race of the missing person? It may be a long list, if you can't narrow down the race."

"I know—but if you could give me a print-out, I'd appreciate it. Try to keep it off the grid, if you will."

"All right; I'll try to get you something today." As he made ready to leave, he asked, "About the suicide-fellow's murder—who's handling the case?"

This was, of course, a good question; it wasn't like they could sweep the whole thing under the rug, what with the church hierarchy keenly involved. "I don't know, Thomas—recall that I'm stuck at home, mopin' about like a dosser."

He stood, and pulled on his jacket. "It's just that it may have some connection to my cascade case, remember? We were wondering if the players who were most likely to grass were being murdered—misdirection murders, so that no one could connect the dots."

"Oh—oh, I'd forgotten that workin' theory." Mainly because now she was convinced that the fellow's murder was a containment murder, to cover up Drake's involvement in the corruption rig. And yet again, she was squarely on the horns of a dilemma, because Acton had killed Drake without Williams' knowing, and her guileful husband may not want these particular dots to get themselves connected.

I hate it, she thought crossly, when the divided loyalties thing rears up to bite me, too. "Ask Acton, if he thinks there may be a connection with your cascade case," she advised diplomatically. "He's the one who fetched Savoie out of prison, to begin with, so I wouldn't be surprised if he knows what the suicide-fellow was up to."

Williams gave her a knowing look, as he walked to the door. "I don't know as I should, Kath; Acton may want to let it all go cold, in light of Drake's death. After all, if it came to light that Drake killed him, it would mean one more black eye for the department."

"Let justice be done, Thomas—although I feel like I'm shoutin' into the wind, sometimes. And in any event, you can't slander the dead." For reasons unknown, her scalp prickled.

At the door, Williams paused. "Have we heard from Munoz? I felt a bit sorry for her—with Savoie showing up, unannounced."

Doyle leaned on the door, and made a wry mouth. "Munoz is well-able to take care of herself, my friend. And luckily, Gabriel was Johnny-on-the-spot, to whisk her away."

With some surprise, he met her eyes. "No—was he? That might explain why Tasza was so bent on talking to me, if Gabriel had gone off with Munoz."

"I suppose," she agreed neutrally, knowing that Tasza wasn't invested in Gabriel in the first place, and that aside from that, Tasza was actually a bit over-interested in the fair Doyle's wedded husband. "Trust Acton to put the cat amongst the pigeons—Gabriel says that Savoie is like the scary hound from that famous story."

Amused, Williams raised his brows. "Which story is this?"

"Faith, Thomas, I always get it wrong, but I think there's someone named Doyle, like me."

"Oh—*The Hound of the Baskervilles.*" Still amused, he shook his head. "I don't think so, Kath; the hound in that story was just a cover for the real murderer."

"Oh," said Doyle, who was not about to inform Williams that the real murderer in the current story was, in fact, Acton. It was almost a shame, because she believed this would be where she could say that the story was 'apt', and it was a pity that the one time she could use the word correctly she had to keep her lip buttoned, instead.

Williams opened the door. "Thanks for breakfast, and I'll try to drop off the print-out before I run Layton to Trestles."

Doyle blinked in surprise. "You're runnin' Layton to Trestles? Whatever for?"

He gave her a significant look. "Now that Sir Stephen's moved out, Layton wants to take a look at the books, to see if there are any irregularities."

Doyle made a face. "Well, Sir Stephen's as crooked as a dog's hind leg, but I'd be very much surprised if Acton didn't keep watch on him like a hawk—Acton is nobody's fool."

"I just do what I'm asked, Kath. Mainly, I think Acton doesn't want Layton to drive up there alone—he's a bit frail, after all. And he's bringing in some furniture from storage for the nursery—family heirloom stuff—so I'll help with that; Acton's not going to want random workers, wandering around."

Doyle stared at him. "The nursery?"

He laughed at her surprise. "Yes, the nursery. You'll need one, Kath—unless you want Edward to sleep in a drawer."

A bit defensively, Doyle retorted, "I know I'll need a nursery, you knocker—Reynolds has got the spare room here all fitted out. I just didn't think about Trestles."

Williams shrugged. "Trust Acton to be on it."

"Yes," she said thoughtfully. "Trust Acton."

"Cheers," he said, and turned to leave.

"Cheers, yourself," she replied, and then scrolled up Munoz's number as soon as the door closed behind him. She'd already decided that she would give her two tasks to two different people, because she didn't want anyone putting two and two together—although to be fair, Doyle herself hadn't yet put two and two together. In any event, she'd the strong feeling that she should hold her cards close to the vest, at least until she figured out what-was-what.

Munoz picked up. "Doyle; I need to talk to you."

Doyle blinked. "You do?" Munoz never wanted to talk to her. "Can Reynolds make lunch?"

Doyle weighed this idea, since on the one hand, she probably shouldn't treat Reynolds as though he were a short-order cook but on the other hand, Reynolds was another one smitten by Munoz's *beaux yeux*, so he'd probably not complain. "All right. I have the children today, though, so let this be a warnin'."

"See you soon."

The girl rang off, and Doyle decided she wouldn't let Reynolds know ahead of time that Munoz was coming over, because he'd just run off to buy some stupid ingredients for some stupid spicy Spanish dish, and Doyle hated spicy food.

With no small effort, she heaved her legs up on the sofa table, and sat back to enjoy the momentary silence, whilst Edward poked about at her ribcage.

Chapter 24

It would be best to stay out of the office, this morning. He'd look into Gemma's situation, and then slip away to Trestles.

When the concierge buzzed in to inform Reynolds that Munoz was in the lobby, the servant straightened up in surprise. "Very good."

"You're supposed to ask if I want to see her," Doyle reminded him, but he was too busy reviewing the offerings in the fridge to respond. "Potato *tapas*," he decided. "It will have to do."

"What's that?" asked Emile, hovering behind the servant with great interest.

"Foreign food," Doyle explained in a damping tone. "Horrid stuff; I'll have peanut butter on toast, instead."

"Me too," Emile decided.

"Me too," offered Gemma, who generally copied Emile in all things.

"Perhaps you might attempt a taste of the *tapas*, Master Emile," Reynolds suggested, as he tied his apron. It is similar to scalloped potatoes, which I know you like."

Emile brightened. "Is it? Can I help you make it?"

"*May* I, and yes you may. You mustn't touch the peppers, although you may slide the potatoes into the pan. Careful, the oil will soon be hot. Miss Gemma, would you like to stand on the stool, just over here, and watch? Just so; very good."

Watching the activity, Doyle asked, "How was the park, this mornin'?"

"Reynolds is allergic to ducks," Emile disclosed, as he carefully watched the servant slice the potatoes. "So, we stayed to the path."

"Well, there's another misery, to be laid squarely at their doorstep," Doyle declared. "The wretched blacklegs; they should all be put in a rope."

Emile giggled, and then Munoz tapped at the door. Reynolds called out, "Would you mind, Lady Acton? I'd rather not leave the children."

Doyle hoisted herself up, because everyone knew that stupid Munoz's stupid potato-snack took priority. "Got it."

Munoz paused on the threshold and lifted her face in appreciation. "*Tapas Española*," she pronounced, throwing down her rucksack. "I haven't had any in forever."

"It will be ready shortly, Miss Munoz," Reynolds advised in a deferential manner.

He's never so willing to cook me up even a small blood pudding, thought Doyle with deep disgust; love is a shameful, shameful thing.

From his position at the stove, Emile turned his head to smile at the newcomer. "Hallo, Isabel."

Munoz walked over to stand behind the boy, and watch him as he carefully stirred the concoction in the pan. "Hallo Emile. I bet it was nice surprise to see your Papa."

"I'm going for a visit, tomorrow." Emile announced importantly.

Doyle offered in a sour tone, "Are you? Faith, the poor guards must need to even the numbers, for their next football match."

Reminded, Emile declared, "I'll make another picture for the wall."

"You could draw a switchblade, Doyle suggested darkly. "I've half a mind to draw one, myself."

"You're in a mood," Munoz noted, reaching to assist the boy as he stranded a potato slice on the pan's rim. "Maybe you should go back to bed."

Doyle collapsed into a kitchen chair. "Sorry. It comes from feelin' like a walrus in a fish tank."

"Cheer up; after lunch, we'll go for a walk around the block. Some fresh air will do you good."

This was of interest, as it indicated that Munoz wanted to speak in private. Come to think of it, the girl was in a remarkably cheerful mood—cheerful for Munoz, that was—and immediately Doyle was suspicious of her motives; a cheerful Munoz didn't necessarily bode well for the fair Doyle. "When's Drake's funeral? Have you heard?"

"No, I haven't. They may want to keep it private."

Doyle considered this. "They'll have to hold a memorial service at headquarters, at the very least. Can't just have a DCI die, without a peep."

Munoz cast Doyle a significant look, as Reynolds saw her seated at the table. "Maybe they're afraid too many grieving girlfriends will show up."

Doyle laughed. "Now, there's a sleeping dog who should be allowed to lie, in every sense of the word."

"Ladies," Reynolds interrupted. "Who would care for lemonade?" He then cast an admonitory eye in the direction of the children, and Doyle duly changed the subject to a less salacious one. "Who's taking over Drake's caseload?"

"I am. They're promoting me to DCI."

Reynolds turned to smile at Munoz, even though he surely must know that such news would not be at all welcome to the lady of the house. "How wonderful, Miss Munoz; my deepest congratulations."

Doyle quirked her mouth. "She's jokin', Reynolds. There's no way on God's green earth that she'd leap-frog Williams."

"All too true," Munoz admitted without rancor, and accepted her plate from Reynolds. "I think they're dividing up the caseload amongst the other DCIs, as a temporary measure. I shouldn't be surprised if they transfer someone in—we're in need of an extra hand, at the top."

"I'd feel sorry for the poor transfer," Doyle noted. "I'd hate to be pitch-forked from some peaceful place into this unholy mess."

But Munoz only shrugged, and lifted her glass. "I imagine there are more than a few who are dying to come to the Met; we've a lot more murders out this way, and so there's a better chance to make your bones."

"I suppose that's a mark in our favor," Doyle agreed. "City-folk are a murderous bunch."

"Ladies," Reynolds interrupted again.

Suitably chastened, the two girls turned the topic, and after they'd eaten, Reynolds enlisted the children to help him do the wash-up whilst Doyle and Munoz made their way downstairs.

It was a lovely, warm day, and Doyle took as deep a breath as she was able, lifting her face to the sunshine. She'd passed another indifferent night, tossing and turning, and had decided—for reasons she couldn't truly name—that she was not going to ask her husband about Drake's murder of the suicide-embezzler. Not just yet, anyways—there was something there—something alarming—and it was hovering just outside the edges of her poor pregnant-brain.

Munoz was quiet, and Doyle could sense that the other girl was trying to decide how best to broach whatever subject it was that she was wanting to broach, and so Doyle prompted, "If you've truly been promoted, Munoz, I don't want to hear it."

"No—no promotion. Gabriel wants to marry me."

Doyle stopped short, and stared at her in open astonishment. "*Gabriel* does?"

Munoz laughed, very pleased with Doyle's reaction. "I know—it's completely crazy. He showed me a four-carat diamond, and told me he'd marry me tomorrow, if I liked."

Shaking her head in wonderment, Doyle could only admire the man's ability to understand what would be most pleasing to her companion. "Well, I'd say somethin' about marryin' in haste, but it would be a case of the pot and the kettle, so I won't."

Munoz laughed again. "Not really; I'm not going to jump, of course. But it's an interesting development, considering he's already got a girlfriend, and we haven't even gone out on a date."

Doyle commenced walking again. "I think—I think his relationship with Tasza is more plasonic, Munoz."

"Platonic, you mean. Yes—he said something about how she'll be moving out, soon. But mainly I wanted to ask what you thought of him." She paused, and then admitted almost grudgingly, "You've got a good sense, when it comes to people."

Doyle frowned, because this was rather a sticky wicket; she wasn't sure what she thought about Gabriel. "I like him," she offered. "And I think he's very sharp."

"Yes," the girl agreed, her beautiful brows knit, as she gazed out over the flower beds. "I don't know if that's a point in his favor."

"You want someone you can respect, Izzy."

"I suppose," the girl agreed a bit doubtfully. "I don't think he's RC."

"I don't think so, either," Doyle conceded. "But he's not said, either way. On the other hand, Tasza's an evangelical, so it's not like he has any objection to religious beliefs."

Now it was Munoz's turn to stare in surprise. *"Tasza* is? I never would have guessed it."

With a small shrug, Doyle agreed. "Me, neither. It's true, though—she told me so herself. Apparently, she's a big fan of the DCS, and follows his prison ministry broadcasts."

Munoz made a derisive sound in her throat. "Just when I think people can't possibly be that gullible, I'm proved wrong."

"It's a low bar," Doyle agreed. "On the other hand, gullible people send a lot of business the Met's way."

But Munoz only shook her head. "I can't believe anyone thinks he's sincere."

"But they do. And it's such a common tale—a prisoner touts a religious conversion in order to get a bit more freedom, and good behavior credit."

Gazing at the sky overhead for a moment, Munoz considered this. "I don't know; in his case, I think it's all about getting attention. It must kill him, not to be running things anymore."

Doyle could only agree—having spent a memorable evening with the man when he'd tried to frame Acton, on that dark and stormy night. "Yes, he's someone who likes the attention. But I suppose—at the heart—you're more of a politician than a copper, anyway, if you wind up bein' the DCS at Scotland Yard."

"And now he's found his next rig."

"You have to hand it to him," Doyle agreed ironically.

Munoz glanced over at her. "It's strange, though, to think that someone like Tasza is a true believer."

Suddenly struck, Doyle frowned. "She's LEO, though; so mayhap she's investigatin' him. Mayhap she's investigatin' the DCS."

Once again, Munoz stared in surprise. "Tasza's LEO?"

Doyle nodded. "Yes, although no one seems to know it—Gabriel's been keepin' her under wraps. She's in forensics."

Munoz gave Doyle a look. "If she's forensics, then she's not investigating the DCS, Doyle—she wouldn't be doing field work, especially undercover field work. Besides, there'd be little point to it; he's already in prison for a long time."

This seemed self-evident, and Doyle felt a bit foolish. "No—you're right, of course. Faith, I hate bein' stuck at home; my brain's gettin' rusty."

They'd come to the end of the block, and now turned around to head back—apparently, Munoz wasn't willing to commit to an entire block-circling excursion. "Well, you should count your blessings. Acton's put an ugly homicide on my plate—a middle-aged male with his genitals cut off, so they think it's a spite murder."

Doyle grimaced in sympathy; spite murders tended to be brutal, messy affairs because the murderer hated the victim, and wanted everyone to know this. These were the murders that were done with dozens of stab wounds, or where the corpse had been tortured, or mutilated. "Any suspects?"

"Not yet, I'm still doing a prelim." With a philosophical shrug, the other girl added, "On the other hand, it shouldn't take much legwork."

This was something they taught you at the Crime Academy; a spite murder almost never went cold, because the killer was so incensed that he—or she—usually left a ton of evidence that pointed a big, shiny arrow directly at themselves.

This seemed an opportune time to ask what she needed to ask, and so Doyle adopted a casual air. "Speakin' of legwork, Munoz, I hope you don't mind if I ask another small favor—it's about that inheritance, again, remember? They need to see the dental autopsy—to verify that the dead woman was indeed the charwoman—before they divvy up the money."

But Munoz, true to form, was not going to buy whatever Doyle was selling without some serious pushback. "That makes no sense, Doyle. Wouldn't the death certificate be all that's needed? It would identify the victim, for legal purposes."

Fortunately, Doyle had anticipated just such an objection, and so she lowered her voice. "It's rather a messy situation, though. Because there's money to be had, some shirt-tail relatives are claiming that it's all a hoax, and that the death certificate was forged. I'm hopin' to save everyone a lot of fussin' and legal fees, and produce the dental report so as to lay all challenges to rest."

Munoz sighed, very much put-upon. "All right; as long as it doesn't involve a big time commitment. And I appreciate it, that you didn't pull the rescue card."

This, in reference to the fact that Doyle had fished the fair Munoz out of the river, once upon a time. "Faith, Munoz; I hate the rescue card as much as you do."

Munoz smiled slightly, and glanced at Doyle. "Gabriel doesn't really look at it as a rescue; he said he couldn't believe that I was strong enough to hang on until you came—that I was one out of a million."

Again, Doyle could only admire Gabriel's courtship-cunning. "I suppose that's true, Munoz; when you think about it, you really rescued yourself."

The other girl made a wry mouth. "Nice try, Doyle. I'm not the one who was given a commendation for bravery."

Doyle made her own wry mouth. "And from the DCS, no less."

"Life is very unpredictable," the other girl observed, and Doyle could see that she was very pleased with the Gabriel-development. So was Doyle, for that matter, as she'd been hoping that the latest Savoie-development wouldn't result in an epic rage-fit; Munoz was a fiery one, and Doyle didn't tolerate fiery ones very well.

As they turned to head back to the flat, Doyle teased. "You may not owe me anythin' for the stupid rescue, Munoz, but please don't marry Gabriel, because the next thing I know, you'll be hirin' Reynolds away."

"I'll make no promises," the girl replied, and it was true.

Chapter 25

"Those who carried burdens took their load with one hand doing the work, and the other holding a weapon."

Acton had texted to say he'd be home a bit late, and not to hold dinner. This was just as well, because Williams had dropped off a copy of the missing persons list, and whilst Gemma was being ferried home by the others, Doyle had a chance to pull it out of the envelope and look it over, to see if anything leapt out.

As always, it was a bit discouraging to see how many women had gone missing in a two-month period, but when Doyle concentrated on the names, running a finger down them, she didn't catch a sense that any one of them was of interest.

It was rather sad, to review the stark list on the government print-out paper, but Doyle comforted herself with the knowledge that someone, somewhere, must be missing them; there wouldn't have been a report filed, else.

As she slid the document back into the envelope, however, she also acknowledged that there were undoubtedly other women who'd dropped out of sight with no one to care, one way or another. Her scalp prickled, and she paused. So—someone was missing, and there was no one to care? The charwoman, who was pretending to be dead? No—her brother cared very much, and was prodding the fair Doyle to ease the woman's mind, somehow. Who, then?

For reasons that she could not explain, she immediately thought of Gemma, and how she'd said the Russian word—but that made no sense; this misdirection murder was a grown woman, and besides, no one was searching for Gemma. And even if they were, it was not as though the little girl would be difficult to trace.

Looking out the window, she frowned, because she felt the answer was tantalizingly close; a woman was missing, it was someone who shouldn't be a surprise, and if Doyle didn't have overly-pregnant brain, she'd probably figure it out in an instant.

Her mobile pinged, and she looked to see that it was Reynolds, returning with Emile from their car-ride. She fingered the phone, and wished it was Acton, instead. He knows who's missing-and-unmourned, she thought, because the wretched man is paying blood-money to keep it quiet. I've got to go to the source, then, and figure out some way to winkle the information out of him, even though my winkling attempts never seem to work out because Acton is a wily one, and he can run rings around me in terms of wiliness.

As she stuffed the list into the empty sugar canister, she braced herself for Emile's re-entry and decided that she'd just go forward without any particular winkling-out plan, since having no plan always seemed to work out best, anyways. Mustering up a smile, she greeted Emile—who literally began leaping across the room—and listened to Reynolds' recommendations for the dinner menu.

Acton returned just after dinner, and she knew immediately that he was tired—a rarity for him, since he never seemed to exert himself, overmuch; he was too well-bred to exert himself. The only time she'd seen him tired was when he was having a pretend-affair, which was definitely not the case at present, because he was too busy cooking-up some plot that involved misdirection murders and long-delayed vengeance.

Reynolds respectfully took Acton's valise. "I have kept your plate warm in the oven, sir."

"A moment, Reynolds, I'll shower, first."

He bent to kiss Doyle, who observed, "A shower? Never say you've had to scale a wall—that's what first-years are for. Did the perp get away?"

With a smile, he continued on his way into the bedroom. "I'd almost rather scale a wall; I am trying to tie up all loose ends before Edward is born, and I'm afraid it is heavy work."

This was true, and it made sense; Doyle knew that he was planning to take a few weeks off from work when the baby was born—a shrine-worthy miracle in itself—and he was no doubt trying to get ahead on his caseload, so that he could hand off the leg-work to lesser personnel, and monitor their progress. It went without saying that Acton wouldn't actually be out-of-the-loop for any appreciable time; the CID was woefully understaffed.

As Reynolds settled Emile in for the night, Doyle kept Acton company whilst he ate, and then suggested that she give him a back-rub—which was something he very much enjoyed, and would hopefully put him into an unguarded mood for a bit of winkling.

Willingly, he collapsed onto their bed, face-down, and Doyle clambered up to sit astride his back, and begin kneading his shoulders. "Let me know if I'm too heavy; don't want to crush you, like an apple in the press."

"No—it feels quite good. A bit to the left, please."

"Faith, you're gettin' old," she teased, and focused her efforts on his left shoulder. "Next you'll be sittin' in a shawl, and drinkin' down a posset."

His voice was muffled, due to the pillows. "Possibly."

"You've no idea what a posset is," she accused. "It just goes to show."

"It does sound delightful."

Doyle looked up at the wall, as she worked her fingers into his shoulders. "I never cared for possets; my mother would warm-up some horrid concoction when I had a chest cold." She paused, thinking about it. "It had rum in it, I think."

"Then I will pass," he replied into the pillows. Acton did not care for rum.

She smiled. "We could trade-out the rum for scotch, pour it over ice, and put all the other ingredients aside."

"Better." He reached behind him to grope until he found one of her ankles. "I missed you, today."

"And I you, my friend. Although I wasn't as hopelessly bored as my usual; I had Munoz over for lunch. Reynolds made her some sort of fried-potato-toppos."

"Reynolds is a good man."

"Well, I'm a bit disappointed in him, bein' as he's all smitten with her, and you'd think he'd be above that sort of thing."

She could sense Acton's amusement. "Surely, anyone is better than Savoie?"

With a great deal of meaning, she disclosed, "Gabriel is doin' his best to take her mind off Savoie."

With interest, he turned his head to the side. "Is he?"

"Yes, but I'll say no more, because I think she told me in confidence. And that also goes to show that I was right, and that Tasza is not what she seems."

He turned his face down into the pillows again. "It would be more surprising if you weren't right, Kathleen."

This, of course, was a fair point, and she decided that she may as well ask, "Then tell me what you know about Tasza, husband. I get the sense you'd met before the confirmation, and that you weren't at all surprised when I told you she was LEO."

Thus confronted, Acton turned his head to the side again, so as to speak to her. "Yes, we'd met. She was researching a cross-jurisdictional case, and interviewed me."

Doyle blinked. "Formally?" Any interview with a member of the CID brass was carefully set-up and controlled, for rather obvious reasons.

"No—she had a few questions, and we met informally."

Doyle waited a moment, and then with a sigh of impatience, bent down to scrutinize her sphynx-like husband's face. "Are you goin' to tell me the name of the case, or is it shrouded in secrecy?"

"Secrecy," he decided.

Doyle sat back up, and commenced rubbing his back again. "Well, you made an impression, I think. Small blame to her; it's a handsome thing, you are."

He did not deny it, but said only, "Absolve me of encouraging her."

"No—she's not your type. Your type is heavily-pregnant Irish girls."

"Which was not something anyone would have predicted, I think."

"Life is a never-endin' basketful of surprises," she agreed. "I suppose Tasza's type is tall and lean superior officers—although this business with Gabriel is a sham, so maybe it's just your title she's after."

"Speaking of which, Lady Abby rang me up, on a fairly transparent pretext."

Doyle frowned, as she kneaded. "Remind me who Lady Abby is."

"Howard's ex-fiancée."

Her hands stilled in surprise. "Oh—oh he's broken it off already? Well, I can't blame Lady Abby, either; she probably thought she'd wind up as a top-tier political hostess, and instead she's been thrown over for a lowly nanny. She needs a revenge-romance, and so it's no surprise that she's sending out feelers to see if you're assailingbull."

"Assailable," he corrected gently. "And to her regret, I made it clear that I am not."

"No," she agreed readily. "You're not. Now, there's one thing I never have to worry about."

With great fondness, he squeezed the ankle he held. "You needn't worry about anything, Kathleen."

"Worry is my middle name," she confessed. "It comes from knowin' too much, even though I'd rather just keep my head down, and ignore it all." She paused, and then added, "As a case-in-point, I know you're very happy about somethin', my friend, despite your aches and pains. You're cock a' hoop, if I may say so."

He couldn't help but chuckle. "Am I so rarely happy, then?"

She had to chuckle too, and lightly traced her fingers down his back. "I know it sounds silly, but it makes me uneasy for some reason—that you're so pleased."

With an effort, he propped himself up on his elbows, and turned to look at her. "What is there not to be pleased about, Kathleen? Everything has turned out very well, I think."

She regarded him with a knit brow, as this seemed a fair point. "Mayhap it just seems wonderful by contrast—not to have the sword of doom, constantly hangin' over our heads. It's been a harrowin' few months."

This was the wrong thing to say, and she knew it as soon as she said the words; Acton didn't like to think that he'd brought a heap of miseries to her doorstep, even though—technically—such was the case. Hastily, she warned, "Don't start apologizin', Michael; I'm pig-sick of it, and you know I wouldn't change a blessed thing."

He turned over to lay on his back, and propped an arm beneath his head. "I will make it up to you."

"Stop, or I'll dig out the rum, and force a posset down your gullet."

"The scotch-and-ice kind," he suggested. "I'll wait here."

Chapter 26

A list of missing persons was hidden in the sugar canister. Hard to believe, that she was suspicious, but she hadn't asked him, and so she must be. He'd have to come up with a plausible tale, which was no easy feat.

The following morning, it occurred to Doyle that she hadn't done any worthwhile winkling with respect to the Holy Trinity misdirection murder, and that she was a sad excuse for a detective, to be so easily distracted by her husband's bare back. To be fair, however, it was no easy thing to introduce the subject of charred corpses and blood-money during a back-rub, so she shouldn't be too hard on herself, and should instead look for another opportunity.

To the good, Acton had drifted off to sleep after she'd prepared his scotch posset, and he seemed much recovered this morning. As was her wont, she was lounging in bed, and watching him check his schedule at his desk.

"Barring an emergency, I can come home for lunch," he offered.

"Any chance I can meet you at headquarters, instead?" she wheedled. Faith, but she was bored to flinders.

"We could walk from here to the pub that's the next street over," he wheedled in turn.

"All right." At least it was a small victory, and a change of scenery might present an opportunity to attempt more winkling—no one ever explained to you that marriage involved so much *sub rosa* work.

With a click, he shut his laptop and swiveled around to face her. "I've made some inquiries about Gemma, and discovered that Blakney's relatives have been contacted by a man who's been asking after her. They'd nothing to relate to him, since they hadn't kept in contact. Description is tall Caucasian man, forties, with silver and black hair. Slavic, someone suggested."

Doyle digested this revelation with no small misgiving. "But he didn't leave his contact information?"

"No."

They exchanged a glance, because the man's failure to identify himself did not bode well, and Doyle put a voice to what they were both thinking. "D'you suppose she was bein' trafficked?"

Slowly, Acton shook his head. "It is hard to imagine—she has none of the signs. It is possible that she was being groomed for it."

Doyle rubbed her eyes with her palms. "It's too horrifyin' to even think about it, Michael. It reminds me of the sex slavery rig, that the players in the corruption scandal were operatin'—such evil, despicable people. There's goin' to be a hard justice for them, sooner or later."

Surprised, she removed her palms because she'd caught a flare of emotion from Acton. "What?"

"What, what?" he asked, regarding her steadily.

Narrowly, she eyed him, not at all fooled by his innocent manner. "It's only that I've the sense that you're itchin' to lay down a bit of home-brewed justice, and sooner rather than later."

"I think any man would feel the same."

This was not exactly a denial, but she comforted herself with the undeniable fact that the principals from the corruption rig were now abiding in prison, and it would be no easy feat to lay down a bit of home-brewed justice in such a situation. Or at least, one would think.

He bent to pack his valise. "I will see if I can get an ID on the man they describe—there's probably a street view, on CCTV. If he is a trafficker, then perhaps we can take him off the streets."

"Just don't stir up any sleepin' dogs," she warned. I'd hate to have to explain to Mary that I'm the one who arranged for Gemma to be snatched away by some Slavic man."

"I'll be discreet," he promised, and kissed her goodbye. Doyle watched him go, knowing that he'd turned the subject. Her remark about the sex slavery rig had evoked an unguarded reaction, and she could only assume that someone, somewhere, was getting their just desserts, and mayhap it was just as well that she didn't know the particulars.

As Doyle mentally girded her loins to spend another day wishing she were doing anything remotely interesting, her mobile pinged, and displayed an unfamiliar number. Since she was desperate enough to entertain even a salesman, she readily answered, only to discover that Tasza was on the other end.

"Lady Acton; I hope I am not inconveniencing you."

"Not a'tall," said Doyle, who'd decided that the day was suddenly looking up. "Thank you so much for comin' to the confirmation—I'm sorry things took such an unhappy turn, what with Drake dyin', and all."

"It was a shock," the other girl agreed, and this was not the truth. "We'd brought along a small gift for your husband, but—under the circumstances—we thought it best to leave. Would it be inconvenient if I dropped it by, today?"

"Not at all," Doyle assured her, and wondered what this was all about. "Just let me know when, so that I can tell the concierge."

"In an hour? Or wherever's most convenient."

"Give it two hours," Doyle suggested, calculating rapidly. "Just before lunch."

She rang off, and stared out the window for a minute, trying to decide if she should be ashamed of herself for laying such a trap for her husband. On the other hand—being how Acton was—he was probably already aware that she'd received a call from the girl, and so was forewarned. Besides, any anxious moments he might experience were wholly his own fault, and let this be a lesson to him.

Doyle could hear Emile and Reynolds in the kitchen, and caught the scent of cinnamon pastries. With a smile, she tied her robe around her girth as best she could, and then lumbered out into the kitchen. "Ho, Emile; I feel like a St. Petersburg duck, hissin' for my bolloki."

"*Bulochki*," he corrected with a giggle. "It sounds funny, when you say it."

"Everythin' sounds funny, when I say it," she acknowledged. "Good mornin' Reynolds; I'll be havin' a visitor in the late mornin'—a young woman who may or may not be a friendly."

Reynolds paused to look at her in alarm. "You are not certain, madam?"

"No," Doyle replied bluntly. "So, I'll give you the high sign, if I want you to think of an excuse to clear her out. You can say the doctor is comin' over sooner rather than later, or somethin'."

Surprisingly, the staid servant emitted a small flare of frustrated emotion as he nodded, "Very good, madam."

With a smile, she teased, "My wretched doctor's comin' over this afternoon—never say you've forgotten? That's very unlike you, Reynolds."

"It may have slipped my mind," he admitted, and it was not true.

With dawning horror, she stared at him. "Holy Mother; he's goin' to take blood, isn't he?" Doyle hated needles, and whenever such an occasion arose she could be counted on to pitch a fit, and thoroughly embarrass herself.

Poor Reynolds, who'd clearly been instructed never to admit to such a thing, could only stammer, "I—I cannot say, madam."

"I should flee the scene," Doyle groused unhappily, and flopped into a chair. "And now I know why Acton is comin' home—he's got to hold me down."

"It's just a pinch," Emile piped up. "It only hurts for a moment."

"It's medieval, and stupid," Doyle insisted crossly. "There has to be a better way, than all this pokin' and proddin'. Why, in the old days, people had babies in the fields, and such."

"I wouldn't recommend such a course of action, madam."

"I had to have a shot," Emile told her importantly, and pointed to an area on his upper arm. "You can still see the mark, if you look closely."

But Doyle refused to be consoled. "Well, you're miles braver than I am, my friend. Mother a' mercy, but childbirth is goin' to be a rare crack."

"I am certain you will handle it well, madam," Reynolds soothed, and it wasn't exactly true.

"Well, Edward better be worth it, is all I have to say."

"I will play with him," Emile pronounced. "I will teach him how to do things."

"Now, there's a comfort," Doyle noted sourly.

Hurriedly, Reynolds steered the boy by his shoulders toward the door. "Come, Master Emile; we'll take a quick walk over to the park."

"We can play Ducks and Drakes again," Emile enthused, bouncing in his excitement. "I can teach Edward how to play it, too."

This remark reminded Doyle that even more winkling was needful, as she was supposed to be finding out why Drake had murdered the suicide-fellow—another subject that doesn't just come up in ordinary conversation.

"We will pick up a pastry for luncheon, madam," Reynolds offered, as he escorted Emile out the door.

"There's no bribin' me, when it comes to needles," she pronounced in an ominous tone. "Nice try."

"What sort of pastry?" asked Emile with a great deal of interest, as the door closed shut.

Chapter 27

Apparently, Tasza was coming for a visit.
The Commander had lost the trail, then, and was
growing desperate. Good.

It was no surprise, of course, that Tasza turned out to be a walking bundle of lies. She was also a bundle of frustration, but that couldn't be helped, as Doyle wasn't much inclined to give her the information she was rooting around for.

They were having coffee on the sofa, whilst Emile sat with Reynolds at the kitchen table, practicing his letters in the faint hope that this would keep him quiet.

"Will there be a funeral?" As could be expected, the two girls were discussing DCI Drake's unfortunate demise, and Doyle had the impression that behind her offhand manner, Tasza was carefully watching the fair Doyle's reactions.

"I haven't heard, although I imagine somethin' will be held at headquarters. He had a long career."

"I'm sorry that we left early, but we thought it best to duck out."

"And small blame to you, it was crackin' awkward." Of course, the fact that Tasza's erstwhile beau had already ducked out with Munoz probably contributed to this decision, but Doyle held her tongue—the girl wasn't aware that Doyle was aware, and it was too complicated to keep it all straight.

Tasza sipped her coffee. "Did you know him well?"

"Drake? No, we traveled in different circles; I was in a different unit."

"He and Acton didn't socialize, then?"

Doyle drew her brows together, and pretended to think about it. "No—they weren't particularly friendly." This was a safe assumption, since Acton didn't socialize with anybody, not to mention that he'd up and murdered the man. Doyle decided it would probably be prudent to turn the subject, and so she offered, "Gabriel says you work in forensic accountin'."

Ah; a small flare of annoyance, which meant that the other girl wished that Doyle didn't know this. "Yes. It's rather dull work, I'm afraid. Nothing as clever as what you do."

Thinks I'm an idiot, Doyle noted, and sipped her coffee.

"Will you return to work, after the baby?"

"Yes," Doyle returned with some fervor, happy to have a subject she could expound upon. "I'm goin' barkin' mad with boredom. And besides, the Met is shorthanded."

Tasza offered up an insincere smile. "Thanks, in part, to your husband. Extraordinary, that he uncovered such extensive corruption, and exposed it all. We're lucky there are a few honest police left, like him."

Oh-oh, thought Doyle, with no small alarm. Oh-oh.

The girl continued to stir her coffee in a diffident manner, "Although there is a silver lining, I suppose; the DCS has found his true calling—he has a holy vocation, I think, and it took a prison sentence for him to find it. God indeed works in mysterious ways."

"Amen," Doyle agreed, after duly noting that Tasza didn't think this was the case, at all. "I was surprised to hear it, I must say—he didn't seem much like a believer, to me."

Beneath her causal manner, Tasza was suddenly alert. "Oh? Did you know the DCS well?"

"Not at all," Doyle confessed. "Although he gave me a commendation, once."

The other girl smiled her thanks to Reynolds, who'd come over to pour more coffee. "Well, I can tell you that there's no mistaking his sincere faith. I've listened to every one of his broadcasts, and I'm even more inspired, every time."

Doyle nodded affably whilst hiding her wariness. It was becoming more and more clear that Tasza was monitoring the DCS for reasons other than religious, that she was working for Gabriel—who hailed from MI 5—and that she knew, apparently, that DCI Acton wasn't all that he appeared to be. I've got to be careful, Doyle realized belatedly, and wondered if perhaps it wasn't the best of ideas to have invited the other girl over.

Thinking to do a bit of probing, herself, she adopted a casual air, and asked, "How does the DCS go about his ministry? I know he's become very popular, but it's hard to imagine how it happened, with him bein' in prison, and all. Does he preach at a chapel, there?"

The other girls lifted her coffee cup, and held it between her hands. "No—the prison ministry hour is put up on the internet, every week, and ever since he's been contributing, it's grown enormously—they're broadcasting into other prisons, now, nationwide." She paused, and took a sip. "He's raised more money than they know what to do with—his story is so inspiring."

Although Doyle knew that she was being watched for a reaction, she wasn't certain why this was. "The evangelicals can raise money like nobody's business," she agreed. "They're a lesson to us all."

"I wonder what they'll do with it?" The girl's eyes slid toward Doyle.

But Doyle had no problem serving up an honest answer. "They'll no doubt create some mismanaged program—church people don't make for very good business people, at least in my experience. Better to give it to some nuns who understand how to work wonders on a shoestring—we're very happy with the nuns who're handlin' the Irish orphanage, at my old school."

But Tasza was not interested in going off-topic. "Have you been over to the prison?"

Doyle blinked. "Me?"

The other girl laughed lightly, behind her cup. "Oh—I heard someone mention that Savoie's son visits him." The girl glanced over at Emile, seated at the table. "Such a sweet little boy."

Doyle wasn't sure which was the more surprising; that Tasza was keeping track of Savoie's visitors, or that she believed Emile to be a sweet little boy. "I'm in no shape to go anywhere; instead poor Lizzie Mathis gets roped into it."

The other girl's eyes narrowed, and Doyle could feel her quick flare of dislike. "Lizzie? Yes, I met her at the reception."

"She works in the forensics lab, at the Met," Doyle offered, happy to have the chance to throw out her own dart. "You would get along well, I think—you have a lot in common."

"I'm sure we do," Tasza agreed, and Doyle noted uneasily that this was true, and not necessarily the good kind of true. Time to change the subject, she decided, lest we start comparing which are the best poisons, and such—although Tasza was an accountant-person, Doyle would not be at all surprised to discover that she knew her way around a poison or two.

Tasza continued, "It was so kind of you to take the little boy in, when there was no one else. Gabriel mentioned that he has an aunt, but that she is not in the picture."

Nodding, Doyle informed her, "Yes, Mrs. Barayev—not a very nice woman, so it's just as well. And she's in poor health, anyway—she's in a rehab center, somewhere."

"Oh, I see." Tasza lowered her gaze and sipped her coffee, carefully hiding the fact that she was thoroughly frustrated, beneath her quiet exterior.

Puzzled, Doyle took refuge in sipping her own coffee and then realized—rather belatedly—that she'd slipped up, in mentioning Solonik's evil sister, because it was not generally known that Emile was Solonik's son, and not Savoie's son.

Tasza's right, she thought in disgust; I *am* an idiot. Although in my defense, Tasza's not one who should be speaking of the wretched Mrs. Barayev in the first place, so it's no surprise that I was caught flat-footed—

Slowly, Doyle lifted her chin to stare out the window. *Holy Mother*, she thought. *Holy Mother*—of course.

"She's never even tried to contact him? The aunt, I mean."

"No." Doyle made a mighty attempt to pull together her scattered wits. "Truly, I've never given her a stray thought." Except that she should have, because she knew—in the way that she knew things—that the boy's evil aunt no longer walked the earth, but instead it was her decidedly non-Filipino corpse that had been deposited amongst the rubble of the burnt-out church.

Doyle bent her head, thinking furiously. Why? Why had Acton killed the woman? It all made little sense—Solonik's sister had been a major player in the corruption rig, but she'd been sidelined by a dose of poison, or something—Lizzie Mathis' handiwork, no doubt—and then she'd been parked in a rehab facility, never to be heard from again. Except that—for some reason—Acton had decided that the evil woman needed to disappear—all these months later— and he'd cooked-up a crackin' fine misdirection murder to do it. Why? And why would Tasza be interested?

The concierge buzzed, and after answering, Reynolds announced to the two girls that Officer Munoz was in the lobby.

And here I was afraid I'd be bored to flinders, Doyle thought, and instructed the servant to send up the new arrival. Tasza may not be romantically attached to Gabriel in truth, but Munoz didn't know this, and it would be a rare treat, for once, to put the Spanish girl on the defensive—Doyle shouldn't be the only one having to weather all the awkward situations.

But as usual, Munoz was well-able to manage any social predicament, and expressed her insincere pleasure upon beholding Tasza. In turn, Tasza made a show of moving over for Munoz, whilst Reynolds served the newcomer coffee, and then left a tray of home-made madeleines on the table—apparently, Doyle and Tasza hadn't been worthy.

Tasza explained her gift-leaving errand, and as a result, the two guests commenced to discuss Drake's death yet again, with a meaningful show of insincere regret.

"Poor man," Tasza offered. "There were those rumors about his lifestyle, of course, and I suppose it finally caught up with him." This, with an arch glance at Munoz.

"Say what you will," Munoz replied benignly. "He was a good detective, and solved a lot of cases."

"Well, it must have been a shock; you dated him, I think?" Tasza smiled sweetly, having decided to take a more direct approach.

"Not recently," Munoz replied, with her own sweet smile. "I've met someone new."

Touché, Munoz, thought Doyle. And if it comes to fisticuffs, I'm not sure who'd win; I hope Reynolds has his gun somewhere handy.

"Lady Acton and I were just discussing the DCS, and his new-found calling," Tasza continued, with another coy smile.

Never say Munoz had a fling with the DCS? thought Doyle with some surprise.

But—judging from the girl's reaction—it did not seem as though this were the case. "He's a charlatan," Munoz opined bluntly. "He's only found another way to get in front of the cameras."

Tanya shook her head, slightly. "Oh, then I'm afraid we'll I have to agree to disagree. I believe he has sincerely converted."

"I only hope he's not duping the gullible," warned Munoz, with all appearance of concern.

Two faint spots of color appeared in Tasza's cheeks. "I suppose time will tell."

Munoz seemed disappointed that Tanya was unwilling to rise to the bait, and so she turned her attention to Doyle. "I'm afraid I can't stay, I just wanted to drop off the autopsy report."

"Thanks, Munoz," said Doyle, who no longer needed it.

"I am willing to prepare a quick lunch, ladies," Reynolds interjected in a hopeful tone.

"What are you going to make?" Emile piped up with great interest.

"I'll pass—I have a lunch date," said Munoz, who slid a sly glance over toward Tasza.

Doyle said with pretend-regret, "I'll have to pass, too, Reynolds; Acton's takin' me for a walk." This was just as well, it was exhausting, having to absorb all the cross-currents, and Doyle was sincerely regretting that she'd invited Tasza over in the first place. I shouldn't make any decisions when I'm out-of-sorts, she decided; mental note.

"Let's have peanut-butter sandwiches," Emile suggested to Reynolds.

"Certainly, Master Emile," replied Reynolds with good grace.

"Take one for your Papa," Munoz suggested, as she hoisted her rucksack. "He's very fond of peanut butter."

Whilst Tasza stared at the other girl in surprise, Munoz waved her hand in a casual gesture of farewell.

Chapter 28

It was time, perhaps, to take a step back, and allow the spite murders to play out.

Reynolds hurried over to hold the door for the departing Munoz, but it wasn't necessary, because the door opened, and Acton walked in.

Oh-oh, thought Doyle, watching her husband take a glance around the room. The illustrious Chief Inspector is not happy with his wayward wife.

"Ladies," he greeted them.

"Sir," said Munoz. "I was just leaving."

"Don't forget about your report," Tasza reminded her.

"I won't," the other girl replied easily, and then walked out the door without leaving the report.

Silently, Doyle blew out a relieved breath; Munoz had remembered that she'd wanted the report on the sly—bless her—although it truly didn't really matter, anymore. The mystery of the misdirection murder had been well-and-thoroughly solved, and the only question that remained was the motive for the aforesaid misdirection murder—that, and why the fair Tasza was so very interested.

"Ms. Kozlowski," Acton said, approaching to politely take Tasza's hand. "A pleasure to see you again."

Again, two faint spots of color appeared in the girl's cheeks. "Chief Inspector."

"We were planning a walk to lunch, would you care to join us?"

"Oh, no," the girl disclaimed, and rose to leave. "I'd just dropped by with your gift—thank you for the coffee, Lady Acton."

"Can I come to lunch?" Emile asked hopefully.

"*May* I go to lunch, Master Emile."

"I'm afraid you may not," Acton answered. "Some other time, perhaps."

"I'll be going—thank you, Reynolds." With a nod toward the servant, Tasza walked over to the door.

Acton held out a hand to help Doyle rise. "We can accompany you out—if you are ready, Kathleen?"

"Lead on." Doyle allowed him to hoist her to her feet, and wondered if Acton—who could barely tolerate sharing a lift with Doyle, let alone anyone else—needed a truth-discerner, to listen in to a conversation.

But this did not seem to be the case, as they spoke of inconsequential matters during their descent—although Doyle did have the impression that the other two occupants were being careful not to speak of something in front of her—sharing a secret, they were. Since she'd no doubt that Acton was thoroughly faithful—and alarmingly so—Doyle decided that he must be baiting a trap of some sort, and the fair Tasza had best watch herself, or she'd wind up as the next smoldering corpse in a ruined building.

On the other hand, Acton had a proven history of enlisting opponents who may be useful to him—Savoie serving as an excellent case-in-point—and so it may well be that he'd decided to enlist Tasza, in some way.

Doyle paused with this thought, because she'd have sworn that Gabriel had already been enlisted for team Acton, but now she wasn't so certain; if Gabriel was Tasza's superior officer, one could presume she was acting on his orders, and that did not bode well for the House of Acton—Gabriel was a sharp one.

After they'd parted from Tasza on the pavement, they began their slow progress toward the pub, which was situated on the next street over. Acton stayed silent, so Doyle decided that she may as well get the ball rolling. "Sorry to set you up like that," she offered.

"Are you?" he replied, in a deceptively mild tone.

But Doyle wasn't having it, mainly because her own marital transgressions couldn't hold a candle to his. "Well, if we're goin' to pull caps, husband, I get to pull the hardest. Tell me what's afoot, that Tasza would want to elbow her way into the flat."

"Why did you allow her to do so?"

Doyle blew out a breath, and contemplated the sky for a moment. "I wanted to see what she was up to. She's lookin' into your misdeeds, I think. And if Tasza is lookin', that means Gabriel is, too."

"Perhaps," he agreed. "But you must allow me to handle it, Kathleen."

Crossly, she retorted, "I'd rather Edward wasn't born in prison, Michael."

"I will endeavor to prevent such an occurrence."

As a result of this lofty syntax, it occurred to Doyle that her husband was as annoyed with her as he allowed himself to be, and that she wasn't exactly free of blame for this turn of events. Softening her attitude, she offered, "I should have told you, Michael, and I was regrettin' it straightway. I'm truly sorry."

He paused, and kissed her forehead, to show that there were no hard feelings. "I'd rather you trusted me."

She tucked her hand into his arm and made a wry mouth, as they began moving forward again. "And I'd rather you weren't discreetly flirting with the opposition—although I can see why you're tempted by the challenge; she's rather an ice-maiden."

"What was the report she spoke of?"

Trust Acton to have caught the reference, and Doyle sighed with resignation. "The autopsy report that shows the dead Filipino charwoman was actually Solonik's sister, Mrs. Barayev."

There was a small pause. "The report will show no such thing, I'm afraid."

She glanced at him in surprise. "Not even the dental records?"

"Nothing out-of-line."

She shook her head. "You're a rare wonder, husband. My hat's off to you."

"I could say the same of you. How did you guess?"

But Doyle was not about to speak of ghostly priests, mainly because she wasn't certain exactly what the aforementioned ghostly priest wanted her to do. "How I guessed isn't important; you can't go about killin' people, Michael—I've told you a *thousand* times."

It was his turn to contemplate the sky for a moment. "I am hoping that very soon, there will no longer be a need."

"But there's *never* a need—it's a terrible sin, Michael. And I know you think you're justified—that you're givin' the system a needed push—but we can't just go about, suitin' our own notions of how everythin' should turn out. We have to think of the greater good."

"I am indeed thinking of the greater good," he replied, and it was true.

Exasperated, she insisted, "But your 'greater good' may be somethin' different than another person's, and who's to say who's right? That's why we go to the trouble to hammer it all out, in the courts." She paused, because they'd gone over this rough ground many a time, and she'd the sneaking suspicion that she hadn't made much of a dent in his take-no-prisoners philosophy. "It may mean we miss the mark, sometimes—but otherwise, no one respects the system, and only the strong will have a say in it."

With a soothing gesture, he pressed her hand with his other one. "I understand the theory, but it assumes a good faith effort on the part of those who wield power. We've recently weathered a scandal that flourished only because of corrupt judges, and corrupt law enforcement."

This was true, and with rare diplomacy, she refrained from pointing out that his own schemes weren't much different from the schemes of those who'd been exposed as blacklegs. "I know, I know. But I still think the justice system is our best bet, despite its flaws. And remember that there'll be an ultimate justice, Michael—that's where it will all work out exactly as it should."

He cocked his head. "There may be an ultimate justice, but I believe the concept of societal vengeance is a valid one. The citizenry must be assured that the worst members of society will be publicly shamed, and publicly punished."

This, of course, was a valid point, and Doyle cast about for a counter-argument. "Then we shouldn't appeal to that instinct—that desire for vengeance. We'd be pavin' the way for even more spite murders, and there's too many of them, already." She winced, thinking of Munoz's grisly case.

He made no response—being diplomatic in his own turn, he was—and she was left to contemplate the rather ominous fact that her husband had mentioned that "very soon" there would no longer be a need for any more misdirection murders, which meant, in Acton-speak, that he was contemplating yet another murder, and very soon. But whose? All the players that could be a target for a hearty helping of Acton-style retribution were either dead, or tucked away in prison, where he couldn't get to them. She frowned, having the feeling—yet again—that she was missing something obvious.

They turned onto the next street, and walked for a few minutes in silence. "How did you know about the charwoman, Kathleen? Can't you tell me?"

Doyle thought it over, knowing that he was worried about a potential breach in security, and so she decided to give him the basic truth. "It was the blood-money. The charwoman feels guilty about accepting it—she was worried that she'd pay a price, and not necessarily in this life. I suppose it circles back to that discussion we were just havin'."

"I don't believe we have discussions," he reminded her, gently teasing.

"Faith, I'd forgotten. Well then, it circles back to the non-discussion we weren't havin'." She glanced up at him. "You're a tough nut to crack, husband."

"Surely not," he soothed. "I do understand all your points."

She sighed, because he was being diplomatic again, and she may as well be a bird, beating her wings against a windowpane. "Speakin' of blood, I twigged on to the fact that the doctor is comin' over to poke me with his vile needle—I can read Reynolds like the back o' my hand."

"I've already canceled Dr. Easton, Kathleen; I am sorry you were upset."

But this was annoying, in its own way. "Reynolds shouldn't be grassin' on me, and lettin' you know that I'm a big baby."

"I'm glad he did; I wish it hadn't ruined your morning."

With a sidelong glance, she reminded him, "Recall that I had Tasza and Munoz over; my mornin' was already well-and-thoroughly ruined."

They'd arrived at their lunch-spot, and he held the door for her. "Surely it wasn't so very terrible?"

"You've no idea, my friend. I just kept my head down, and tried to avoid the cross-fire."

He chuckled, and then placed a hand on her back, as they headed toward a table. "The doctor wanted to take a sample of your blood to make certain they have the correct blood-type available, in the event a transfusion is necessary."

But she scorned such a suggestion. "Not at all necessary, Michael. I'm Irish, remember? I can have a baby anywhere, at any time. It's built into the genetics."

Amused, he smiled. "Nevertheless, it is considered a necessary precaution."

He'd been gently persistent, which meant she'd probably have to give in. "I'll need to be bribed, then."

"Name your price."

"Tell me why you are so wary about Tasza."

There was a pause, as he saw her seated, and then came around to seat himself. "I'm afraid the less you know, Kathleen, the better—particularly at this point in time. I would ask that you trust me."

The remark only confirmed her feeling that something was coming to a culmination, and—judging from Acton's general mood, these past few days—Katy bar the door against whatever it was. Perhaps it was just as well that she stay in the dark; she was about to have a baby—lest she forget—and hopefully, this happy event would take Acton's mind off murder and mayhem for a few moments, amen.

"All right," she said, because she knew that was what he wanted to hear. "But please keep to mind what I've said, Michael, and take no chances; I'm in no shape to mastermind a prison-break."

"Nonsense," he teased. "I have every confidence."

Chapter 29

He was reluctant to bring up the subject. She didn't enjoy staying at Trestles.

After Acton had returned to work, Doyle's day continued eventful, because Williams dropped by, on his way home from work. "Where's Reynolds? I was hoping for another meal."

"Reynolds is not here. Emile's gone to visit Savoie, and so the poor man's got a few hours of blessed silence to do whatever it is he does in his spare time. You are welcome to forage for yourself, if you'd like."

Williams swung down his rucksack, and removed his jacket to throw it over the back of the sofa. "I might scramble-up some eggs, then. Want any?"

"No—I'll watch. I've lost my appetite, lately."

He looked through the cupboards until he came across a pan, and then removed the eggs—along with a bottle of beer—from the refrigerator.

"Thanks for comin' by," she said, watching him roll up his sleeves. "It's that rough, when you can't wander about at will. I've half a mind to take up croquetin'."

He smiled, as he lit the stove burner. "I think you mean crocheting."

"Both," she declared flatly. "And whittlin', besides. Faith, I hate all this doin' nothin'; I'll never make a decent aristocrat."

Cracking the eggs with a spoon, he broke them directly into the pan. "Not much longer, Kath. And you could always take up cooking."

Resting her chin on her hands, she watched him over the back of the sofa. "There'd be little point in learnin' to cook; in a very strange twist of fate, there's people who cook for me, now—although the new cook at Trestles hasn't had much of a chance."

"She's good," he confirmed, as he added a splash of milk to the eggs. "She served me up a very nice brisket on a moment's notice, when I was over there with Layton."

Doyle smiled. "D'you see what I mean? Who has brisket for lunch, I ask you?"

"Well worth the trip," he confirmed, as he turned up the heat. "Although Acton missed it; he was overseeing something on the grounds, with Hudson."

Doyle stilled for a moment, because this was a surprise—Acton had been there at Trestles, too? Surely, he hadn't mentioned it—had he? With a knit brow, she lowered her gaze and thought about it. No—she was certain he hadn't mentioned it. That was the day he came home tired, and needed his back rubbed.

Her scalp prickling, she lifted her face. "Was Tasza there, by any chance?"

He looked up in amusement as he stirred the eggs. "No. Why on earth would Tasza be at Trestles?"

"I don't know—just a thought. She came by to visit here, earlier today, even though she's not the pop-in-for-a-visit type."

With a small smile, Williams turned his attention back to the eggs. "Acton is not having an affair with Tasza, Kath."

"I know, I know—please don't think I'm havin' pregnant-lady paranoia, Thomas. Tell me, what do you think of Tasza?"

"No, thanks."

She made a face. "I don't mean in *that* way—men; honestly. I meant what do you think about her in general—I got the impression when she was here that she was rootin' around for information, of some sort."

He shrugged as he stirred the eggs. "I can't help you; I really haven't interacted with her much at all."

Doyle frowned, and watched the stove-top flames. "It just makes me uneasy; it's never a good idea to cross swords with Acton."

He raised his brows in surprise. "*Tasza* is crossing swords with Acton?"

Doyle decided that she should snabble it, as it seemed clear that DI Williams was yet again being kept out of the loop—and there was no shame in it, as the fair Doyle was also a left-out-of-the-looper. Instead, she offered vaguely, "I don't know what I think, just now, but I've got one of those feelin's I get when I think there's a common thread, runnin' through all these different things, but I can't quite pluck at it."

With an amused expression, he glanced over at her. "Welcome to my world, DS Doyle. Although I finally have a promising lead on the cascade case."

This seemed of interest, and she was more than willing to divert her thoughts to another topic. "You do? What's happened?"

He cast her a meaningful glance. "For a short time, all the money was parked in the prison ministry account at Wexton Prison."

She met his gaze in surprise, and then decided that she truly wasn't much surprised, after all. "The DCS was in on the cascade scheme? What—was he launderin' the corruption rig money?"

"Something like that. The money's gone, now, but at least I've picked up the trail again. I should be able to trace what happened to it—it's a huge sum of money, so it's not easy to hide."

Doyle made a sound of derision. "Trust the DCS to be up to his eyeballs in it—and that would explain his sudden conversion, too. The evangelicals are famous for raisin' bushels of money at the drop of a hat, so it's the perfect cover for movin' large sums around." She paused, thinking about the DCS, who'd also crossed swords with Acton, and had come up well short. "Will they prosecute him?"

"It depends on what we find. I'll keep you posted, but in the meantime, keep it under your hat."

"Right. Well, that's good gossip, DI Williams, and I'm much obliged."

He turned off the stove, and scraped the eggs onto his plate. "I've another one I've got to keep as quiet as I can. A spite murder—man was groin-shot."

"Wife," Doyle guessed immediately. A groin-shot was usually administered by someone who was familiar with that area.

"No; he's never married. But here's the fun part—he was a Health Professions Council member." He shot her yet another significant glance.

"Oh-ho," she said, raising her brows. "The plot thickens, it does." The council members had been involved in the corruption rig, but there hadn't been enough evidence to go after any of them. That, and there was the obvious problem in going after such worthy public servants; any case would have to be airtight.

Their discussion was interrupted when the concierge buzzed to say that Mathis and Emile had returned from Wexton Prison, and were looking to come up.

"Brilliant," said Williams, sitting down with his eggs.

"Be nice," Doyle warned. "She's doin' the work of the angels, takin' Emile to see his Papa."

"Savoie is not his Papa," Williams advised, in between bites. "That whole situation seems a little smoky, to me."

Doyle had to concede that this was a fair point—that Solonik's son had been taken in by an underworld rival in the first place, not to mention that the boy was currently living the high life, here at castle Acton. "I know. But Savoie does love him, Thomas—I am certain of it."

He glanced up at her. "Just be careful, Kath."

"'Careful' is my middle name," she teased, as she walked over to get the door. "You—of all people—must know that."

He gave her a look, as Lizzie and Emile made their entrance—Emile immediately running over to greet Williams and inquire if there were any more eggs.

"I'll make more," he agreed with good grace, pushing his chair out. "How hungry are you?"

"I'll do it," Lizzie offered, taking off her coat. "And I'll see if there's bacon, or sausage."

"You shouldn't wait on us," Williams protested. "It's not PC."

"I like to cook—I do it all the time, at Trestles," she countered. "I don't care if it's not PC. How about you, Lady Acton?"

"I'll pass, Lizzie. What did Savoie have to say for himself?"

"My Papa says we will go home soon," Emile disclosed excitedly. "I have to be patient."

"That's you," Doyle agreed. "'Patient' is your middle name."

"I don't speak much with Mr. Savoie; instead, I sit in the waiting area during their visit," Mathis explained. "Although I complained about one of the guards, who was a little too friendly."

Because Williams looked as though he was winding up to make a smart remark, Doyle hastily observed, "The guards there are awful. Cheeky, and full of themselves."

"You've been to Wexton?" Williams asked with some surprise.

"Yes—in connection with the corruption case," Doyle answered vaguely. In truth, she'd gone on an off-the-record visit with Solonik, whilst he was being held there. She'd been hoping to ferret out the Russian's evil plans, but instead, she'd walked—

like an idiot—straight into a trap, which went to show you that she should keep her off-the-record activities to a bare minimum.

"One of the Wexton Prison matrons was a player in the corruption rig," Williams explained, for Mathis' benefit. "She was at Trestles, that night."

"I remember her," Mathis noted in a neutral tone. "She fell ill."

Since Doyle was convinced that Mathis had poisoned the woman, she hurriedly turned the subject. "And the DCS was exposed as a blackleg that very night—the miserable gombeen."

"A lot of drama," Mathis agreed, in a monumental understatement. "Not what we're used to, there."

"And I argued with you about tactics, Mathis," Williams reminded her, teasing. "I don't think you're used to that, either."

"Not at all," the girl agreed evenly, and dished out eggs and bacon without further comment.

Oh-ho, thought Doyle, smiling to herself. It's smitten, she is—or as smitten as she allows herself to be. It's like a soap opera, around here, what with Howard after Mary, and Gabriel after Munoz, and Mathis—well, Mathis was not exactly after Williams, but the girl wouldn't protest if the man made a move, not that it seemed likely to happen. Idly, she watched them, as Williams listened to Emile's chatter, and Mathis walked over to replace the boy's rucksack on the closet hook, and hang up his jacket.

Wait—there it was; the boy's jacket. Doyle stared, as Mathis casually closed the closet door, and returned to the sink. Doyle was certain that Emile had lost the jacket at the confirmation reception, but now it had re-appeared, coming back from Emile's prison visit. So—whatever it was they were smuggling had made another round trip.

"When do you start school?" Williams asked Emile, with the air of someone hoping that it was sooner rather than later.

"Next month," the boy pronounced importantly. "I will wear a uniform, and there are rabbits, in a cage."

Mathis looked up from doing the wash-up. "Oh—Lady Acton, Mr. Savoie asked if you would see to it that Emile has all the required inoculations."

Doyle looked up in surprise. "I thought Emile already had his shots."

"Mr. Savoie mentioned that he needed them; I've no idea, either way." Mathis dried her hands, and then checked the messages on her mobile. "I'll have to get back to the lab."

"Well, thank you, Lizzie. When's your next visit to the prison?" Mainly, Doyle was thinking about the next round of smuggling.

"I don't believe there is anything scheduled," Mathis replied in a neutral tone, and Doyle's scalp prickled.

Chapter 30

The final act was slated for tomorrow, and then all accounts would be settled.

Doyle could barely contain her impatience as she waited for Williams to leave, and nearly pushed him out the door when he showed an inclination to linger—probably was angling for another beer—but she'd some sleuthing to do, and best get it done before Reynolds came back. After closing the entry door, she pulled Emile's jacket from the closet, and carefully examined it; checking the seams until she saw what she was looking for. Doyle's mother had taught her to sew a fine seam, and a small section of the jacket's inner lining had been hastily tacked.

Squeezing, she systematically went over the garment, and concluded that whatever it was, it had been taken out at the prison, which only made sense; something was going in, not coming out. What was surprising, though, was that the tacked seam area measured two inches, at most. Not a mobile phone, then? Cigarettes would fit, but it was hard to believe that Acton had gone to all this trouble for cigarettes, and she was certain that the smuggling operation was Acton's—there was a plot afoot.

Thoughtfully, she re-hung the jacket, and considered what was best to do. Acton was up to something—faith, the day Acton was *not* up to something should be declared a national holiday. He was in a good mood about whatever-it-was, and she'd the impression that he was crossing swords with someone—she knew the signs, by now—and that he was winning, which was not a surprise.

And—according to Mathis' last remark—no further prison visits were planned, so presumably the smuggling of small objects into the prison was at an end. Savoie was still there, though—he'd been held for an unusually long time without being charged. Savoie, who had the crooked guards at Wexton Prison in his back pocket, and was promising Emile that they'd go home, soon.

The most logical conclusion—when you added it all up—was that a prison break was planned, and indeed, Acton had admitted as much. The puzzling thing was that if the mechanisms for a prison break were being put in place, Savoie would presumably have to flee the country, but it seemed clear that Savoie was going nowhere. He'd enrolled Emile in school, here in London, and now he was fussing about his inoculations.

Doyle's scalp prickled, and she turned her gaze toward the boy, who was standing at the window and watching the scene below, with his hands and forehead pressed against the glass. "Emile," she asked. "Remember when you told me you got a shot? When was this?"

He lifted his head to look at her. "I needed to have a shot to go to St. Petersburg. It pinched, but I didn't cry." He looked down below again. "But then I didn't even go."

Doyle walked over, and stood beside him, as they gazed out the windows. "Do you remember what the doctor's name was?"

The boy shook his head, and then breathed on the glass, creating a circle of moisture. "No—it wasn't a doctor, it was a guard at the prison. He took my picture, too, for the important papers."

Doyle stared at the top of the boy's head, completely flummoxed. "Your Papa was goin' to take you to St. Petersburg?" Perhaps Savoie was indeed departing these shores—although it seemed very strange that the notorious Frenchman would choose to go to St. Petersburg—one would imagine that the

Russian underworld would not appreciate the likes of Philippe Savoie lurking about, trying to muscle in on their territory.

Smiling, the boy shook his head, and turned to look up at her, amused that she was so perplexed. "No, no, no—the lady was going to take me. The lady who is your friend—yours and Papa's. She was going to take me to meet Papa in St. Petersburg, but it had to be a secret, and I mustn't say." He paused, then added fairly, "I don't think it needs to be a secret anymore, since I'm not going."

The puzzle didn't seem to be getting any clearer, and so Doyle guessed, "Was the lady named Tasza? Was she tall, with blonde hair?"

The boy laughed at the absurdity of this. "No—it was the old lady; the *babushka*."

Suddenly, the puzzle pieces began to fall into place, and with a sense of relief, Doyle remarked in a casual tone, "Oh— that's right; the lady who was at Trestles, that night when we were all there."

The boy nodded, and returned his scrutiny to the scene below them. "I played with the toy animals," he remembered.

"Yes—that's right. Are you sure it was the same lady, who was helping with your shot at the prison? I thought she was very sick."

He sucked on his finger for a moment, before tracing in the wet image on the window. "Yes—it was her. Her hair is white, now." He giggled. "She called me Jonathan—she didn't know that was my old name, not my new one. She had a cane, and she let me hold it."

Doyle nodded, and said no more. So; one mystery solved; Solonik's evil sister—the boy's aunt—must have resurfaced to try to seize the boy, and this move had no doubt resulted in her winding up under the rubble at Holy Trinity. There was not the smallest chance that Savoie was going to relinquish Emile to her—even though she was probably the only person with a legal claim to the boy—and Acton had been happy to assist in a little misdirection murder, to ensure the boy's future.

This thought gave her pause, though, since Acton was not the type of man who would be over-concerned with someone else's loose-end child. More likely he needed Savoie's cooperation in whatever scheme was currently going forward, and this was the best way to guarantee it. Strange, though, that he'd gone to such lengths; if Mrs. Barayev had suddenly died at her nursing home, it wouldn't have been much of a surprise, after all. There was no need, one would think, to go to the trouble of disguising her identity, and paying off a charwoman to disappear back to the other side of the world.

The concierge buzzed to say that Reynolds was below, and so Doyle decided that she'd postpone thinking about this niggling loose end; why had Acton staged such an elaborate misdirection murder, for someone he could murder in a much more plain-vanilla fashion? Mayhap he was showing off, or something. Or turning the tables—Acton was the grand master at turning the tables.

Emile immediately began debriefing Reynolds about his prison visit, and the servant—upon beholding the boy racing about the kitchen in his excitement—decided that a walk to the park might be just the thing. Doyle shot the man a grateful look as the two made their way out the entry door, Emile describing the prison's barbed-wire-topped walls with ghoulish relish.

The sudden silence was a welcome relief, after such a ragged day, and Doyle decided that she'd very much like to behold her wayward husband, if for no other reason than to try to test out her theories.

"Come home?" she texted, then added, "Not in labor," just so he didn't panic. She'd the sense, despite his calm façade, that he was worried about the upcoming blessed event.

"On my way, have some news," he replied, and with a fond smile, she brushed her thumb across the screen. A doting man, he was, and she loved him, despite his many and troubling faults. After all, his many and troubling faults seemed to be rooted, lately, in his outsized devotion to his unlikely bride—it was one of those paradonces, or whatever you called them; he was constantly masterminding some scheme to supposedly better her life, and she was constantly telling him that he needn't—all she needed was his fine self. The poor man had fixated on the wrong girl; mayhap if she started acting like a demanding shrew, he'd have less time to stir up trouble amongst the citizenry.

Blowing out a resigned breath, she put her mobile away, and acknowledged something she'd truthfully realized long ago—Acton was not about to stop his masterminding; he enjoyed it too much. He wasn't exactly what you'd call a normal man, and all his various schemings helped him to feel that he was in control—that he could control the uncontrollable, as if there were such a thing. If he had a true faith, then perhaps he wouldn't feel the need, but he didn't have a true faith—few people did, it seemed—and so she should help him with his need-to-be-in-control issues, as best she could.

She'd been hoping that the happy rhythm of their life together might soothe him enough to tone it down, but apparently, she'd been too optimistic about the depth of the problem. Faith, it was a little disquieting to realize that he'd had Mrs. Barayev murdered just as he was preparing for his confirmation—really didn't speak very well for the holy catechism, when all was said and done.

I'll keep trying, she thought; I'm the only one who can, and I've got to think about that whole hellfire scenario—although Acton would probably give them a run for their money, down there.

With a sigh, she settled in to wait.

Chapter 31

It was extraordinary news, and he still wasn't certain he believed it.

A short while later, her husband came through the door, bearing a latté generously topped with whipped cream. "To tempt your appetite," he suggested, as he leaned to kiss her. "You didn't eat much, at lunch."

"Done," she said readily, and started sipping. "We've got the blessed place to ourselves; Emile was jumpin' about like a jackdaw, and so Reynolds went to run him ragged in the park."

"A good strategy," Acton agreed, as he made his way toward the kitchen. "I confess I do not recall having half as much energy."

She had a glimpse, for a moment, of a lonely little boy, immersing himself in books to escape the reality of his terrible parents, and she suddenly decided she wasn't going to give him the third degree about whatever was going forward at Wexton Prison. I'm truly not very brave, despite what everyone thinks, she thought, and I'm afraid if I have it out with him about the smuggling—and the murder of Mrs. Barayev—it will wind up as somehow being a call-to-action for me to fix the situation, and I'm in no shape for a call-to-action, just now.

Acton pulled the orange juice bottle out of the fridge, and then loosened his tie, as he sank down beside her on the sofa.

"What's your news?" she asked with interest. "It's a simmerin' brew, you are."

For once, Acton seemed uncertain as to what he wanted to say, and he contemplated the orange juice bottle for a moment. "I don't like to impose upon you—you know that."

Teasing, she asked, "Is this about sex? Text Reynolds then, and tell him to take the long way home, again."

Smiling, he tilted his head. "Unfortunately, not. I've come across something of interest, and so I've invited a visitor over. He has a fantastic story, and I'm not certain I believe it."

"Then I stand ready to help," she said lightly. Acton needed a truth-detector, then, to sort out whatever-it-was.

He met her eyes with all sincerity. "I'm sorry, Kathleen, but I think it is necessary."

But she wouldn't hear any apologies. "Whist, husband; this used to be our stock-in-trade, back when we were doin' field-work together, and clearin' out the villains like so much brushwood." She smiled fondly, and leaned in against his arm. "Those were the days, weren't they? 'Terrified' was my middle name, back then—I was that nervous around you."

He smiled. "And mine was 'frustrated'."

Laughing, she teased, "That's as may be, but look how well it's all turned out."

"It will be even better," he assured her.

This seemed a golden opportunity to bring up the Acton-improvement topic, and so she gently reminded him, "Life is an unendin' series of unplanned surprises, my friend, both pleasant and unpleasant. There's truly not a lot you can do about it."

But Acton—being Acton—was not about to admit to such a thing. "I must disagree; a bit of planning can tilt the field immeasurably."

With a smile, she lifted her head to look at him. "Is that so? Well, good luck to you—I can think of a few fields that tilted in the wrong direction, right off the top o' my head. Greyfriars Bridge comes to mind. And a certain detective trainee." Running her hand up his arm, she offered, "I appreciate the attempt, Michael—truly I do, but you can't try to control the uncontrollable. You'll only go down to certain defeat."

He rested his head against the top of hers. "Nonetheless, I can tilt the field."

With a mental sigh, she decided that she'd beaten her wings enough today, and so said no more.

Her husband lifted his arm to look at his watch. "Our visitor should be arriving, soon."

"Sounds a bit ominous," she ventured, wondering why he was being so mysterious.

He gazed into the fireplace for a moment. "I don't think he's a threat of any kind, but I cannot be certain."

"Is he in the database?"

"No," Acton replied slowly. "He is not."

Straightening up, she declared, "Well then; that's why you need me, and my apt-ness. What's the case?"

"There is no case." He hesitated. "I think I'd rather not say anything more; it may be best if you listen in to our conversation, and draw your own conclusions."

"Right then." Privately, she hoped she wouldn't be subject to yet another emotion-fraught conversation, today—she'd already had a bellyful. Of course, it went without saying that he wouldn't ask it of her if it weren't important; he tended to be more circumspect about her perceptive abilities than she was.

The concierge buzzed, and then announced, "The gentleman is here to see you."

"Please send him up."

Acton stood, and Doyle asked, "Shall I do pretend-work at the computer, whilst I listen in?"

"No—there is no need to get up; it shouldn't take long." Again, he looked at his watch.

The visitor came through the door—a rather somber man, late forties, perhaps—who emanated a combination of weariness and wariness. Not a danger, she decided immediately, but he's not sure if we're a danger.

After greeting Acton, he walked over to bow over Doyle's hand, briefly. European, she guessed—and perhaps a minor aristocrat; he had that old-world air about him.

"Would you care to sit?" Acton asked. "It may take a minute."

With a stiff nod of acquiescence, the visitor perched on the edge of the chair he was offered, and waited.

Acton began, "I understand that you are in a difficult situation, and that you cannot simply trust me."

Doyle blinked, because Acton's manner was conciliatory, rather than his usual interrogation tactic, which was to frighten the poor detainee to within an inch of his life. So—she thought; we're not doing an interrogation, then.

"What can you show me?" the man asked. Wary, he was.

"I think I can help you, but first I need assurances that you mean no harm." Acton paused. "You must admit, it is an extraordinary story. I would not like to think that it hides a more sinister purpose."

The man's gaze rested on Doyle for a moment, and she could see that he was worried about speaking openly in front of her. "I have told you nothing but the truth. I swear it to you."

There was another pause, whilst Acton gave Doyle a chance to brush the hair from her forehead—the signal that she used to tell him that lies were being told. She didn't, though, because the man spoke the truth. He had the trace of an accent, and Doyle tried to identify it; she wasn't good with accents, but this one seemed both familiar and unfamiliar, in a strange way.

"It is a delicate situation," Acton continued. "And I must be concerned about her safety."

Doyle hid her sudden uneasiness. Whose safety? Hers? What did this fellow have to do with her?

Bowing his head, the man agreed. "Her safety is my first concern. Of course."

Doyle's hands remained in her lap, and she sensed that her husband was immensely relieved.

"Then I believe I can be of help."

To Doyle's surprise, she could hear a card-key in the slot, and the door opened to reveal Mary, looking a bit confused, as she held Gemma's hand at the threshold. "Oh—Lady Acton, I was so worried. The concierge asked us to go straight up, and I was afraid—"

But the woman paused in astonishment, because the visitor had leapt up, and after taking several long strides across the room, knelt before Gemma.

"Your Serene Highness." Overcome, the man blinked back tears.

Gemma smiled. "The army-man," she pronounced, in her little voice.

Chapter 32

This was probably what she would call an unplanned-for surprise.

"Didn't see that one comin'," Doyle observed. "Tell me what's goin' on, here, husband."

They were watching the visitor speak in quiet tones to a clearly bewildered Mary, as the three of them sat together at the kitchen table, Gemma happily eating pretzels and coloring in her book.

Acton rested his gaze upon the trio at the table, and said softly. "Her true name is Georgievna. Most of her family was killed, over a hundred years ago." He paused. "She is one of the only survivors of the male-line Romanovs."

Doyle eyed her husband. "Haven't a *clue* what that means, Michael."

"The Romanovs were the Tsars of Russia."

Frowning, Doyle followed his gaze. "You're tellin' me that Gemma's Russian *royalty*?"

Acton nodded. "After a fashion. The Russians follow Salic Law, which means females cannot rule. And aside from that, after the Russian Revolution, all the direct heirs were killed, so it's all rather uncertain. She's a rare survivor, and probably a Grand Duchess."

Doyle smiled. "Then you're sayin' she outranks you, husband?"

Acton smiled in return. "I suppose she does."

Shaking her head in wonder, Doyle asked, "How, by *all* the holy saints, did a 'serene highness' wind up bein' a loose-end child?"

"In recent years, a new royalist party has emerged in Russia—an attempt to re-establish the traditional monarchy. But those who do not wish to relinquish their power are very much opposed to any suggestion that the Romanov line be re-established."

Doyle tried to sort this out. "Because Gemma's a royal, she's in danger? Where are her parents?"

"Her parents died rather mysteriously, and she was immediately spirited out of the country, and placed with Blakney, where no one would think to look, until it would be safe for her to return."

Taking a guess, Doyle ventured, "Was it Solonik, who did the spiritin'?"

"Yes. Solonik and his brother-in-law were affiliated with the new royalist group, and were undoubtedly promised a high position, if the group was ever successful in coming into power." Acton tilted his head in concession. "None of the players are very principled, I'm afraid. This man—" he nodded his head in the direction of the army-man, "is one of the military officers who would not be averse to restoring the old order."

"He seems very sincere," Doyle ventured. "He truly loves her."

"No doubt. But theirs is a dangerous gamble, and he must keep a low profile, for fear that anyone who could make a challenge will be assassinated. That's one of the reasons he dared not advertise what he was doing, or even identify himself."

Frowning, Doyle observed, "So—Solonik stashed her away with Blakey, thinkin' it would be a good place to hide her. But then Blakney got himself murdered, and Mary—who had not taken Blakney's last name when she married him—moved elsewhere, and the little girl was lost."

"Correct. And no one knew what had happened to them, because—"

"—because you moved them into a better neighborhood," Doyle completed. "Faith, it's amazin' he found her at all."

But Acton examined his hands for a moment. "He only found her, because I found him, first. And I found him because you were alarmed when Gemma said a Russian word, and you insisted that I look into it."

Doyle paused, much struck. "I'm spooky," she admitted.

Acton lifted her hand and kissed its back. "Sometimes."

"Edward's not spooky," she assured him. "Just in case you were wonderin'."

"Oh? I did wonder."

She decided she'd turn the subject—she didn't like to speak of her perceptive abilities, and despite his calm façade, she knew that the subject made her husband uneasy, too. "So; what happens now? Poor Mary's been gob-smacked."

"We've agreed that Gemma should remain with Mary, for the time being. She'll be safe—especially since she'll take up residence with us, when the baby's born. If Captain Kolchak couldn't trace her, it's unlikely that anyone else can, either."

Doyle nodded in agreement. "Then she'll go to St. Margaret's, as planned?"

"She will. All in all, it is unlikely that she'll go back to Russia any time soon. We must keep it quiet, of course."

Smiling, she lifted her palms. "No problem there, my friend. I can scare believe it, myself."

"The Captain will monitor her well-being, of course, and he would like to make certain she doesn't forget the language. I think it may be best to put it about that she and Emile are cousins, so that she can practice with him, and no one will think it strange."

"They do practice," Doyle informed him absently, as she watched the girl concentrate on her coloring. "I just didn't realize it, at the time." She rubbed her eyes. "Saints, Michael; it's all very symmet— symetro—"

"Symmetrical?" he offered.

"Yes—thank you. Emile's father stepped up to help, and then after he was killed, so did his son, all unknowin'."

Acton tilted his head. "I think Emile may have purer motives."

"Aye." Doyle quirked her mouth. "Despite the fact he's a basketful of trouble, he does mean well." Teasing, she glanced up at him. "There's a lesson for you, there."

"Now, there's an astonishing thought," he observed, and bent to kiss her.

Chapter 33

He couldn't help but feel a deep sense of satisfaction. As an added bonus, the Commander was thoroughly stymied, and he'd a Romanov, living under his roof.

"I'm afraid," the Filipino priest informed Doyle gently, "that it is a call-to-action, after all."

Faith, I'd completely forgotten about this little side-serving of spooky, Doyle thought a bit guiltily. "Oh—hallo, Father. I guess I haven't been thinkin' about you lately, because I solved the puzzle about the blood-money Acton's payin' to your sister."

"Yes," he agreed, and nodded.

Since he seemed disinclined to speak further on the subject, she admitted, "I'm not sure what to do about it—it's water under the bridge, now, and I imagine your sister could use a bit of extra money."

Again, he nodded in understanding, but disclosed, "She is forwarding the money to the bishop, for the church's rebuilding fund."

Doyle stared at him for a moment. "Is she? Well, there's irony and justice, shakin' hands."

"Yes." He smiled his benign smile.

Doyle found that she wanted to draw the conversation to a close, and as quickly as possible. "Then all's well that ends well, I suppose. I'll keep workin' on Acton—I'm tryin'; truly I am—and I appreciate the tip-off about the blood-money." Not certain what one said, she added, "I hope you have a nice eternity."

But he shook his head slightly. "You know what must be done, my child. We sometimes must go where we'd rather not."

This comment sparked a heated response, and she retorted, "No—I haven't sworn obedience, and I'd rather not go anywhere. Look at you—you went to Africa, and then died, for your pains. It's such a waste—that someone like you dies in—in absturity—"

"Obscurity," he corrected gently.

"—in obscurity, and an out-and-out charlatan like the DCS is *stupidly* famous."

"It is not ours to judge," he reminded her in a mild tone.

But Doyle wasn't having it, and blew out a breath in exasperation. "Well, that one's not at all hard to judge, my friend. He's a blackleg, through and through, and it's not fair *at all.*"

The priest did not respond, but regarded her with his usual benevolence.

Something in his gaze inspired Doyle to rein in her temper, and so she conceded, "I suppose it's a good thing that he's bringin' in believers by the bushelful—and in this day and age, that's quite the accomplishment—but it's not the right way to go about it, by swindlin' people. Faith, that's as bad as blood-money, if you ask me, and mayhap you should go visit him in his dreams, and tell him so."

"Greed is a terrible sin," the priest agreed, a bit sadly.

"A primary motivation for murder," said Doyle, who realized that she was quoting what Acton had said, for some reason.

"But the blood-money is not sinful in and of itself, my child. It is the sinner, who stands for judgment."

Doyle stared at him in surprise. "Never say there's more blood-money, on top of the last? For whose blood?"

But there was no response, and then she gasped, as her eyes flew open and she stared into the darkness of her bedroom.

"Is it time?" Sleepily, Acton reached for the light.

"No," she replied, and stayed his hand. "I'm that sorry I woke you, Michael."

He sank back down into the pillows, and drew her to him. "Need anything?"

"A good night's sleep," she teased, and kissed the face so close to hers. She couldn't tell him that what she truly needed were some answers—the Filipino priest may be a kindly man, but she recognized a scolding when she heard one.

It was a call-to-action, he'd said. And apparently—surprise of surprises—there was even more blood-money being paid over to someone else, which apparently meant that the fair Doyle had to shake her stumps yet again, and find out what was afoot.

Frowning at the dark ceiling, she tried to decide what the priest had meant. At first, he'd said that she knew what had to be done, but then instead of telling her plainly—faith, they *never* spoke plainly—he'd wandered off-topic by talking about the crooked DCS, and about even more blood-money. Who was Acton paying? And for what?

Thoroughly frustrated, she decided she'd think about a protocol in the morning, when her head was a bit clearer. After intertwining her fingers in her husband's, she then—almost surprisingly—fell immediately to sleep.

Chapter 34

He arranged for her the doctor to visit that afternoon.
She was tired, and hadn't eaten much.

Doyle was no further along with a protocol the following morning, as she sat at the table and watched Emile poach her breakfast egg under the careful direction of Reynolds.

"It's turned white," whispered Gemma, who stood atop her chair, observing the proceedings with wide eyes.

"Indeed, it has, Miss Gemma, and so we must take the ladle—carefully, Master Emile; the water is very hot—and slide it onto the toast."

With a great deal of pride, Emile solemnly carried Doyle's plate to her, and Gemma was entrusted with the small glass of orange juice, which was only sloshed a bit when it landed at its destination.

"Thank you, Emile, and you are an excellent assistant, Gemma."

"My mum will bake cookies, when she comes home tonight," Gemma disclosed in a rare burst of words. "She says a nice man will come to visit us."

Reynolds advised a bit hurriedly, "Now, Miss Gemma; you mustn't re-tell private conversations—"

But Doyle smiled. "It's all right, Reynolds; Mary's mum has indeed met a nice man, and I imagine it won't stay a secret long." She smiled to herself, thinking about Reynolds' reaction when he found out about the Howard-and-Mary romance; the servant would have to reshuffle his deck of who-was-important, and who-was-not. A shame, that she couldn't mention Gemma's secret; that would be a reshuffling for the ages.

The servant took this opportunity to send a meaningful glance in Emile's direction. "I think you should tell Lady Acton your own secret, Emile; I promise she won't take it away."

Doyle looked upon the boy with interest. "Have you a secret, Emile? Can you shoot ducks with it?"

The boy smiled, but Doyle could see that he was suddenly wary. "No—it was something I found at the park."

Interestingly enough, this was an out-and-out lie, and so Doyle's interest was piqued—Emile was usually too forthright for his own good. "Can I see it?"

"*May* I see it," the boy corrected.

"You must not correct Lady Acton, Master Emile."

"It's a thankless task, and better men than you have tried," Doyle agreed. "May I see the secret, Emile?"

At Reynolds' nod, the boy ran to his room, and then came back, holding something in his hand. With palpable reluctance, he opened his fingers to reveal a gold coin, nearly the size of his small palm.

Doyle stared at it, her scalp prickling like a live thing.

"You may hold it, Gemma, but only for a minute," the boy offered importantly. "You mustn't say anything to your mum, though; it's a secret."

"Where did you find it, Emile?" Doyle already knew the answer, but decided she'd double-check, on the off-chance that her call-to-action wasn't staring her in the face.

"On the pavement, at the park," the boy lied, his cheeks turning a bit pink.

"He wasn't going to tell me, but I saw it in his hand," Reynold disclosed. "In exchange for his confidence, Lady Acton, I assured him that he could keep it."

"Of course, you may keep it, Emile; besides, it'd be a sleeveless errand to try to find the true owner." The coin was about two inches across, and sported an unfamiliar language, but if it had said "blood money" in capital letters, it couldn't have been more clear. Here was the answer to all mysteries, and the reason for her soft-voiced scolding from the night visitor.

She was tempted to interrogate the boy, to see what he'd say, but she decided it was hardly necessary—they weren't smuggling cigarettes or mobile phones to Savoie; they were smuggling gold. But why? Presumably, Savoie was rich—faith, he was probably swimming in blood-money, and lots of it.

"Impossible, to trace the owner," Reynolds agreed. "A very lucky find, Master Emile."

Doyle watched Gemma hold the coin with careful little hands, and realized this was an important point—money could be traced, particularly if was the police who were doing the tracing. But coins like this one could not be traced.

She lifted her gaze to the window, trying to decide whatever-it-was that she was trying to understand. Savoie was sitting in prison, larking about with the guards, and promising Emile that he'd be home soon. For some reason, Acton was smuggling gold coins to him, in Emile's jacket—although more correctly, it was Lizzie Mathis who was smuggling the coins. But wait—Doyle should be a good detective, and not leap to conclusions. It seemed clear that Mathis was facilitating the smuggling, but she may not know its object—she wasn't allowed in the room, when Emile visited Savoie.

Indeed, it was possible that Acton himself didn't know about the coins—but of course he did; Mathis was following Acton's orders, that much seemed evident. There was no other reason to recruit the unlikely Mathis to escort Emile to visit his father; Mathis could be trusted not to grass about whatever was going forward, and Acton trusted very few people.

With a twinge of annoyance, Doyle contemplated the unpalatable truth that Acton trusted Mathis more than the wife of his bosom with whatever-this-was. He doesn't trust me, she realized—at least not in this—because he thinks I'll try to throw a mighty wrench into the works, and then beat him with a nightstick, for good measure.

Slowly, she lowered her head, a bit ashamed of herself. Acton's concern was unwarranted, though—his fair bride wouldn't have tried to throw a wrench, because she was too busy putting her head in the sand, and trying not to face what needed to be faced: Acton had one more misdirection murder to commit, and the victim couldn't have been more obvious. As the Filipino priest had pointed out—in his gently scolding way— Doyle knew what had to be done.

She lifted her head to watch Emile tell Gemma something about the coin's origin that Reynolds had told him—she wasn't listening, because she was trying to come up with a protocol. Rescuing the wretched DCS from Acton's bloody-minded vengeance seemed a tall order—given her present condition— but as she'd a saintly priest urging her on, she'd no choice in the matter, and best get crackin' on a plan, because she truly should have a plan before she did something impulsive. She'd the feeling, she did, that she was about to do something impulsive.

If the blood-money was being delivered to the prison, it was probably not going to Savoie as much as it was going to bribe others at the prison—certainly the cheeky guard, which would explain his cheeky attitude. Faith, when you thought it through, it all made complete sense; she'd thought it odd that Acton hadn't killed Mrs. Barayev and the DCS outright, on that Hound-of-the-Baskervilles night, and now it seemed that he'd just decided to delay his revenge a bit—mayhap he didn't want to make it too obvious that it was his own hand, behind these misdirection murders.

But Doyle frowned slightly, because try as she might, this theory didn't piece together very well. Acton was nothing if not efficient, and it seemed the height of inefficiency, to take such pains to disguise the Russian woman's death, and pay off a Filipino charwoman, to boot. Not to mention it was no easy thing to arrange to have someone murdered in prison—or at least, one would think. Much easier to do the deed before the villain had been locked safely away. "It doesn't make sense," she mused aloud.

"I beg your pardon, madam?"

Pulled from her thoughts, Doyle replied, "Sorry, Reynolds—I was woolgatherin'. It comes of nearly goin' mad, havin' to sit here, when everyone else is pickin' up gold off the streets." She noted that Emile and Gemma had decided to make a game of tossing the coin back and forth, and so Doyle made a show of placing an arm across her forehead, and leaning back into the sofa.

As could be expected, almost immediately Reynolds addressed the children. "Perhaps, Master Emile, you should put the coin away now, and we'll go for a walk. It is a fine morning."

"By all means, put it away," Doyle agreed. "You wouldn't want the ducks to seize it—the wretched thieves."

The boy giggled. "These are London ducks, not the St. Petersburg ducks. It's the St. Petersburg ducks who are the thieves, remember?"

"I wouldn't trust a single duck a single inch," Doyle advised darkly. "Mark me."

"I'd no idea that ducks were such a hazard," Reynolds remarked, and went to fetch the children's jackets.

But Doyle wasn't listening, because she'd suddenly stilled, reminded that Solonik's evil sister had planned to take Emile back to St. Petersburg, for reasons unknown. Now, there was a niggling loose end to beat all the other niggling loose ends. Emile had said that the woman was at the prison when he'd visited Savoie—the same prison where Mrs. Barayev used to work as a matron, doing evil deeds behind the scenes—and that she'd seen to it that Emile had the requisite shots, and travel documents—faith, she'd even had the guards involved in the preparations.

Try as she might, she could make no sense of it; Doyle knew that the woman had no fondness for the boy—she was as cold as an ice shard, through-and-through. And besides, she must have known that Savoie would do whatever it took to fetch Emile right back again, and exact a terrible revenge, in the process. It seemed a very foolish thing to do, to make plans to steal the boy away, right there in the prison. Unless—

Slowly, Doyle lifted her head to gaze out the windows and contemplate a terrible, terrible thought. What if—what if Savoie had been allied with Mrs. Barayev, and was planning to take Emile to St Petersburg along with her, and thus take up the reins of the Solonik underworld? After all, the woman had been deeply involved in her brother's evil deeds, but now that all her men-folk had been killed, she was in no shape to handle it herself. Why not recruit Savoie, and promise him riches, as well as an unfettered right to Emile?

Was it possible? It would mean that Savoie was willing to double-cross Acton—which ordinarily, wouldn't be much cause for alarm, since half the villains in London would like nothing more than to double-cross Acton. But Savoie was not your usual villain; Savoie was dangerous, because he was—inexplicably—another one of those rare persons Acton apparently trusted. Although—although, it wasn't *truly* inexplicable—it was because of Doyle; because Savoie had saved her life, once, and Acton knew they were friends. And now Savoie knew that Acton was arranging to murder the DCS, and was—perhaps—secretly planning to abscond to Russia, all without Acton's knowing. Perhaps he was meaning to expose Acton, as well—leave him holding the bag. The implications were alarming, and Doyle tamped down a flare of panic.

Reynolds paused at the door. "We should return before lunch, madam; please phone, if you require anything."

Doyle pulled herself together, and mustered-up a smile. "Right then. Emile, I'm countin' on even more gold, so please keep a sharp eye out."

The boy's laughter could be heard as the door shut, and Doyle immediately took the opportunity to press her fingers to her temples—she needed to convince her poor pregnant-brain to start thinking, and to start thinking fast.

If Savoie were double-crossing him, then there was nothin' for it; she'd have to warn Acton. But—if she warned Acton that she'd twigged on to him, she'd probably not have another opportunity to rescue the wretched DCS. Instead, Acton would nod understandingly whilst she scolded him about not going about killing people, and then the erstwhile minister would probably be transferred to some far-afield Irish prison, and disappear from there.

The ghost-priest was right; I *do* know what needs to be done, she admitted to herself with deep regret. I've got to go to wretched Wexton Prison, and speak with Savoie, to sound him out. Then I've got to figure out some way to save the stupid DCS—depending on what Savoie has to say, and how bleak the situation is. It shouldn't take but a few minutes, and I can't see any other way out—there's no one else who can do it.

As she gathered her feet beneath her, she remembered what the priest had said—that we sometimes must go where we'd rather not—and she made a wry mouth, now that she knew what he meant. I've got to stop the last misdirection murder, she thought with resolution; there's no bunkin' it, and shame on me, for thinking there was nothing I could do to stop it.

With grim determination, she hoisted herself up, and prepared to answer her call-to-action.

Chapter 35

Today was the day. "Whoever sows injustice will reap calamity."

"Mathis," Doyle said into her phone. "I'm that sorry to bother you at work, but I wanted to ask you about somethin' Emile told me about his prison visit. It may not be important, but I wanted to double-check."

"Certainly," said Mathis, who was probably rolling her eyes.

"It's somethin' I'd rather discuss face-to-face," Doyle added. "It's a delicate matter, and I'm not sure whether I should bring Acton into it."

There was a small pause. She knows I'm up to something, thought Doyle; a wily one, was Mathis.

"Of course; I'll be happy to come by at your convenience, Lady Acton."

"I'm truly sorry, Mathis; it shouldn't take more than a minute, and you won't even have to park; if you'll just pick me up at the front door, I'll ride around the block with you."

"I'll be there shortly, then."

On her way out the door, Doyle left her mobile on the sofa table, double-checked her ankle holster, and then grabbed Emile's jacket from the closet, wincing because she'd moved too fast, and she must have tweaked her back, somehow. Once down in the lobby, she smiled at the concierge, and then watched out the revolving doors for Mathis, hoping the girl wouldn't be long.

When Mathis pulled up, Doyle allowed the doorman to open the passenger door, and then settled in, as Mathis pulled away. "Thanks a million, Mathis. I'm truly grateful."

"Is that Emile's jacket?" the other girl asked, and Doyle knew that behind her impassive exterior, she was very wary.

"Yes. It's actually an excuse-in-disguise, because I've lured you in under false pretenses. We're goin' to Wexton Prison, and you're goin' to take me in to speak with Savoie."

To her credit, the girl didn't swerve into a tree, but instead, glanced at her passenger with a hint of incredulity. "*What?*"

Hurriedly, Doyle continued, "I can't explain the details, but I'm worried that Acton's in some sort of danger, and I have to speak with Savoie, in order to sort it out."

"Lady Acton—"

"There's no arguin' with me, Mathis; I'm worried that Acton isn't aware of somethin' important."

There was a pause, whilst Doyle could see that the girl was reconsidering an outright refusal. "Why can't you tell Lord Acton?"

"Because Savoie's a very good liar, but he won't lie to me." Doyle was aware that this was a mighty lame explanation, but it was as close as she could come to the actual one. Inspired, she added, "It has to do with Emile—and I can't say more."

But Mathis only shook her head, slightly, and turned to regard her companion with all sincerity. "Then I would trust Lord Acton, Lady Acton. I'm certain he can deal with whatever the problem is."

"I can't tell him—not as yet. Please believe me when I say that he may be in danger—it may be a trap."

Although they weren't yet heading toward the prison—as far as Doyle could tell—at least Mathis hadn't pushed her out of the car, which seemed a promising sign. And the girl's next comment seemed another promising sign.

"Perhaps we should enlist Williams, to assist."

Doyle couldn't help but smile. "Well, as thrillin' as it would be to re-enact our favorite car trip, I'd rather not, because he'd queer the pitch, at the prison. You're the one the guards are familiar with, and it would raise all kinds of eyebrows if I had a DI, taggin' along."

Into the other girl's thoughtful silence, Doyle played her trump. "If you won't take me, I'm afraid I will go all on my own, by hook or by crook."

"Right then; I will take you."

There was a small silence, whilst Doyle mentally breathed a huge sigh of relief. "It's not like he'll fire you, Lizzie," she offered. "You're one of the only people he trusts."

As could be expected, this compliment evoked a small burst of pleasure, and Mathis rallied enough to disclaim, "Then I'm caught between the devil and the deep blue sea; if I don't go, you'll be the one to fire me."

"Never," Doyle proclaimed stoutly. "And besides, I wouldn't know how to go about it; we peasants have no experience in such things."

In an even tone, the girl observed, "And yet, Sir Stephen and the dowager are both gone from Trestles."

Doyle turned to stare at her in laughing surprise. "I didn't do *that*—for heaven's sake, Lizzie, give Acton credit, where credit is due."

But Mathis only countered, "It wouldn't have happened, save for you."

Doyle paused, because this was true; it wasn't until he'd married his Irish bride that Acton was suddenly inspired to clear all grifting relatives out of his ancestral home. "Well then; I'll take full credit, and must warn you never to dare cross me."

Mathis smiled her dry little smile. "As you see."

But Doyle only smiled in return, as she shifted to try to find a comfortable position—faith, she'd wrenched her stupid back. "You're only comin' along on this hare-brained scheme because you think it's what Acton would want you to do."

Mathis didn't bother to demur to this very valid point, but only asked, "What is the plan?"

Doyle considered her companion for moment, and then decided there was nothin' for it. "I'm guessin' that when you took Emile on your prison visits, you weren't required to check in, or go through the metal detectors. I've brought the jacket along, hopin' for the same treatment."

If Mathis knew why the jacket never went through the metal detectors, she gave no indication. "But won't they recognize you?"

"Everyone recognizes me," Doyle admitted, a bit glumly. "Never rescue anyone from the river, is the advice I would give to you."

Mathis lifted a corner of her mouth in amusement. "What will you tell them, as the reason you're there with me, then?"

"I am meetin' with Savoie and the DCS, since they are producin' a program together for my church's Everyday Heroes outreach. It's goin' to be about the perils of criminal behavior."

Mathis thought this over, then nodded. "That's a good one."

"Thank you," said Doyle, who was rather proud of it, herself.

"They'll give you an escort, you know."

"I know. I'll just need a minute to speak with Savoie, on the side. Mayhap you could distract the guard." This, with a sidelong glance. That Mathis was perfectly capable of such a subterfuge went without saying; she'd flirted with Drake, after all, so that he wouldn't notice he was being well-and-thoroughly poisoned.

"I will do my best."

"Thanks, Mathis. I truly, truly, appreciate it, and I wouldn't have asked, if it weren't so important."

"Let's keep it brief."

"No argument, here."

They drove the rest of the way in silence, and Doyle wondered whether her companion would take her first opportunity to squeak to Acton about his wayward wife. Perhaps she would, but so long as Doyle could manage two minutes with Savoie, it would be worth it—she'd happily take her lumps once she'd sorted out what-was-what, and figured out how she could save the DCS from his fate. Hard to believe—that Savoie would turn coat—but on the other hand, something was definitely afoot, what this morning's gold coin staring her in the face, and the Filipino priest sounding the alarm. It needed only to be sorted out, and then she'd be home in time for lunch. Acton would be very unhappy with her for this unsanctioned field trip—especially if she threw a spanner in his wheel-of-many-schemes—but she was doing it for his own good, and let this be a lesson to him. Besides, now that she'd determined on a plan of action, she was hugely enjoying having slipped her leash; there was only so long a body could stare at the four walls, for the love o' Mike.

Mathis turned into the prison's guest lot. "And here we are, Lady Acton."

Doyle smiled at the girl. "Since we're havin' an adventure together, d'you think you could call me 'Kathleen'?"

"No," Mathis replied, and secured the gear shift. "I'm afraid I couldn't."

"Fair enough," said Doyle, who'd only expected as much.

Chapter 36

He texted, to inform her of the rescheduled appointment, but she did not respond.

As Doyle had anticipated, the prison guards at the reception desk gave Mathis a knowing look, and then waved them through.

I'd forgotten that the guards here are all bent, she thought, as Mathis explained their errand to the visitors' desk. And I suppose I mustn't be surprised that this sad situation hasn't been remedied, since my better half has obviously decided to take advantage of it, himself.

This actually gave her a moment's pause, in that she'd presumably have no backup on site if things went awry—for example, if Savoie were indeed a turncoat, and decided he'd like nothing better than to take Acton's foolish wife as a hostage.

I hope I'm not making a monumental mistake, here, she thought, and braced her hands against her back, because her stupid backache refused to go away. But I can't believe it of Savoie; more likely he's working with Acton—as opposed to against him—and no doubt he's been enlisted to murder the DCS, since that would explain why he's been so content to sit in prison, biding his time and counting out gold coins.

The only factor that made her uneasy was Emile's tale of secret inoculations and passport papers. If the now-dead Mrs. Barayev planned to spite them all by whisking Emile back to Russia, why would she make the clandestine arrangements here—on the prison premises—where word would certainly get back to Savoie? More likely Savoie knew about it in the first place, which did not bode well, and she should not make any foolish assumptions by pretending that Savoie couldn't possibly mean her harm. He was a dangerous man, after all.

Doyle straightened her shoulders with renewed resolution, as a rough-looking guard was given the task of escorting them to the prison ministry's office. The man spoke to Mathis in a familiar way, but didn't give Doyle more than a passing glance. That's exactly what I get, for thinking I'm world-famous, she thought. Although I'm hugely pregnant, which means that no one is bothering to take a close look.

As they walked down the linoleum hallway, the guard openly eyed Mathis in appreciation, and Doyle was reminded that the stupid guards were cheeky and horrid—as she'd discovered herself, when she'd visited the evil Solonik the first time she was here. Faith, she hated this place—no one here was happy, and decades of human misery practically emanated from the very walls. Abandon all hope, ye who enter here, she thought, and then couldn't suppress a shudder.

"Mr. Savoie will be here shortly," the man explained, as they paused before a door in the hallway. "Allow me to take your jacket." With a knowing smirk, the guard lifted Emile's jacket from Mathis.

Oh-oh, thought Doyle; no gold in there, today. And now that she thought about it, she realized the obvious—the gold coins had been going to bribe the guards. After all, there was no need for Savoie to receive cold hard cash in prison, but the guards were another matter.

Doyle had only a moment to worry about the guard's reaction when the jacket came up empty, because the security door had swung open, and they were escorted into the small prison ministry office.

The former DCS of Scotland Yard was seated behind a cluttered wooden desk, and, after a moment's astonished surprise, he rose to greet them. "Why, DS Doyle; it is good to see you again."

But Doyle was too astonished to speak. *Holy Mother of God*, she thought, completely thunderstruck; there was no need to abandon all hope, because hope was right here, like a candle in the darkness.

He'd offered his hand, and she took it as she managed to find her voice. "Sir."

It was force of habit, because he wasn't a ranking officer any more—indeed, the last time she'd seen him, the net was closing in, and he was desperately trying to figure a way out of the trap that Acton had set for him. But this deceitful leopard had indeed changed his spots, and now radiated a palpable and holy goodness. The former DCS of Scotland Yard could not have had less in common with the ghostly Filipino priest, yet they were entirely the same.

"I am Lizzie Mathis," Mathis prompted into the silence, and offered her hand in turn. "We've come to discuss an upcoming episode for the Everyday Heroes program." Mathis slid a meaningful glance in the direction of the guard.

There was a small pause, but the DCS replied, "Of course, of course. Please be seated, ladies—I'm afraid we've only the one chair."

Mathis turned to bestow a flirtatious glance upon the guard. "I'll wait outside with you, then." With some eagerness, the guard approved of this plan, and Mathis smiled up at him as he held the door for her, even though she was emanating loathing and disgust.

Good one, thought Doyle, as the door shut closed, and she wondered if perhaps Mathis had also realized that their failure to come bearing gold gifts might arouse suspicion. Hopefully, the girl could stall the fellow long enough to allow Doyle to fulfill her task, because suddenly her task had become very clear; small wonder the ghost-priest was urging her on—saints weren't exactly thick on the ground, nowadays.

"How can I help you?" The DCS leaned forward, and clasped his hands on the table. "I'd be happy to collaborate on an outreach, although my resources are limited."

"They're going to murder you," Doyle said without preamble. And they mustn't.'"

Her companion was understandably puzzled by this outburst. "Are you quite all right, DS Doyle? May I fetch some water?"

"We've got to get you out of here, and quickly," Doyle repeated. "No one is goin' to protect you, here—and this is no place for the likes of you."

But the man only smiled at her—the same benign smile she'd seen from the ghost-priest. "On the contrary; I think this is exactly the place for me. When Jesus Christ is in my prison cell, every stone shines like a ruby."

Doyle blinked; leave it to the evangelicals to be spouting off about Jesus Christ, when any self-respecting RC knew that you kept your head down as you slid in and out of the back pew, as God intended.

Rapidly re-assessing her strategy, she offered, "Well—be that as it may—you're slated to be killed, and you'll not want anyone committin' mortal sins in the process."

He considered this, and nodded. "Right. I imagine the exercise yard is where they plan to strike; I think there was a dry run, just the other day." He paused, and bent his head for a moment, thinking, as Doyle duly observed the nasty, purple bruise on his temple. In a low voice, he asked, "How many assets on site, and how many on back-up?"

Doyle decided she'd gloss over this rather discouraging information, and instead hurriedly warned, "Savoie is comin' in any minute; let me do all the talkin'."

Understandably, the man raised his brows. "*Savoie* is coming here?"

"He is." Again, Doyle hurried past an explanation. "I'm afraid it's a rather long story, but we're to pretend you're collaborating with him on a program about turning your lives around."

The DCS regarded her with gentle incredulity. "If that's the case, you've got a hard row to hoe, Sergeant. If there is a plot to murder me, it is undoubtedly Savoie's plot—he's very unhappy about his missing money."

Because her scalp had suddenly started prickling, Doyle paused at this disclosure. What missing money? Was he talking about the gold coins? Then she remembered Williams telling her about the cascade scheme, and how it had passed through the prison ministry's account. A bit taken aback that the battered-but-holy man seated before her would have the remotest interest in filthy lucre, she chided, "Well, it just goes to show you that it's not very smart to cross someone like Savoie. And you mustn't steal, in the first place." Drawing her brows together, she added, "I think that's one of the commandments."

With a small sigh, the DCS shook his head. "Oh, I didn't steal his money, Sergeant. He remains unconvinced, however."

Further discussion was curtailed when the door swung open and Savoie himself entered, accompanied by another guard who seemed to be more along the lines of Savoie's assistant, than his escort. It was clear that the Frenchman was a bit taken aback, upon beholding the fair Doyle, and she could sense the wariness behind his impassive expression. "Yes? What is it you wish?"

Reminded that her original task was to find out if Savoie was double-crossing Acton, Doyle knew a moment's extreme exasperation—faith, everything had suddenly got a lot more complicated, and her back hurt like the dickens, to boot. Next time a ghost pesters me, she promised herself, I'll pull the covers over my head, and say something rude.

The DCS filled in the silence. "Good morning, Mr. Savoie. Thank you for offering to help with the program."

Savoie's pale gaze slid to Doyle for a moment, and then he made a gesture with his head, and the guard who was with him turned to step out of the door, and close it behind him.

"Shall we pray?" the DCS continued, and stood to place an arm around Doyle's shoulders, pulling her in toward him, as he held out the other arm to Savoie.

Trust the evangelicals to want to huddle, and get all touchy-feely in the midst of a crisis, Doyle thought with irritation. A bit angrily, she shook off the man's arm and said to Savoie, "I don't know what's been cooked up, Philippe, but you mustn't kill this man. It's very important that I get him out of here."

Surprisingly, she could feel the dismayed reaction to her words from the other two. They didn't respond, and so with some insistence, she repeated, "I've got to get him out, and you've got to help me."

But into the silence, the door was flung open, and Mathis was marched in; the guard she'd been flirting with holding her firmly by the elbow, and the floor's desk supervisor accompanying the other two.

"All right; what's going on, here?" the supervisor asked in an ominous tone.

The usually unflappable Mathis was emanating extreme concern as she informed Doyle, "I'm afraid there is a surveillance camera, in this room."

And I'm roundly an idiot, Doyle realized in acute dismay.

Chapter 37

Worried, he phoned the concierge to ring her, and discovered that she'd left with Mathis. Strange, that neither had mentioned it.

There was a tense moment, whilst Doyle went through her options, none of which seemed very good.

"*Être prêt à prendre son arme,*" said Savoie, into the silence.

"What?" The supervisor glanced at him. "Do you know these two, Mr. Savoie?"

Her mouth dry, Doyle forced a giggle, and tried to sound a bit stupid. "Of course, he does—after all, I asked him to come here. I think we're havin' a misunderstandin' is all—we are going to produce a program about a prison break, and I think you heard us practicin' our lines."

But it seemed apparent that the supervisor wasn't buying what Doyle was selling, and he addressed Savoie again. "I don't like this—what do you want to do?"

"*Moment,*" Savoie instructed, and stepped forward to push Doyle rather roughly into the chair. He then bent over her, with a hand on each of the chair's arms so that his face was close to hers, his manner menacing. "You will tell me what your purpose is, here."

The DCS interrupted, "Say; that's quite enough—there's been a misunderstanding, and there's no need to frighten the poor woman."

"We were playactin'," Doyle quavered. "Please, please believe me." If it came to it, she could clench her fists and attempt an upward throat-punch, but she doubted she could get the drop on someone like Savoie—not in her current condition.

But his next words were unexpected. "I do not think so; I had the meeting with you before. At the projects."

With a show of extreme nervousness, Doyle nodded, and wished she could see where this was going. For some reason, he was referring to the night she'd first met him—the night she'd been attacked, and he'd rescued her.

"Enough; please—"

But Savoie ignored the DCS, and continued to fix Doyle with his pale, menacing gaze. "That was a fine weapon."

There was a small pause. "It still is," she answered in a frightened whisper. So—he was asking if she was wearing her ankle holster, which she was, but it wasn't at all clear whether she should allow him to have her weapon, or whether she should try to shoot him, instead. "I was afraid there was a wolf, wearing sheep's clothes."

"*Non*," he answered, and lowered his head even further, so that his face was an inch from hers, his posture sinister. "Not the wolf. The Saint Bernard."

Nothin' for it, Doyle thought; I hope I'm not making a monumental mistake, here. In a semi-hysterical voice, she waved her hands a bit wildly, and began to plead, Oh, please—please, sir; my baby—"

With a swift movement, Savoie pulled her weapon from its ankle holster and turned to shoot the supervisor directly in his face, then pivoted to shoot Mathis' guard, who had pulled his own gun in abject surprise, but was thwarted when Mathis leapt to pull his arm down just as he fired. The resulting shot went wild, and then that guard collapsed also, a bullet hole centered on his forehead.

Savoie swore in French, and staggered, grasping the edge of the desk before taking careful aim at the surveillance camera in the upper corner, and hitting it directly in the lens.

There was an astonished silence, and then Mathis, her face spattered with blood, scrambled to reach for the fallen guard's weapon.

"Back," ordered Savoie, as he turned Doyle's gun on the girl.

"Don't shoot Mathis," Doyle pleaded. "She's a friendly." Then to clarify, she addressed all of them. "No one should shoot anyone else."

"Amen," said the DCS, with some irony.

With a grimace, Savoie inspected the bleeding wound on his leg, where the guard's bullet had wounded him. "Tell me what you do here. Quickly."

"There's a plot afoot to murder this man." Diplomatically, Doyle didn't mention that it was no doubt Acton's plot, with Savoie providing the assist. "I'd like to extract him; is there anyone here that's not utterly corrupt?"

"My assistants—the people who work in the ministry with me," the DCS offered.

"They're probably not very good in a fire-fight," Doyle reflected doubtfully.

Mathis spread her hands in a disarming way at Savoie. "Let me have a look—you may need a tourniquet."

Jerking his head in acquiescence, Savoie hoisted his leg onto the desk. "Who else is on the floor?" he asked the DCS, and then grimaced and swore, when Mathis probed his wound.

"No one—since this floor isn't for incarcerations. But there will be a security check-in at the top of the hour, and the central command will notice when no one checks in."

Savoie glanced up at the clock on the wall. "Do you know how to do this check-in?"

"No," the DCS confessed.

"I can try to do it, by looking at the history on the laptop," Mathis offered, "but if I don't do it correctly, it may trigger an alarm. I'm rather surprised the disabled camera hasn't triggered an alarm."

Savoie made no comment, and Doyle belatedly realized that the alarm probably hadn't been triggered because everyone knew Savoie was in the room, and they were all carefully trying not to notice that he was murdering the DCS.

Savoie asked Doyle. "Any extra rounds?"

"Just the one cartridge," she admitted. Truly, she wasn't of much use, and unless she very much missed her guess, she was asking Savoie to turn coat on his own people, and they were not the sort of people that handled such things very well.

"There's an exit wound," Mathis pronounced. "And the bone's not impacted."

"*Bien*," said Savoie, as Mathis firmly pressed his bloody leg between her hands.

Doyle spoke up. "A through-and-through is nothin', truly. I've been shot in the leg, myself." Best not to mention the circumstances, of course—talk about awkward, that would be the topper.

His jaw clenched, Savoie glanced over at Doyle. "Acton, does he know you are here?"

"No," Doyle admitted, and then realized a bit glumly that there was no way she would be able to sweep this little contretemps under the rug.

Without comment, Savoie pulled a disposable mobile out of his prison jumpsuit's pocket, and pressed the call button.

With a touch of gallows humor, Doyle remarked to Mathis, "I'm betwixt the devil and that sea person."

The devil and the deep blue sea," Mathis corrected, lifting a hand to take a glance at the oozing wound.

"Quiet," said Savoie. He began to speak rapidly in French, and then paused. Doyle couldn't hear the words, but she could hear the sweet, sweet tones of her husband's voice, and suddenly had to blink back tears.

Rather to her surprise, Savoie handed the mobile over to her.

Doyle swallowed, and pulled herself together. "I walked into a rare randyrow, Michael, all unknowin'. I'm truly sorry."

"No matter, Kathleen. If you would, please give me a report."

"We've two guards down, and Savoie's been wounded. Mathis is here, and we reckon we've got six minutes before someone realizes somethin's amiss."

There was a small pause. "Is your hair in your eyes?"

He was referring to the signal they used when she knew someone was lying, which meant he was apparently wondering if it was a trap. Small blame to him, what with the DCS and Savoie figuring prominently in this little holy show.

"No," she replied steadily, and hoped it was true—she hadn't had a chance to sound out Savoie's loyalty to the Russian contingent as yet, since that concern had suddenly dropped down in her list of priorities.

"Are you hurt?

"I am hale and hearty," she lied. Her back felt like it was set to break in half.

"Tell him I can access the roof," the DCS offered, in the background. "I conduct baptisms on the roof, and now we have the guard's security access card. The stairwell is across the hall."

"Did you hear?" Doyle asked Acton.

"Put him on," Acton said, and Doyle handed the mobile over.

It was apparent that Acton began asking about schematics. "C-3," The DCS responded. "Bars on the windows, and reinforced glass. A security door on the stairwell and at each end of the hall, but otherwise minimum security, since it's an administrative floor. Can you pull it up on your screen?"

There was a pause, whilst he listened to Acton. "I don't think we should wait; they will employ tear gas through the vents, as a riot-control tactic. DS Doyle probably shouldn't breathe tear gas." He paused, and then lowered his voice. "And I'm afraid it may be a GBH." This was a police term—grievous bodily harm—that referred to a highly dangerous situation, where the suspects were willing to do their worst.

Then to the roof we go, thought Doyle, mentally girding her loins. "Best to move quickly," she said aloud, trying to sound confident.

Suddenly, they could see flashing lights through the glass panel in the door, and a blaring alarm sounded. With one accord, they all leapt to their feet, and Doyle's water broke.

Chapter 38

He signaled to his assistant,
and started issuing rapid-fire orders.

"We should move," the DCS said. "Once they realize these two are down, they will turn off all security card access and institute a lockdown. Then they'll turn on the tear gas—it's what I would do."

"We go, then," said Savoie, as he held out his hand for the mobile. "Come, come."

The DCS willingly handed it over, and Mathis asked, "Should we leave it on, so that Acton can track us, and hear what's happening?"

"*Non*," Savoie replied succinctly, and lifted the phone to his ear. He listened for a moment, said "*Bien*," and then rang off to shove it into the desk drawer.

"It's a burner phone," Doyle explained. "Can't keep usin' it, or they'll hone in."

"Give me a gun, then," Mathis said to Savoie. "I'll stay behind, and fire at them down the hall when they try to approach. It will buy some time."

While this seemed an excellent plan, Doyle knew she couldn't allow such a thing. "No, you're comin' with us."

"I'm sure they won't shoot me," the girl insisted, and it was not exactly true.

"*Non*," said Savoie, who was apparently willing to back Doyle. "*Allons*."

But the girl's heroics had triggered an idea in Doyle's semi-panicked brain. "They'll be reluctant to shoot—or even use the gas—if they think Savoie's a hostage. I'm sure there's a camera in the hall, and they don't know Acton's on the way. It might buy some time."

"Good idea, Sergeant," said the DCS with a nod. "He's already been shot, so that will add authenticity." The DCS held out a hand to Savoie. "Here; I'll hold a gun to your head."

As could be expected, Savoie flatly refused to hand a gun over, and so the DCS suggested, "Take the ammo out, then; they need to think you're at risk, and that I've already shot you."

There was a tense moment, and so Doyle offered, "It's that deep-sea-devil-person, again, Philippe. Nothin' for it."

With a grim expression, Savoie pulled the cartridge out from one of the guard's guns, and then handed the weapon to the DCS.

"Thank you," the man said. "Now, put your hands behind your back, and I'll wrestle you across for the cameras."

"*Bien.*"

"Here," Mathis stepped forward to smear her bloody hands on Savoie's face. "We have to make it obvious; they may not be able to see the leg."

It's all very ironic, thought Doyle, and if I weren't dying to lie down somewhere, I think I'd appreciate it miles more.

"Got the security card? Good. Everyone ready?" The DCS paused. "*My God is my rock, in whom I take refuge.*" He kicked the door open, and then made a show of manhandling the bloody Savoie down the blaring and flashing hallway. In a menacing manner, he gestured with the weapon toward Mathis, who hurried over to the stairwell access door, with Doyle close behind.

There was a tense moment when the card didn't seem to activate the heavy iron door, but then the green light flashed, and Mathis began to pull down on the handle. "I'll need some help, she shouted at Doyle over the noise. "It's heavy, and if it re-locks it may not let us activate again."

Galvanized by this potential disaster, Doyle grabbed the handle and pushed with what little strength she could muster, but was surprised to find another hand impatiently pushing hers; a man's hand, encased in a thick, leather glove.

With some surprise, Doyle looked up to see the Trestles knight, heaving the door open in a manner that left little doubt that he was very unhappy with the fair Doyle.

"Sorry," she shouted at him over the din, as Mathis braced herself against the heavy door to prop it open. "I didn't realize I was in labor."

"You're in labor?" Mathis stared at her in alarm, as the DCS pushed Savoie through. The girl glanced down the hall toward the empty security desk. "Go; I'll stall them. We've got to give Acton enough time to get here."

"No," Doyle shouted. "Everybody who works here is bent; you come with us."

But the girl had stood back, and was allowing the door to automatically swing shut. In vain, Doyle clutched at her arm, but Mathis yanked it away. "Go—I'll be all right."

But then, Mathis jumped forward with a small yelp. "Ouch; what was that?"

A sword, thought Doyle, as the door clanged shut behind them, the tip of the sword getting caught in the process. Yet another sin to be laid at my door; the stupid knight was very fond of his stupid sword.

The closed door had the benefit of muffling the alarm, and they paused to recover for a moment, whilst Savoie immediately demanded the empty gun back—it was apparent he didn't want the DCS to have any type of weapon.

"Lady Acton is in labor," Mathis announced, carefully suppressing her extreme alarm.

"It's early," Doyle disclaimed in an airy tone. "Nothin' to speak of." She was then subject to a wave of pain that caused her to bend over and cry out, before she bit her lip, embarrassed.

They all stared at her in dismay for a moment before the DCS took her elbow. "Then let's move up to the roof, while you still can." They began to climb the stairwell, and he smiled at her in a reassuring manner. "Not to worry; I've delivered a few babies, in my days as a field officer. It's not something you forget how to do."

This was true, and much appreciated, but Doyle was ready to change the subject. "What now? Should we block the vents, just in case?"

"The command will re-assess," the DCS said, as they climbed the stairs. "They'll be worried about Savoie, and they'll think we're contained with no way out, so that they have a few minutes to think it over. It should be enough for Acton to scramble a helicopter SWAT—it takes about twenty minutes."

This was said with more certainty than he felt, but Doyle took comfort in the fact that she knew her husband, and knew that he'd move heaven and earth to get her out of this mess. And besides, there was an angry knight doing his best to gum up the works—although it wasn't clear what a fifteenth-century specter could actually accomplish. He'd poked Mathis, though, which was certainly a mark in his favor.

They clanged up the stairwell, Savoie grimacing, as he leaned heavily on the railing, and the sound of their footsteps echoing off the walls. At the top, they came to the roof access door, which required a security card to exit.

"We wait here," said Savoie. "Acton, he will unlock it from his computer. That is how we will know it is safe to move."

Doyle decided she wasn't going to stand on ceremony, and sank down on the top step, as another wave of pain washed over her. "Grand."

Mathis pointed out the flaw in this plan. "How will we know it's Lord Acton, and not prison personnel doing the unlocking?"

"We will not know," the Frenchman replied briefly, and then swore, as he bent to examine his wound.

"They saw I have a weapon," the DCS assured the girls. "Unlikely they'd try to storm us, and put Savoie at risk—it would be poor tactics."

"They may be panicked, and not very interested in tactics," Doyle declared a bit grimly, as she clutched at the railing. "They're a passel of blacklegs, with a lot to hide."

The DCS glanced at Savoie. "We just need to stall—and not much longer, I imagine. If it comes down to it, I can negotiate— I'll tell them I know where the money is, and that I was trying to escape to get to it."

Savoie met his gaze, and then nodded. "*Bien*. Go stand by the door, and see if you can hear anything." He handed the DCS the empty gun again.

"May I have a gun?" Mathis asked again.

"*Non*," Savoie replied shortly, and then crouched beside Doyle. "You must tell this baby to wait, yes?"

"Yes," Doyle agreed, and clenched the railing until her knuckles showed white.

Savoie made a sympathetic sound. "We have the deep blue devil, yes?"

"We do," she agreed, then swallowed—the mention of the missing money reminded her that she hadn't yet found out what she needed to know. The situation was hair-raising enough as it was, but if Savoie was planning to double-cross Acton, it would immediately get worse—faith, she may have to shoot Savoie herself, when all was said and done. "I wanted to ask you somethin', Philippe."

"I may not answer," he advised fairly. "Me, I do not answer the questions." Thinking about this, he amended, "For Emile, and for you, sometimes I do."

Doyle could appreciate this attitude, and ventured, "I understand that Mrs. Barayev—Emile's aunt—was here at the prison, when Emile was visitin'. Emile says she was arrangin' to take him back to St. Petersburg."

"Yes," said Savoie, his mouth suddenly thinning. "This is so."

Nothin' for it. She continued tentatively, "I was worried—I suppose when Emile told me this, I was worried that you were in cahoots with her. That you were plottin' against Acton."

He stared at her with open incredulity. "Fah—you do not trust me, still?"

"I truly can't be blamed, Phillippe," she defended herself. "You're an out-and-out blackleg, yourself."

Savoie gave her a very put-upon look, and said as though speaking to a simpleton, "I do not plot against Acton. Me, I did not know about this plan, but Acton, he found out, and he stopped her. He stopped *la chienne* from taking Emile away, *remercie la sainte mère*." He paused, and lowered his gaze for a moment, as emotional as Savoie ever allowed himself to be. "Acton, he kept Emile safe from her."

This was of interest, as Doyle was aware of no such abduction attempt. Not to mention it suggested that Savoie didn't know that the woman had been shuffled off this mortal coil. Carefully, she offered, "So—she's fled to St. Petersburg, then? A good riddance, I say."

"*Non,* he replied in a grim tone. "*Non*—it is bad rid-dance. The money, it is gone."

Doyle stared at him, her scalp prickling, and a terrible, terrible thought forming in her mind. Swallowing, she asked, "So—it's Mrs. Barayev, who has the money that everyone's chasin'?"

But the Frenchman seemed to recall his answer-no-questions philosophy, and said only what was presumably a very bad word, in French.

It didn't matter, however, because suddenly, everything that hadn't made sense began to make sense, and Doyle rested her forehead on her knees for a moment, to hide her reaction. Mother a' mercy, the irony was thick on the ground—it wasn't Savoie who was double-crossing Acton, it was Acton who was double-crossing Savoie.

Serves me right, she thought, clenching her teeth against another wave of pain. And I'm roundly an idiot, yet again. This time, the pain did not recede right away, but instead increased in intensity, so that she groaned aloud, "Jesus, *Mary* and Joseph."

"You mustn't blaspheme," the DCS gently admonished. "Here, hold my hand."

Chapter 39

Don't let her die. Please.

The group waited in the tense silence, Doyle trying to think about anything other than the unfortunate fact that the heir to the House of Acton was bound and determined to be born in a miserable prison stairwell.

"You hear nothing?" Savoie asked the DCS at the door.

"No—although I don't know as I'd hear anything in the first place—it's a double-sealed door. But I imagine very soon, they will try to parlay with us. Since we don't have a phone, they'll use the loudspeakers."

"This is not your normal situation, though," Doyle pointed out, which seemed a massive understatement. "The brass may not want anyone else to know what's goin' down, and if they use the loudspeakers, they can't very well keep it quiet."

She didn't add that it was unlikely even Acton wanted anyone to know what was going down, now that she'd finally figured it out. Suddenly, it was all clear-as-glass, and all the puzzling loose-ends had tied themselves up in a neat little bow. After all, Acton had—uncharacteristically—held off from murdering the main principals in the corruption rig—Drake, Mrs. Barayev, and the DCS—even though he was definitely not the forgive-and-forget type. Faith, the DCS had stormed into Acton's beloved Trestles and tried to arrest him; that her husband hadn't yanked a sword off the wall and dispatched him on the spot should have been the obvious tip-off that he had some scheme afoot. And now she knew why he'd behaved with such uncharacteristic restraint; he wanted to get his own hands on the fortune that the corruption rig had gathered up, and he wanted to do so without anyone's realizing what he was doing.

Therefore, he'd put the worthy DI Williams on the embezzlement case, and then had implemented his own, parallel, cascade scheme, which had worked out like a charm. When Williams started getting close to solving the embezzlement crimes—as Acton knew he would—the main players began to panic, and kill the lower-echelon types who were the most likely to confess to the police—Drake's list, the ghostly priest had called it.

This necessarily required them to keep consolidating the fortune so that it ended up in one place—they couldn't risk any new people with knowledge—and so it was a simple thing, really, for Acton to spring his trap at the very end; to seize the fortune, arrange for it to pass through the prison ministry account, and then arrange for the matron to mysteriously disappear—along with all the money—just after she spoke openly of fleeing to St Petersburg.

Only the matron hadn't fled at all; she'd been buried under the rubble at Holy Trinity Church, a misdirection murder that no one would mourn—or even be very interested in—save for the fact that a charwoman living in the far-away Philippines was uneasy about taking blood-money. And now the DCS was slated to be murdered by the angry prison guards, who would be convinced he'd conspired to rob them of their ill-gotten gains, since the final stop for all the money was the prison ministry's account.

I almost feel sorry for the blacklegs, Doyle thought, as she rubbed her face against her knees, and waited for the next contraction. It was a perfect plan—not that Acton would ever concoct an imperfect one. To all appearances, the money was gone, and the players were not about to go crashin' about in Russian mob-land to get it back. And—as the icing on the cake— the only people who might guess that Acton was behind this particular larceny-by-trick were the law enforcement players—Drake and the DCS—who'd both be conveniently dead.

Suddenly, they could hear a banging clang down below, as a lower door was flung open, and then they could hear several loud explosions in quick succession, sounding over-loud in the contained space.

"Flash-bangs," shouted the DCS, as the noise echoed up the stairwell. "They'll be coming up floor by floor, to clear us out. The front line will have riot shields, and try to draw fire, since they think I've only the ammo from the guards."

But Savoie had already figured out this ominous plan, and he'd put his hand under Doyle's arm to help her up. "Come, come, little bird; we go outside."

"Is that wise?" Mathis asked in confusion. "Won't they have someone cutting off any escape on the roof? We should wait for Acton."

There was a small silence as the two men herded them over to the door. "They've decided to cut their losses," the DCS advised in a level tone. "Their CO must have looked at the tape, and realized that DS Doyle came here on a rescue mission. They've decided we are all expendable."

"They'd—they'd kill Savoie?" asked Mathis in surprise.

"*Oui*," agreed the Frenchman in a grim tone. "They cannot allow the questions to be asked."

They assembled at the security door, and Doyle closed her eyes briefly. I can't allow everyone to be killed because I'm roundly an idiot, she thought, tamping down panic. Think, Doyle; think.

"Another minute," Savoie said, and focused on the door's red light, waiting for Acton's signal. "We wait as long as we can."

"*The Lord is my shepherd, I shall not want,*" the DCS recited steadily. He then paused, and advised, "Look for cover on the roof—there are vents, and storage modules."

Doyle tried to remember her close-quarters-combat training at the Crime Academy. "Who's front line? I'll need a gun, and we should set-up our angles."

"I'm front line," said the DCS, without hesitation. "I'm their main target, and I'll try to convince them I'm more valuable alive. *He maketh me to lie down in green pastures—*"

"No, I'm front line," Mathis interrupted. "I'll hide a gun, and pretend to break free. When they allow me to approach, I can shoot whoever's in command."

"They won't let you approach," said the DCS. "If they're willing to sacrifice Savoie, they're desperate. *Yea, though I walk through the valley of the shadow of death—*"

But this gave Doyle an idea. "I don't think they know who I am," she said, and pressed a hand against her side to ease another burst of pain. "I never checked in at security. If I tell them who I am, and that Acton's on to them, their plan to wipe out all witnesses is ruined. They'll know they can't just add a few more bodies to the count, and sweep it all under the rug."

They all jumped, as another series of explosions could be heard below them, coming ever closer.

Thoughtfully, the DCS met Savoie's eyes with his own. "A fair point. What do you think?"

"They'll take her hostage," Mathis pointed out impatiently.

"That's to the good," Doyle explained. "Then they'll be stuck with that deep-blue-devil person, and have to try to negotiate their way out of this mess. I'd take Acton's odds in that situation, any day of the week."

"*Oui,*" Savoie decided. "I will speak to them."

"No," Doyle insisted, pulling her hair out of its ponytail. "It has to be just me—I'm recognizable, and they have to see this red head straightaway, especially if there are shoot-to-kill orders. If they see the bridge-jumper, everyone will have second thoughts."

"Agreed," the DCS said. "But the rest of us should follow her out and secure the door behind us; the stairwell team won't have the benefit of seeing her, and they may start firing."

With one accord, they all jumped in alarm as another series of explosions could be heard, closer below them, this time. "Everyone ready?" the DCS asked, and then held the security card to the door. *"Thy rod and thy staff, they comfort me."*

"Bien," said Savoie.

With a fierce push, the DCS and Savoie swung the heavy metal door outward, and Doyle strode outward onto the roof with her hands held out from her sides, as high as she could lift them. Naturally, it was raining—as befitted the situation—and for a few tenses seconds she tried to get her bearings, and hoped that the rooftop personnel hadn't actually been given shoot-on-sight orders.

Loudly, she shouted, "I am Lady Acton." She squinted against the rain, and it took her a few seconds to see the prison riot personnel, their weapons drawn as they crouched behind vents and other structures. She added for clarity, "I am Lord Acton's wife." She figured she'd better throw that in, just in case they didn't connect the dots. "The Chief Inspector is on his way, and you are all under arrest. You do not have to say anything. But, it may harm your defense if you do not mention when questioned something which you later rely on in court. Anything you do say may be given in evidence."

There was a moment of surprised silence. She pointed to the nearest man and added, "I will need to borrow your flexcuffs. officer."

"Hold, right there," another man shouted. He bent his head, and she could hear his rapid-fire conversation over the comms with whoever was directing the operation, the words indistinguishable, but his tone a bit panicked.

Good one, Doyle, she thought; and let go of the breath she'd been holding. You've managed to throw the cat amongst the pigeons in the deep blue sea.

Chapter 40

There. There she was.

"Hold in place, I am awaiting orders," the comm officer shouted, and Doyle dutifully waited, a flash of lightning illuminating, for a brief moment, the Trestles knight, who stood beside her, his broken sword at the ready.

"Lay down your weapons," Doyle shouted, and hoped another labor pain wasn't about to unleash its fury—embarrassing, is what it would be, if she had to lie down whilst trying to attempt a mass arrest.

And then faintly, in the distance, Doyle could hear the sound she'd been straining to hear—the blessed, blessed sound of a helicopter's rotors. "Acton's comin'," she shouted. "And hell's comin' with him. Surrender your weapons—whoever turns first will probably get a conspiracy plea deal."

"Seize her," the comm officer shouted in a panicked tone, but no one moved, and Doyle could sense their confusion and dismay. Much heartened, she drew a deep breath and congratulated herself; when it came to turning the blacklegs against each other, she'd learned a lesson or two at the feet of the master.

The helicopter hovered above them, and a loudspeaker announced, "Throw down your weapons. Hands up, or we fire at will."

There was a tense moment whilst the outcome hung in the balance, and then the man closest to Doyle suddenly dropped his weapon. "Ow," he exclaimed, and rubbed one of his hands in surprise. The others, seeing this apparent capitulation, followed his example in short order, holding their hands on their heads and kneeling as commanded by the DCS, who shouted himself hoarse, trying to be heard over the noise as the chopper landed on the roof.

Acton leapt out before the skids had even touched down, and ran over to Doyle, who tried to present a calm appearance, but then sank down to sit on the roof, unable to stay upright despite her best efforts.

"Kathleen," he said urgently, as he cradled her shoulders and head. "Are you injured?"

Poor man, she thought, as the rain pelted down; he's a wreck. "No—I'm fine, Michael," pronouncing it 'foine'. "Edward's comin', though. And sooner rather than later." She then gritted her teeth, unable to speak, as she descended into a miserable well of pain.

The DCS knelt beside them. "Have you called in a field unit? I don't think we can trust anyone on the premises to help with the arrests."

"Not necessary; MI 5 has a unit on the way up," Acton replied. "Help me carry her to the copter, please."

"I weigh too much for any one mortal man," Doyle managed to joke.

As Acton locked his hands under her arms, the DCS turned around and lifted her legs, so that the two men carried her toward the waiting copter. It was a strange tableau, as they hurried past the prison guards, who now lay spread-eagled on the roof, wrists cuffed to the next man's ankle, as was the protocol when there were more perps than flexcuffs. The rain pelted down, and Doyle could see Mathis, brandishing a guard's weapon over the group. Almost without surprise, she also noted that Savoie was nowhere to be seen.

One of the helicopter personnel watched them approach from his post at the sliding door, and shouted, "Injured? I can start an IV."

"She's in labor," Acton shouted in return. Then, to Doyle, "How far apart are the contractions?"

"I haven't had a chance to pay attention," Doyle panted. "But I think they're close."

"Resist the urge to push, Kathleen," Acton instructed in a firm tone.

Doyle couldn't help groaning aloud, and then gasped, "What d'ye think I'm *doin'*, ye foolish man? D'ye not know 'tis bad luck, to birth a babe in the rain?"

"Go," Acton shouted to the copter pilot, as the other officer scrambled in after them.

But as the man turned to pull the slider shut, another figure ran up to the copter, and Doyle recognized Tasza, who shouted, "Report, please."

Mother a' mercy, I must be hallucinating, Doyle thought, but to her surprise, Acton complied. "I do not know the particulars, Commander, but it appears the prison personnel were afraid they'd be grassed out, and were planning to eliminate all potential witnesses."

"That about sums it up," Doyle gasped, and then went silent, when Acton met her eyes. Oh, she thought; doesn't want me gabbling to Tasza.

"I'll need a full report in an hour, if we're going to put a hold on all of them," the woman shouted.

But Acton said only, "My wife is in active labor, and I am taking her to Trestles. I will be available by phone."

Trestles? Thought Doyle. Faith, I *am* hallucinating.

"Let's go," Acton said again to the pilot.

Mathis suddenly appeared behind Tasza, her hair plastered flat by the rain. "Wait—shall I come?

"No," said Acton, who signaled that the door should be shut.

Well, she's in the doghouse, thought Doyle, as the helicopter lifted away from the building. My fault again, and I'll see if I can fix it, once I'm not trying to crawl out of my skin, here.

"As quickly as you can," Acton shouted to the pilot. "I'll show you where you can land, on the south lawn."

"Are there lights? Visibility is not very good," the pilot ventured.

"That's an order," said Acton.

"Yes, sir."

"The one time I wouldn't have minded an ambulance," Doyle joked. Her poor husband was in a state, he was.

He bent his head and took her hand. "You don't have to try to make me feel better, Kathleen. Just hold on."

"I love you," she gasped out. "And I'll try to make you feel better if I feel like it—just try to stop me, you *knocker*." There was a small pause, and then she prompted into the silence, "And you're supposed to say that I don't have to say."

"You don't have to say," he offered, with the ghost of a smile. "Not to me."

"That's better," she retorted. "And this childbirth business is for the birds."

"Hold on," he repeated. "We'll be there soon."

But Doyle wasn't listening, because she was wracked with such pain that she wasn't sure she'd survive it, and heard a strange groaning sound that she realized was coming from within herself. Then—almost like a miracle—the pain was gone, and she stared at the chopper's ceiling, where Acton's face used to be.

"He's here," said the officer excitedly.

"He's here," Acton repeated in wonder.

"He's here?" Doyle asked in astonishment. And then she could hear a tiny wailing sound, and promptly burst into tears.

Chapter 41

*The gamut of emotions, from desperation to
wonderment. Strange, that a short time ago
he'd despaired of ever feeling anything, ever
again.*

D
oyle woke because Dr. Timothy McGonigal was trying to
take her blood pressure without waking her, and as the
device discreetly pumped on her arm, she opened her
eyes. "Ho, Timothy. Where's that baby?"

"Here," said Acton, who was seated by her bedside, and
holding Edward in the crook of his arm. He reached to take her
hand. "How are you?"

"I am crackin' excellent," Doyle observed, and it was the
truth. "But you look a bit ragged, my friend."

"There's nothing wrong with him that a little sleep won't
fix," McGonigal observed with a smile. "And I'm sorry I woke you,
Kathleen, but perhaps we should try to put the baby to the breast
again. Shall I call for Mary?" When they'd all arrived the night
before, the good doctor had been surprised to discover that
they'd hired a nanny who had no experience with infants, and so
he'd ably stepped into the breach.

"No—let me find my bearings for a few minutes, Tim, before
we call in an audience. Although if Nanda's here, I suppose I
should listen to a veteran."

There was a small silence, as Acton carefully deposited the
sleeping baby in Doyle's arms. "No, no—Nanda did not come
with me." The doctor offered nothing further.

Oh-oh, thought Doyle, watching McGonigal gently pull on Edward's tiny jaw; there's trouble in paradise—although they were an odd pairing to begin with, and the cultural differences may have been just too hard to overcome. Of course, I'm one to talk—it's that pot and kettle thing, yet again.

"Ouch," she exclaimed suddenly. "Sweet baby Moses, that hurts."

"You'll get used to it," the doctor assured her. "Good—he's latched on."

Now, here's a surreal experience, thought Doyle, as she watched the baby open his eyes, briefly, and then close them again.

"I think he'll have blue eyes," said McGonigal. "Although it's too early to tell. Unusual, with both of you brown-eyed."

"Green, Tim. He'll have my mother's eyes." For a brief moment, Doyle raised her gaze, and met her husband's. "And note that I didn't need you or your paltry needles—did it the old-fashioned way, I did."

"Very impressive," the doctor agreed with a smile, but she could see that he was troubled—she shouldn't have mentioned Nanda. Poor man, he hadn't much experience with women, and was no doubt suffering his first real heartbreak.

"I'll leave you three alone," he offered, after a moment. "He looks to be doing well."

"Hudson will see to your breakfast," Acton said. "And a room has been made up—I hope you will stay for the fête."

"Don't worry; I wouldn't miss it."

"What's a 'fate'?" asked Doyle. "Sounds a bit ominous, and I've had my fill of ominous."

Acton explained, "It is traditional to hold a celebration for the staff, when an heir is born."

"Ah," said Doyle. "Will there be a maypole, and wassailin'?"

"Blood-oaths, instead," he teased.

She made a wry mouth. "You laugh, husband, but everythin' would have been miles easier if there'd been a few blood-oaths required from the very beginnin'."

With a smile, McGonigal closed the door behind him.

"I am that sorry I gave you such a scare, Michael," Doyle said as soon as they were alone. "Please, please forgive me."

"There is nothing to forgive, Kathleen," he replied, and it was true—she was lucky he was that besotted with his wrong-headed wife.

She reached to squeeze his hand. "I'm roundly an idiot, and I beg your pardon fastin'."

"You are impulsive," he corrected. "You are not an idiot."

"Tasza thinks I'm an idiot," she ventured, watching him. When he made no reply, she continued, "Is she a friendly, Michael?"

This seemed a valid concern; Tasza was a Commander—which made her Gabriel's superior, not the other way 'round. And—rather ominously—Tasza had been taking a pretend-interest in the prison ministry, which everyone thought was ground zero for the money-laundering operation. Small blame to them, since that was exactly what Acton had intended, in his plot to doom the DCS, and seize all the money for himself—quite the two-for-one, it was. Her devious husband had hijacked the cascade scheme, and had served it up with a generous side-helping of vengeance, as an added bonus. He'd waited for Williams to put the fear of God into the villains, and then had waited patiently whilst they killed all the lower-level people in a panic, leading him, like that scary misdirection-hound, to the stolen treasure—although she was mixing the two stories, and she shouldn't. While it was true that Acton's scheme may have involved a few misdirection murders, here and there, the more pertinent fact was that there was a fabulous treasure to be stolen. Faith, Acton himself had said it was more like that stolen-treasure story, and like a gobbin' fool, she hadn't taken him at his word.

She realized that he was speaking to her, and so she pulled her wandering thoughts back to the conversation at hand. "So, Tasza's not a friendly?"

Acton chose his words carefully. "I would advise against giving her any information, and if she asks any questions of you, please refer her to me."

With a speculative look, Doyle lifted her gaze from the baby at her breast. "D'you think she's on to you?"

Her husband met her gaze in surprise. "About what?"

"About all the gold that's sittin' in the vault here—or the dungeon, or whatever it is."

There was a moment of astonished silence, and then he lowered his head for a moment, trying to decide what to say. "How did you know?"

She readjusted the baby, and sent him a look. "I know you, my friend, like the back o' my hand—that's how I know." This was basically the truth, and the fact that a ghost had prodded her a bit need not be mentioned—best that he didn't know her methods, after all.

And anyways, it hadn't been that hard to piece it all together, once she'd seen Emile's coin. The fortune from the massive corruption rig had gone missing, and Doyle knew that the counter-terrorism people kept careful tabs on any large and unexplained deposits that went into banking accounts. Acton, of course, knew the same, and therefore he'd had Layton convert the money into the world's oldest currency—untraceable, and easily stored away for centuries, if necessary. And—as it so happened—he had just such a centuries-old storage place, himself.

There was a long pause. "You are extraordinary," he said, and meant it.

"And impulsive," she added, and then winced as the baby tugged too hard. "Don't forget impulsive, husband, else I never would have married you in the first place. You, on the other hand, are the opposite of whatever impulsive is, and you are due for a monumental scoldin'. Mother a' mercy, Michael; if I didn't have to hand you the baby to do it, I'd brain you with the nearest joint stool."

Acton tilted his head. "Ah. A shame, to think that just a moment ago you were begging my pardon fasting."

But she was not going to let him jolly her up, because she'd had yet another brush with disaster, and was getting mighty sick of staring disaster in the face. "We're past that part; now we're at the part where I lay into you, yet again."

With an attitude of resignation, he sat back and met her eyes. "I am all attention, then."

She was struck, for a moment, with how out-of-character it was for him to allow anyone to browbeat him, and confessed in a rush, "I hate it, that I'm the one who always has to trim your sails."

"There is no one else who could," he replied honestly.

The subject hung in the air between them for a moment. Acton hated letting anyone within his fortress, but he'd made an exception for her, because he couldn't help it, poor man. And— since she was the only person who could possibly influence him—this didn't seem to be a coincidence; it seemed evident that she'd been steered his way, or he'd been steered her way, depending on how you looked at it. Faith, it was one of the reasons she kept after him—it was her role to keep after him, apparently, and she shouldn't shirk it just because it always seemed a sleeveless task. Not to mention that she loved the man, and was very uneasy about that whole hellfire scenario— mayhap she was turning into an evangelical, after all.

Doyle gathered up her thoughts for a moment, and then began, "You think it's about the money, and the power that money provides. You were powerless, once, and I think havin' a lot of money—by hook or by crook—makes you feel less powerless. But that's not what it's truly about, Michael. Money can't take the place of faith—or family. My mother used to say that before they invented money, they invented family."

She paused for a moment, distracted by this thought. "Although her family ditched her when she turned up pregnant, so I suppose that didn't hold true, in her case. Come to think of it, I should go track them down, whoever they are, and throat-punch every last one of them."

"Only say the word," he offered.

Despite her attempt at having a serious discussion, she had to smile. "It is so very gratifyin', Michael, to have such a champion. I don't tell you near enough."

"Shall we take Edward to Ireland?"

"He's too young to do any throat-punchin'."

"I'm not."

"No spite murders," she warned. "They're the worst." There was a pause. "Where was I? I've forgotten."

"You were telling me that I must try to be a better person."

"Same old song," she sighed. "I'm such an archwife."

He leaned forward, and lifted her hand to kiss the back. "You are the greatest and best thing that has ever happened to me."

"Tell me I'm makin' a dent, at least."

"You are—I give you my word. But please—" He paused, thinking about what he wanted to say. "I would ask, Kathleen, if you have any concerns in the future—any concerns at all—if you would please bring them to me, rather than attempt to remedy the situation yourself. I don't know as I could withstand many more days like yesterday."

But Doyle only shook her head. "I'll give you no such assurances, my friend, because I want you to be worried that I might up and storm Wexton Prison at any moment. It would serve as a small check on your schemin' ways."

He had the grace to bend his head in acknowledgment. "Yes. You are indeed extraordinary, and I don't know why I continually underestimate you."

As Doyle knew she wasn't as extraordinary as much as she was plagued by ghosts and assorted proddings, she decided to gloss over that part. "That's not the point, Michael; the point is that you shouldn't have been workin' such a scheme to begin with. Although I suppose you did tell me, when you said it was like *The Four of the Sign*."

He kept his gaze on the coverlet, as he nodded his head in agreement, but she laughed. "All right; what was it, again?"

He smiled slightly. "*The Sign of the Four*."

"Whatever, Michael—the point is this; you can't keep the money. It's blood-money, and besides, you've got to learn your lesson, and I'm at my wit's end."

But Acton met her eyes. "Much of the money will go to build a new diocesan school, Kathleen. Along with a new free clinic, to replace Holy Trinity's."

Adamant, Doyle continued to shake her head. "No. You can't go and build things with it; not with blood-money."

He contemplated her hand, as he played with her fingers. "If I recall correctly, the original blood-money was put to good use. They used it to purchase a potter's field, I believe."

She stared at him in stark disbelief. "Holy Mother, I've created a monster."

"And besides, a good deal of the corruption rig money was diverted from the Health Professions Council. I would hesitate to return it to them."

"They're a bunch o' blacklegs," she agreed, seeing his point. "Not to mention they're gettin' themselves spite-murdered, left and right."

He lifted his gaze to meet hers. "The nave at St. Michael's should be enlarged, to accommodate the new parishioners."

There was a long moment whilst she stared at him, frowning—never let it be said that she didn't know when she was on the losing end of an argument. "If you throw in a bell tower for Father John, I'm sold."

"Done." He leaned forward—careful not to interrupt Edward, and kissed her.

With a sigh, she sank back into the enormous four-post bed, and closed her eyes. It went without saying, of course, that a significant sum was going to be left in the vault at Trestles—Acton was Acton, after all, and couldn't seem to help himself. All and all, I can claim a moral victory, she decided, and I think even the ghost-priest would pat me on the back for a job well-done.

Chapter 42

The spite murders were bothersome, but he'd not stand
in the way—he'd no doubt do the same, himself.
It would be beneficial, perhaps, to leave town for a time.

They day progressed, and Doyle found that it was rather nice, to be settled into the sumptuous bed with the baby, and with no pressing tasks hovering on the horizon. She wasn't certain how long they'd be at Trestles, but it seemed that Acton was in no hurry to return to London. Reynolds had been brought over to help out, and from what Doyle had seen, he'd assumed a subservient role without turning a hair, humbly taking instruction from Hudson, the steward. Not for the first time, it occurred to Doyle that Reynolds was nobody's fool.

Mary and Gemma had been moved in, also—Gemma allowed to come in briefly, so as to gaze upon the baby with wide eyes, whilst Mary listened to a highly-edited version of Edward's dramatic birth. We'll have to get our story straight, Doyle realized; I imagine Acton would rather the exact circumstances of Edward's birth were not made public.

Doyle was settling Edward into his crib—and trying to decide which end of the elaborate, silk-swathed structure was the head—when she heard a discreet knocking at the door jamb, and turned to see Reynolds, standing correctly at attention.

"Excuse me, madam, but Lord Aldwych is below, and begs a moment of your time to meet Master Edward, and convey his congratulations."

Doyle straightened up, as this was of interest; Acton was Lord Aldwych's heir, but the two men thoroughly despised each other. The fact that the old man had made the effort to come pay a formal call was nothing less than an olive branch, and Doyle could only be grateful—Edward had a very nasty set of relatives, after all, and the fewer blood-feuds, the better.

Beneath his respectful manner, Reynolds was radiating a deep satisfaction—nothing like taking a gander at the ancestral estate, to raise a butler's spirits. "Lord Aldwych will be unable to attend the fête, it seems, but would like to meet the heir, if it is convenient." He paused. "Lord Acton wished me to say that I can relay your excuses, if that is your desire."

Doyle braced her hands on her back. "Heavens, no, Reynolds—as if I'd let you miss the chance to kowtow to a genuine earl."

The servant entered the room with a brisk step. "I hope I do not kowtow to anyone, madam," he replied with a tinge of disapproval. After taking an assessing glance around the room, he then walked over to the windows to straighten-out the tail of a velvet curtain. "May I fetch your dressing-gown and slippers, madam?"

"You may," she agreed, hiding a smile. "Anythin' to make me look like less a pretender than my usual."

"No such thing, madam—but as he is from a different generation, he may look askance, if you entertain him *en déshabillé*."

"Can't have that," agreed Doyle. "No askancin' allowed."

The servant cast a critical eye over the sleeping baby. "Have we something a bit more dignified, for Master Edward to wear?"

Doyle eyed him with amusement. "I don't know how you can make a one-day's baby look dignified, Reynolds. We'll have to stick to the T-shirt, I think."

"As you wish, madam," the servant said smoothly, but nevertheless draped a lace-edged blanket over the sleeping Edward.

Watching him, Doyle decided that she just couldn't resist, and there was nothin' for it—besides, he'd have to find out, sooner or later. "Here's a wrinkle, Reynolds. It turns out that our Gemma's a Romanov."

Reynolds bent to fetch Doyle's slippers. "I believe, madam, that you haven't found quite the right word."

With no small satisfaction, Doyle related, "No—it's true. Gemma's real name is Georgievna, or somethin' complicated. She's a Romanov—the ones from Russia, who were mostly killed, a long time ago. She's a super-duchess, or some such thing."

Slowly, Reynolds turned to stare at her for a long moment. "Who told you this, madam?"

She smiled at his amazement. "Acton himself, my friend. It's true as true can be."

Reynolds drew his brows together, still trying to assimilate this extraordinary news. "Great heavens. Then she is related to our royal family, too."

Now it was Doyle's turn to be surprised. "Is she?"

"Oh yes—they were all cousins."

But Doyle could only shake her head. "*Such* a pack of nonsense. I have it on good authority that the only kingdom that matters is the kingdom of heaven."

His brow knit, Reynolds slowly lowered the hands that held Doyle's slippers. "If I may ask, madam, why is she here?"

"I'm not exactly sure, but I think she may be in some sort of danger, so please keep it under your hat—no boastin' at the butler's pub, or wherever it is you go to swap tales."

"Certainly not, madam." He frowned out the windows. "If no one is to know, then what will become of her?"

"Honestly, I haven't a clue. But at least she knows how to poach an egg, which will stand her in good stead."

Recovering his poise, Reynolds nodded, briskly. "I appreciate your confidence, madam, and I will say no more." Recalled to his task, he advised, "I will fetch Lord Aldwych, now."

As he turned to leave, Doyle asked, "Speakin' of loose-end children, Reynolds, where's our Emile?"

In a neutral tone, the servant paused to relate, "Emile is having a holiday in France, madam."

"I'm not even goin' to ask," she decided. "It's a gift horse, is what it is."

"Exactly," the servant agreed, and bowed his way out.

A few minutes later, Doyle was greeting Lord Aldwych, who was Acton's great-grandfather, although each of them wished it weren't the case. Acton had accompanied him, and behind his perfect-polite manner, Doyle could sense her husband's suppressed desire that the ceremonial meeting take place and then be over and done with—no love lost, between these two.

Self-consciously, the elderly man held up a mobile phone, and took a snap of the sleeping baby, his arthritic, gnarled fingers holding the mobile in the manner of someone who's only recently learned.

"A fine boy," he whispered, with the slight rasp of the very aged.

Not long, now, thought Doyle.

"We are indeed very pleased," said Acton, in his public-school voice.

The old man nodded, but didn't move for a moment; gathering himself. "I would seek a boon from you, sir."

"Willingly," said Acton, who hid his wariness.

Without taking his gaze from the baby, the other man began, "There was a child I'd lost track of—a child from the wrong side of the blanket. I've found him, now, and he's married, with his own children. I would ask—" He paused. "I would ask—

if you could—perhaps help them, in some way. Schooling for his children, perhaps."

"Of course," said Acton immediately. "Only leave me his information."

Lord Aldwych nodded, and then turned to begin his painstaking way toward the doorway. He paused, for a moment, before Doyle. "Madam," he said, and inclined his head carefully. "I am grateful to you."

"Cheers," said Doyle

The old man did not look at Acton, but his next words were clearly intended for him. "We have much in common, sir. We were both victims of your father."

Acton, who never spoke of his father, made no reply.

The old man nodded again, as he stepped forward. "I suppose we can only hope that he is burning in hell."

"Oh, he is," Doyle assured him. "Believe you me."

Chapter 43

He was tentatively hopeful that she didn't mind staying here, at least for the time being.
It rejuvenated him, to be here.

Doyle spent the remainder of the day alternating between dozing and feeding the baby, and Acton had retreated to catch some sleep—he'd be expected to preside over the celebration, and needed to rest-up. She could hear activity and muted voices below stairs, as the preparations were made, and thought yet again that the whole situation was utterly surreal, and that she rather wished her mother were here, to goggle alongside her.

Hard on this thought, she realized that the knight was standing in the far corner, his broken sword resting on his shoulder as he gazed at Edward, asleep in his mother's arms. There was something in that hardened gaze that moved her to tears, and she said aloud, "I'm truly glad it all worked out for you, after all this fussin'. It hasn't exactly been a slice o' heaven, mind you, but I'm glad you got what you wanted." She paused. "And I'm sorry about your sword—although that was Mathis' fault. Can't you get another one, from that King Hal person?"

"Kathleen?"

She smiled as Acton slipped into the room, no doubt thinking that she'd lost her mind, and truly, it wouldn't be much of a surprise, after everything that had happened.

"Who were you speaking to?" Her husband asked the question with the air of someone who is not certain that he wanted to hear the answer.

"Well, he's gone now, but I was speakin' to the knight, who is that pleased with Edward, and the way that everythin's landed as it should have. It turns out that the lost Acton heir—the one that everyone was bangin' on about—was the RAF pilot, after all. The same fellow your grandfather substituted as the false heir—although he didn't know he was the true heir, at the time. Neither one of them did." She paused. "Ironic, is what it is."

Acton stared at her, speechless.

She laughed at his reaction—not often that Acton was at a loss for words. "It's true, and let this be a lesson to you stupid aristocrats with all your stupid bloodlines, and such. The RAF officer was the lost heir, all along, and the knight cooked up the scheme to throw them together—the heir and your great-grandfather—whilst they were workin' at the airbase durin' the war. Poor ghost, he's been doin' a journeyman's job, gettin' it all worked out correctly." She added, "Gave him a scare at the prison, I did."

Slowly, Acton raised his gaze to stare at the grounds, out the diamond-paned windows. "And so—I was the true heir, all along."

"Edward's the true heir; you are yesterday's news, my friend." Still coming to terms with it, the poor man was, and small blame to him. It occurred to her, suddenly, that perhaps Acton's ways—the way he was—could be traced to his belief, all along, that he was an imposter. Overcompensation, Dr. Harding would have called it.

Acton bent his head, and gazed upon the sleeping baby for a moment. "Shall we do something to show the knight our appreciation? Put his portrait in pride of place over the mantel, perhaps?"

"He's not a portrait sort of person," Doyle advised bluntly. "But he would like to see Mathis married off to someone nice; she's related to him, too. Somethin' about a buxom maidservant."

There was a small silence, and Doyle eyed him. "Not to mention that Mathis needs a raise."

He met her gaze. "Does she?"

"Please don't be angry with her, Michael. I'd the bit between my teeth, and she did the best she could, under the circumstances. Faith, Savoie will probably try to hire her away; she spent the entire time tryin' to get the drop on 'im." She paused, and then added with some emphasis, "You can't be blamin' her; neither one of us knew what we were walkin' into—and that, my friend, is thanks in large part to you."

He ducked his chin in concession. "Yes, I suppose it is. I'm hoist by my own petard, then."

She laughed aloud. "Not a *clue* what that means, Michael. Is that from the other Doyle person, again?"

He leaned in to kiss her soundly. "Someone else entirely."

"And you'll not lay waste to the poor DCS, will you? He was a brick."

"No."

"Well, that's a relief. Would you like to hold the baby?"

"I would," he said, and carefully lifted Edward from her arms, before settling into the chair.

Doyle continued, "Now, there's a true conversion, if I ever saw one—the DCS, I mean. Like St. Paul on the road to Damascus—only even more unbelievable."

"I confess I am very surprised to hear it."

In a diffident tone, she ventured, "His ministry could use a bit of money, I think—they're fightin' the good fight, too."

Acton pulled his gaze from his new son, and met her eyes with some amusement. "You are catching me at a weak moment."

"My mother didn't raise a fool, my friend."

"All right—I'll see what can be done." He lowered his gaze to Edward, again.

It occurred to Doyle that Acton hadn't asked about the events at Wexton Prison, and she decided she'd wait a bit—a bit unsettled about it, he was. She couldn't have asked for a better demonstration of not being able to control things, and hopefully it had given him pause.

They sat together in companionable silence for a small space of time, and then Acton lifted his head to speak again— amused, he was. "I must tell you something, and I'm not certain how to go about it."

She teased, "I'm too much of a burden to bear, and so you're leavin' me for the fair Tasza."

"Definitely not. Brace yourself; you're getting another commendation for bravery."

She laughed aloud. "Truly? Am I allowed to refuse?"

"I'm afraid not."

"Then ring up the *London World News*," she sighed with mock-resignation. "Faith, I'm a legend in my own time—and Munoz will want to slay me, for dredgin' it all back up again."

"Very true. You should perhaps consider her feelings first, the next time you are tempted to make a mass arrest."

"I should consider yours, too. I see a few grey hairs, Michael."

"Nonsense. You are worth every grey hair."

She smiled at the sleeping Edward. "We're parents, Michael. Can you imagine?"

"No," he confessed with a smile, and it was the truth.

CPSIA information can be obtained
at www.ICGtesting.com
Printed in the USA
FSHW011601280421
80934FS